HOME FOR CHRISTMAS

It's September 1940 and the London Blitz has begun. For the four girls living at number 13 Article Row, life must go on, despite the nightly trauma inflicted by Hitler's raids. Underground employee, Agnes, is working to deal with people seeking safety from the deadly hail of bombs. Dulcie is trying hard to make peace with her mother after her sister, Enid's death. And nurses, Sally and Tilly both work at Bart's Hospital where they witness the terrible toll inflicted on ordinary Londoners. As the bombs continue to rain, all the girls want this year is to be home for Christmas.

HOME FOR CHRISTMAS

HOME FOR CHRISTMAS

by

Annie Groves

Magna Large Print Books
Long Preston, North Yorkshire,
BD23 4ND, England.

British Library Cataloguing in Publication Data.

Groves, Annie
 Home for Christmas.

 A catalogue record of this book is
 available from the British Library

 ISBN 978-0-7505-3606-6

First published in Great Britain in 2011 by HarperCollins*Publishers*

Published in Large Print 2012 by arrangement with
HarperCollins Publishers

Magna Large Print is an imprint of Library Magna Books Ltd.

Printed and bound in Great Britain by
T.J. (International) Ltd., Cornwall, PL28 8RW

The memory of the late Tony Bosson.

Acknowledgements

Susan Opie, and Victoria Hughes-Williams, my editors at HarperCollins.

Yvonne Holland, copy editor extraordinaire, who, as always, has done a magnificent job.

All those at HarperCollins whose hard work enabled this book to reach publication.

Tony, who contributed so much to my books via the research he did for me.

PROLOGUE

Just After Christmas 1936

'Darling, oh, your face is so cold.'

Sally Johnson, eighteen years old and near the end of her first year as a probationer nurse at Liverpool's Mill Street Hospital, laughed at her mother's loving complaint as she reached up and kissed Sally's face.

'That could be because it's trying to snow out there and my face is the only bit of me you can't tell me to wrap up warmly,' Sally teased her affectionately. Standing in the delicious beef-scented warmth of the family kitchen, she unwrapped herself from her gloves, scarf and hat, and then the good warm coat that her mother lovingly insisted on her wearing.

The kitchen table, with its blue-and-white-checked oilcloth, had already been set for their evening meal. Above it, the light from the blue and white glass ceiling light, burnished Sally's dark red curls. She had inherited her hair colouring, so her father often said, from his own mother, whilst her oval-shaped face, with its high cheekbones and good skin, came from her petite fair-haired mother.

Sally knew how lucky she was to have grown up in such a close and loving family. Her parents – her tall, dark-haired, handsome father and her

13

pretty mother, adored one another just as they did her, and she loved them both dearly in return. Life was pretty good in the Johnsons' smart semidetached house in the middle-class Wavertree area of the city.

'Morag said today how much she and Callum had enjoyed spending Christmas here with us,' Sally told her mother as she went to hang up her outdoor clothes in the hallway, glad of the brief moment of privacy so as to conceal the soft blush that had burned her face just because she had spoken Callum's name.

Callum. Sally would never forget the kiss he had given her under the mistletoe on Boxing Day when they had been alone in her parents' front room.

'Morag's always telling me how lucky I am to have you and dad as my parents,' Sally added, as she returned to the kitchen. 'Not that she needs to remind me.'

Morag and Sally had met when they were doing their initial three months' training together at Mill Street Hospital. Morag and her brother, Callum, an assistant teacher, had lost their own parents in a boating accident on Loch Lomond two years before Callum's work had brought them to Liverpool. The two girls had hit it off straight away, and once Sally had told her mother about Morag and Callum's sad loss, Sally's mother had made them both very welcome at number 28 Lilac Avenue.

Sally could still remember that dizzy breath-catching-in-her-throat feeling she had had when Morag had first introduced her to her brother.

14

Callum had come to walk Morag home from the hospital after they had been on nights, and the minute she had seen her friend's tall, good-looking brother, with his thick dark hair and his warm smile, Sally had been lost. Callum also was kind and considerate and, well, just everything Sally had ever imagined herself finding attractive in a man. She knew that her parents liked him, from the way her mother fussed over him, and her father took him off down to his garden shed to talk about whatever it was men did talk about in such male havens.

Callum, with his worn Harris tweed jacket with leather patches on the elbows, his tattersall shirts, and the warmth in his piercing blue eyes whenever he looked at her, had stolen Sally's heart completely. And by kissing her as he had done on Boxing Day evening he had shown that he cared about her too, even if he had said aftewards that he hadn't intended it to happen and that, as a poorly paid assistant teacher with a sister to support, 'he was the worst kind of a cad for kissing her when he knew he had nothing to offer her.' But then he had paused and looked at her and said huskily, 'At least not at the moment.' Sally had known then that those words, coming from Callum, were every bit as good as a request to go steady from another young man, and her heart had swelled with gratitude to whoever was responsible for her meeting him.

No one could possibly have a better friend than Morag. She and Sally were closer than sisters. They did everything together: worked; complained about their poor aching feet and their raw

15

hands; went dancing together at Liverpool's famous Grafton Ballroom, 'oohed' and 'aahed' over the newest pictures to be shown in the cinemas; and Morag even thought that Sally's parents were every bit as special as Sally did herself.

One day they would be sisters, when she and Callum were ... but no, Sally couldn't even think the word 'married' because she knew if she did she would blush and then her mother would ask her why.

As Sally had discovered this Christmas, some things were too new to tell even the most loving of mothers and the closest of friends, some things were so special, so magical and so longed for that they could only be shared with one special person, and thought about in private.

'That will be your father,' her mother announced now, her face lighting up as she heard the sound of a key in the front door.

Sally's father had a good job working as a senior clerk at the Town Hall. As always when he came home, he put an arm round his wife and his daughter, drawing them close, as he asked, 'And how are my best girls?'

Oh yes, she was one of the luckiest girls in Liverpool, Sally acknowledged with so much to be thankful for.

And it had been the most wonderful Christmas, starting two days before Christmas Eve when she and Morag had decorated the Christmas tree her parents had brought home from St John's Market, along with a large turkey and enough vegetables and treats, her father had teased her mother, to feed them all for a month. Whilst her

16

mother had sat and watched, and her father had tested the pretty Christmas tree lights from the previous year, Sally had lovingly explained to Morag the family significance of each precious tree ornament. There had been the delicate tin candle holders that held the bright red wax candles, which were never lit in case they caused a fire. The candle holders had originally belonged to her grandparents, and it took a steady hand to clip them securely upright onto the tree's branches. Then there had been the glass baubles, some of them predating Sally's own birth, others bought new each year of her life, and with so many happy memories of previous Christmases that unpacking them was like rediscovering old friends.

As the afternoon light had faded into evening and her mother had switched on the lights in the comfortable sitting room – with its dark green damask-covered three-piece suite, its curtains and cushions made from paisley-patterned fabric, bought on special order from Lewis's in Liverpool; the dark green and gold patterned fitted carpet that her father had insisted on, even though her mother protested that it was far too expensive – Sally had seen the tears in Morag's eyes.

But it had been her mother who got up from her chair to come over to them and put her arm tenderly round Morag, telling Sally quietly, 'Darling, go and put the kettle on, will you?'

When Sally had come back into the sitting room, Morag had been smiling, albeit somewhat tremulously, and later, when they were back at the hospital, Morag had told her emotionally,

'You have the most wonderful parents, Sally, especially your mother.'

On Christmas Eve they had all gone together to the church where Sally had been christened and confirmed, and after Midnight Mass, with the crispness of frost in the air, neighbours and friends had been warmly welcomed back to number 28 Lilac Avenue for a glass of sherry and the mince pies that Sally and Morag had helped to bake. With Sally sharing her own room with Morag over Christmas, and Callum sleeping in the small boxroom, the house had been full, but in the most wonderful way. Sally's father and Callum insisting on cooking breakfast on Christmas Day after church, laughing and joking with one another, her mother keeping an eye on the turkey, before they had all settled down in the front room to open their presents.

Then there had been Christmas lunch itself. Her mother was a wonderful cook and, of course, Sally and Morag had been set to work helping with the veg, and decorating the table in the morning room, extended for the guests, and looking very bright and Christmassy with its white napery and the red and gold crackers purchased in Lewis's Christmas department earlier in the month.

The house had been filled with the scents of Christmas, roasting turkey, the sharp smell of the sprouts grown in the Johnsons' own garden, the scent of the pine needles from the tree, the hot smell of the multicoloured tree lights, her mother's lily of the valley perfume and the very grown-up Nights in Paris perfume both Sally and Morag were wearing in honour of the special occasion.

18

The paper garlands her father and Callum had put up over the ceiling moved in the draught from the constant opening and closing of doors, and the sound of laughter and lively conversation filled the air.

Of course, Sally's mother had been at the centre of all the activity, a commanding officer quietly managing her troops as they all worked to get the best lunch of the year onto the table.

Then on Boxing Day some of the neighbours had come over, and there had been a singsong round the piano, Sally listening with pride and love to Callum's good strong baritone.

Oh, yes, it had been the very best of Christ-mases, though with even happier Christmases to come, Sally was sure of it.

December 1938

Sally couldn't bear to look as she walked past the cemetery on her way home to Lilac Avenue, increasing her pace and turning her face from the place where her mother was buried. She could still hardly accept that her mother was dead.

It had been such a long hard road from those early days of hope that somehow the doctors were wrong, followed by the disbelief, despair and even anger that someone as special as her mother should be struck down by such a cruel illness, the long-drawn-out days, weeks and then months of her decline and the terrible pain she had suffered with that decline. Then – and Sally could still hardly bear to think about this – those

19

last days when it had seemed impossible that the emaciated tiny human frame – tortured by pain and trying so bravely not to betray the extent of her suffering – lost in the bed that she and Morag kept immaculately hospital pristine and neat, could actually be her mother.

Her mother had tried so bravely not to distress those she loved by revealing how much pain she was in, but of course Sally had known. How could she, as a nurse, not know?

Morag had been so wonderful – the best of good friends, truly an angel – taking over the most intimate nursing of Sally's mother as though she had been her own when Sally had needed to leave her mother's bedside to give way to her tears. Sally's heart lifted now with the knowledge that when she got home, having unexpectedly been told that she could finish her shift several hours early, she would probably find Morag already there.

'You are so kind,' Sally had told Morag.

'It is a privilege to do this for your mother, Sally, after all she has done for me,' Morag replied.

And Morag hadn't just helped with the nursing. Whenever she was off duty, and Sally still working, she'd gone round to Lilac Avenue to cook a hot meal for Sally's father, and take over some of the chores that Sally's mother could no longer do. Just as though they had indeed been sisters they had worked together to nurse Sally's mother and give her father what comfort they could. Callum had played his part too, sitting and talking with her father in the evenings.

Sally was past the cemetery now and could

20

allow herself to breath normally again although that felt wrong when her beloved mother was no longer breathing. She and her father would never stop mourning her and missing her, Sally knew.

As she turned into Lilac Avenue through the windows of its houses she could see Christmas trees and Christmas decorations. Christmas was only a matter of days away but Sally couldn't bear to think about it. She couldn't imagine ever wanting to celebrate Christmas without her mother.

Rather than use her front door key Sally went round to the kitchen. As she put her hand on the door knob, what she saw through the frosted glass in the top half of the door froze her in shocked disbelief. The image of two people embracing might be fuzzy and distorted by the thick glass, their features obscured, but for Sally there was no mistaking what they were doing and who they were.

Morag and her father were in one another's arms and Morag was kissing her father – not com- passionately as the best friend of his daughter, but intimately on the mouth, in the manner of a lover.

Filled with revulsion, trembling with disbelief, Sally stepped into the kitchen as Morag and her father moved apart.

Sally looked at them both in silence. Morag's face was white, her dark brown eyes shimmering with tears, her guilt plain for Sally to see. Behind her father's sadness Sally realised that she could see a glint of another horrifying emotion in his eyes. He was happy. Happy that Morag had kissed him.

'Sally, please don't look like that. It isn't what you–' Morag was saying, trying to catch hold of her arm, but Sally moved back. She was trembling so much that she had to lean on the wall to support herself.

'No.' She shook her head. 'No don't touch me ... don't come anywhere near me. How could you? How could you do this?'

'Sally.' Now it was her father trying to reach for her, his familiar face – the kind loving face she had known all her life – creased in distress. 'I'm sorry you had to find out about Morag and me like this. We were going to tell you...'

Sally felt as though her heart were being wrenched out of her body when her father reached for Morag's hand and held it tightly, giving her the most tender and protective of looks.

'I wanted to tell you,' he continued, 'but Morag wanted to wait until after Christmas. She thought it would be easier for you then.'

'Easier for me to be told that my father and my supposed best friend were betraying my mother's memory in the most grotesque and horrible way?' Sally demanded on a choking breath of disbelief that was getting close to hysteria. 'Dad, how can you think that? How can you do this, when Mum... She's not even been dead two months yet. Two months and yet already Morag has somehow managed to worm her way into ... into the place that should only ever belong to my mother.'

'Sally, that's enough!' The stern note in her father's voice shocked Sally into fresh despair. 'I will not have you blaming Morag – for anything.' The loving look her father gave Morag made

22

Sally feel as though someone were squeezing her heart painfully hard. 'If you must blame anyone, then blame me. I love Morag and I know that the love I have for her would have had your mother's blessing.'

'No!'

The denial was torn from Sally's throat as she pulled open the back door and ran out of the house, ignoring her father's plea for her to stop.

It was dark now and Sally didn't know how long she'd been crouching here beside her mother's grave, anger and grief spilling from her with the tears she had shed.

In two days it would be Christmas, but there was no place in Sally's heart now to celebrate that special season.

'Sally.'

The sound of a much-loved voice saying her name had her crying out in relief. She turned to him as he crouched down next to her, the scarf her mother had knitted for him last Christmas twisting in the ice-cold wind blowing across the bleak graveyard.

'Oh, Callum...'

She was in his arms and he was holding her tight, the warmth of his embrace thawing her emotions, so that fresh tears fell.

'I suppose you know what's happened?' she asked him when the tears had finally stopped and she was drying her face with the handkerchief he had offered her.

'Yes. I've just come from the house.'

'Callum, how could they betray my mother like

that? My father and your sister, my best friend – I still can't believe it. I don't want to believe it. I don't want to see Morag ever again. I don't want her coming to the house or having anything to do with my father. I blame her more than I do him. I–'

'Sally, I know you've had a shock, and I can understand that right now you feel a certain amount of betrayal, but I promise you that the only reason they didn't tell you about their feelings for one another was because they didn't think you were ready. When they discussed it with me–'

Whilst he had been speaking to her Callum had stood up drawing Sally to her feet as he did so, and now he was holding her cold hands in the warmth of his, but for once she was barely aware of his touch.

'You knew? You knew about this and you didn't tell me?' she demanded angrily.

'They asked me not to, although... Sally, we all know how much you loved your mother, and how much her death has upset you, but you are an intelligent girl and, to be honest, I'm surprised that you didn't see the love growing between them for yourself. I know that your mother did, and that she welcomed it, knowing that two people she loved so much would find happiness together.'

'No, that's not true. My mother would never have wanted... She loved my father.'

'Yes, she did, and in my view it was because of the great love she had for both him and for Morag that she welcomed the knowledge that your father would not be left alone after her own death.'

'You're on their side, aren't you?' Sally accused him.

'It isn't a matter of taking sides.'

'It is for me.' Sally pulled away from him, adding bitterly, 'And I know now whose side you're on, Callum. I wish I'd never met either of you. I trusted Morag. I thought she was my friend, but I realise now that I never knew her at all. No one who was a true friend to me would have done what she's done, betraying my mother, stealing my father, and you taking her side. I never want to see either of you again.'

'Sally, please don't be like this.'

'Don't be like this? How do you expect me to be? Am I supposed to be glad? Am I supposed to welcome the fact that my best friend has been making up to my father behind my back whilst my mother has been dying?'

'Sally...'

Callum was reaching for her, his dark hair, tangled by the cold wind, flopping over his forehead, as he held out his arms. The pain she was feeling was more than she could bear. She had loved him so much, and she had thought that he loved her, just as she also believed that Morag was her friend and that her father was devoted to her mother. But all of them had deceived her, and betrayed her mother, and she would never be able to forgive them. Never. She stepped back from him.

'Don't touch me. Don't come anywhere near me.' Her furious words were raw with bitterness and pain.

25

ONE

12 September 1940

Sally Johnson pushed back her mop of dark red curls, briefly freed from the constraint of her starched acting sister's nursing cap, and slipping off her shoes, wriggled her toes luxuriously.

She was sitting in a small windowless room close to the sluice room of the operating theatre where she worked. In this small haven the nurses were unofficially allowed to have a kettle, tucked away, when not in use, in the cupboard above the sink along with a tin of cocoa and a caddy holding tea so that they could make themselves hot drinks. The place was more of a large cupboard than a room, the dark brown paint on the skirting boards like the dull green on the walls, rather faded, although, of course, both the floor and the walls were scrupulously clean. Staff nurse would have had forty fits if her juniors hadn't scrubbed in here with every bit as much ferocity as they did the theatre itself.

When it had three nurses or more in it there was standing room only. Right now though as she was in here on her own, Sally had appropriated one of the two chairs for her tea break. Nurses always had aching feet when they were on duty. They'd had a busy shift in the operating theatre: a list of patients with all manner of injuries from

Hitler's relentless bombing raids on London.

Thinking of their patients brought home to Sally how much more responsibility she would have when she got her promised promotion to sister. She was very proud of the fact that Matron thought she was ready for it, even if there were times when she herself worried that she might not be. Sally loved her work, she was a dedicated and professional nurse who always put her patients first, but right now she couldn't help thinking longingly of her digs in Article Row, Holborn, and the comfort of a hot bath. What a difference time could make – to some things. Article Row was her home now and the other occupants of number 13 as close to her as though they were family. Family... Sally's expressive eyes grew shadowed. What she had left behind in Liverpool no longer had the power to hurt her. And besides, Sally reminded herself as she replaced her cap firmly over her curls, there was a war on and she had a job to do.

On Article Row another member of the household at number 13 was already on her way home, or rather she had been until she'd bumped into a neighbour.

'Tilly, let me introduce you to Drew Coleman,' said Ian Simpson. 'He's an American and he's going to be my lodger.'

Tilly smiled politely as Ian turned from her to the tall, broad-shouldered, hatless young man, whose open raincoat was flapping in the breeze.

'Tilly's mother knows all about lodgers, Drew. She's got three of them. All girls too,' Ian grinned.

Article Row possessed only fifty houses, all built by the grateful eighteenth-century client of a firm of lawyers in the nearby Inns of Court, whose fortune had been saved by the prompt action of a young clerk articled there.

Number 13 had belonged to Tilly's paternal grandparents originally. Tilly and her parents had moved in with them when Tilly had been a baby because of her father's ill health. Tilly couldn't remember her father. He had died when she was a few months old, his health destroyed by his time in the trenches during the Great War. Her mother had nursed first Tilly's father, then later her mother-in-law, and then her father-in-law through their final illnesses. It had been after the death of Tilly's grandfather, just before the start of the current war, that Tilly's mother had decided to take in lodgers to bring in extra money.

'Four girls all living under the same roof?' the young American queried with a smile. 'Oh, my. I've got four sisters at home, and they fight all the time.'

'We don't fight,' Tilly informed him reprovingly, shaking her head so that her dark brown curls bounced, indignation emphasising the sea green of her eyes and bringing a pink flush to her skin. 'We're the best of friends. Sally – she's the eldest, she works at Barts Hospital – St Bartholomew's, the oldest hospital in London – like I do. Only she's a nurse, and I work in administration for the hospital's Lady Almoner. And Agnes, she...' Tilly hesitated, not wanting to tell this stranger that poor Agnes was an orphan who had never known her parents. 'Agnes works at Chancery Lane

28

underground station, in the ticket department. Then there's Dulcie, who works in the perfume and makeup department of Selfridges, the big department store on Oxford Street. She's ever so stylish, although she's got a broken ankle at the moment.' A small shadow crossed Tilly's face at the still raw and frightening memory of what had happened only a few nights earlier, on her own eighteenth birthday, when the four of them had been caught in a German bombing attack on the city on their way out to celebrate. Dulcie had caught her heel in the cobbles of the street and had fallen over, breaking her ankle and banging her head. As all of them had admitted to one another afterwards, they'd thought they were going to be killed, but they had stuck together, determined not to run for safety and leave Dulcie to her fate. Now, because of that, a bond had been formed between them that they all knew they would share all their lives. Tilly really felt that she had grown up that night.

'Drew here has been sent over to London by the newspaper he works for in America to report on the war,' Ian explained to Tilly.

Tilly nodded as she surreptitiously studied Ian's lodger. He looked as though he was in his early twenties, his thick mid-brown hair slightly sun-bleached at the ends. He had warm brown eyes that crinkled at the corners when he smiled, his smile revealing white, even teeth. On his right hand he was wearing an impressive-looking gold ring with what looked like a crest on it. Not wanting to seem too curious, Tilly looked away politely.

Ian Simpson worked as a print setter on Fleet Street, for the *Daily Express*. His wife and their four young children had evacuated to Essex at the start of the war, and Tilly's own mother had often said that it must be lonely for Ian living in the house on his own during the week.

Tilly had heard American accents before, but Drew was the first American she'd met in person. She gave him a friendly – but not too friendly – smile. At just eighteen, and with the experience of several months of war behind her, which had included her foolish crush on Dulcie's handsome army brother, Rick, Tilly now considered herself wise enough not to pay too much attention to a good-looking young man, and Drew *was* good-looking, she had to admit.

Tilly glanced back in the direction from which she had come, at the pall of dust hanging on the air, the result of nightly bombing raids on London's East End by the German Luftwaffe.

'Well, you'll certainly have had plenty to write about for your newspaper, with the bombings we've had these last few nights,' she told the young American gravely.

'Yes.' Drew's voice was equally grave. 'I went over to Stepney in the East End this morning. I thought I had the makings of a good journalist, but finding the words to describe the devastation and horror of what's happened there so that the folks back home will understand...' He shook his head, and Tilly knew exactly what he meant. As they talked Tilly resisted the temptation to look up at the sky. These last few days of relentless air raids had left everyone's nerves on edge, but she certainly wasn't going to give in to her fear in front of this young American.

'I've heard there were over four hundred killed on Saturday night, and three hundred and seventy on Sunday in the East End with over sixteen hundred injured,' Ian told them. 'And I've lost count of the number of air-raid alarms there's been. Three times this afternoon we heard the air-raid warning go off, and had to leave the printing presses to get down to the shelter.'

'It was the same with us at the hospital,' Tilly agreed. 'Our shelter is down in the basement of the hospital, and they've got the operating theatres down there as well. We can hear the bombers, even down in the shelters, though.'

'I think you British are being magnificently brave,' Drew told her with great sincerity.

'It's all very well being brave, but what I don't understand is why we don't hear our own anti-aircraft guns firing at the Germans,' Tilly said with some concern.

'Well, I might be able to answer that question for you,' Drew told her. 'You'll have heard of Ed Murrow?'

Tilly nodded. Ed Murrow was a well-known American radio broadcaster.

'Yes,' she confirmed. 'He does the nightly *"This is London"* wireless programme to America doesn't he?'

Drew beamed her a smile of approval. 'That's right,' he agreed. 'Well, I heard him talking to some other journalists last night in the American Bar, and he was saying that the Government has left the skies open for your own fighter planes to

31

blow the Germans out of the air.'

Tilly gave him a wan smile. She knew he had wanted to cheer her up, but as far as she could see from the terrible damage being inflicted on the city, their own fighter planes didn't seem to be doing very much to stop London being blitzed by German bombers. Not that she was going to say so, of course. She was far too patriotic to do that.

Being patriotic, though, did not mean that there were times when she didn't feel afraid.

All the occupants of number 13, with the exception of Sally, who was on duty, had spent the last two nights in their Anderson shelter in the garden, all of them pretending to sleep but none of them actually doing so, Tilly was sure. They had lain in their narrow bunk beds, listening to the dreadful noises of the assault on the city. The worst, in Tilly's opinion, were those heart-stopping few minutes when all you could hear was the approaching relentless menacing purring sound made by the engines of the German bombers coming in over the city. Your stomach tensed terribly against what you knew was going to happen when the bombs started to fall. She could feel herself holding her breath now, just as she did at night when she lay there waiting for the full horror she knew was imminent: the whistle of falling bombs; the dull boom of huge explosions, which shook the ground. Somewhere in the city houses were being destroyed and people were being killed and injured. In Article Row they had been lucky – so far – but she had seen at work what was happening to those whose families and homes had been blown apart by the bombs: numbed, disbelieving white-faced people visiting their injured relatives; or even worse, those poor, poor people who came to Barts hoping against hope that the loved one who was missing might be there and alive.

Tilly, like everyone else in the department, had had to put her normal routine to one side because of the work involved in recording the details of the patients now flooding into the hospital.

You could see the tension in people's faces. When you were out on London's streets, crunching through the broken glass littering the pavements, you hardly dared to look at the fearful shapes of the destroyed buildings – and certainly not towards the river, where the docks had been bombed night after night and where, in the morning, some of the fires were still burning. If you heard a loud sound fear automatically gripped you, but you pushed it aside because you had to, because you didn't want Hitler thinking he was beating down your spirit, knowing how afraid you really were.

'Oh ho,' Ian warned, interrupting Tilly's thoughts, 'here comes Nancy. Nancy likes to keep us all in order,' he told the American. 'She's a bit of a stickler for making sure that none of us does anything that might lower the tone of the Row. Isn't that right, Tilly?'

'Yes, I'm afraid it is.' Tilly was forced to admit ruefully. 'Nancy likes to disapprove of things. She's also a bit of a gossip,' she felt obliged to warn Drew.

'She certainly is.' Ian pulled a face. 'When I

brought my cousin home with me the night she'd been bombed out, Nancy was on the doorstep first thing the next morning wanting to know who she was and if Barb knew she'd stayed the night. Lena soon put her right and told her what was what.'

'I'd better go,' Tilly told Ian. 'Mum will be wondering where I am.'

'It sure was nice to get to meet you,' Drew told her with another smile.

He seemed a decent sort, Tilly acknowledged as she hurried towards number 13. Not that she was remotely interested in young men, not since Dulcie's elder brother, Rick, had taught her the danger of giving her heart too readily. That had simply been a silly crush, but it had taught her a valuable lesson and now she intended to remain heart free.

In the kitchen of number 13, Olive, Tilly's mother, was trying desperately not to give in to her anxiety and go to look out of the front window to check if she could see her daughter.

Although it was unlike Tilly to be late home from work, normally Olive would not have been clock-watching and worrying, but these were not normal times. When the Germans had started bombing London night and day almost a week ago, they had bombed normality out of the lives of its people, especially those poor souls who lived in the East End near the docks.

As a member of the Women's Voluntary Service Olive had already been to the East End with the rest of her local group under the management of

34

their local vicar's wife, Mrs Windle, to do whatever they could to help out.

What they had seen there had made Olive want to weep for the occupants of what was the poorest part of the city, but of course one must not do that. Cups of hot tea; the kind but firm arm around the shaking shoulders of the homeless and the bereaved; giving directions to the nearest rest centre; noting down details of missing relatives to relay to the authorities, the simple physical act of kneeling down in the rubble of bombed-out houses to help shaking fingers extract what looked like filthy rags from the carnage, but which to those pulling desperately at them were precious belongings – those were the things that mattered, not giving in to tears of pity for the suffering.

From the window of her pretty bright kitchen with its duck-egg-blue walls, and its blue-and-cream-checked curtains, Olive could see out into the long narrow garden, most of which Sally had converted into a vegetable patch. But it was their earth-covered Anderson shelter that drew her attention. They had spent the last four nights inside it, and would probably be inside it again tonight, unless by some miracle the Germans stopped dropping their bombs on London.

Where was Tilly? No air-raid sirens had gone off during the last couple of hours, so she should have been able to get home by now, even given the delays in public transport the bombing had caused. Perhaps she should go and check the street outside again?

Olive had just walked into the hall when she

heard the back door opening. Quickly she hurried back to the kitchen, relief flooding through her when she saw Tilly standing there.

'Oh, Tilly, there you are.'

'I'm sorry I'm a bit late, Mum,' Tilly apologised immediately, seeing her mother's expression.

The resemblance between mother and daughter was obvious. They both had the same thick dark brown curls, the same sea-green eyes and lovely Celtic skin, and even the same heart-shaped faces, although Tilly was already nearly an inch taller than her mother.

'I was just walking into the Row when Ian Simpson called me over to introduce me to an American reporter he's got lodging with him.'

'An American?' Olive's voice held a hint of wariness. America was a neutral country and had not taken sides in the war, unlike the British Dominions, such as Canada, Australia and New Zealand, who were all offering 'the mother country' support in their fight against Hitler.

'Yes,' Tilly confirmed as she went to give her mother a hug.

Olive put down the knife with which she'd been about to resume scraping the thinnest possible covering of butter onto some slices of bread.

'I thought I'd make up some sandwiches to take down to the Anderson with us later, unless Hitler gives us a night off.'

'Huh, fat chance of that,' Tilly responded. 'We've had three air-raid warnings already this afternoon, but at least we've got the hospital basement to go to. We're ever so busy, Mum,' she added, 'and if you could see some of the poor souls we've had come up to our office, looking for family they've lost ...'

Tilly's voice broke, and Olive hugged her tightly, smoothing Tilly's curls with a loving hand.

'I know, Tilly. Our WVS group went over to the East End today. Everyone's doing their best, but no one expected that there'd be so many made homeless so quickly. All the rest centres that haven't been bombed have been overwhelmed. They're trying to get more opened as quickly as they can, but the conditions in some of the shelters people are using are so squalid and unhealthy...' Olive released her daughter to look at her. 'I should have sent you away out of London, Tilly. It would have been much safer for you.'

'I'm glad you didn't,' Tilly told her determinedly, adding when she saw her mother's expression, 'I'm not a child any more, Mum. I want to be here, doing my bit. It wouldn't feel right, running away and leaving it to others. Only this morning Miss Moss, the office manager, said how hard we were working and how proud she was of us. And, anyway, where would I go? We haven't got any family I could go to. Besides, I want to be here with you, and I know that you wouldn't leave.'

It was true, Olive was forced to admit. She would never leave London whilst her house was still standing. Olive was very proud of her home and of living on the Row, in the small area that took such a pride in its respectability and its standards. People who lived on the Row felt they had made something of themselves and their lives, and those were things that no one gave up lightly. But much as she loved her home, Olive

37

loved her daughter more, and she knew there was nothing she wouldn't do to keep Tilly safe.

'Where are Agnes and Dulcie?' Tilly asked, wanting to divert her mother's anxious thoughts.

Of the three lodgers, Agnes was the closest in age to Tilly, though her start in life had been very different. Abandoned on the doorstep of the small orphanage close to the church, Agnes had no mother that the authorities had ever been able to trace, nor any other family. Because of that, and because of Agnes's timid nature, the kindly matron of the orphanage had allowed Agnes to stay on well beyond the age of fourteen when most of the orphans were considered old enough to go out into the world, employing her to help out with the younger children in order to 'earn her keep'. When it had become obvious that the country could be going to be at war and the orphanage had had to evacuate to the country, Matron had managed to get Agnes a job with the Underground, and Olive had been asked to take Agnes in as one of her lodgers. By the time Agnes had plucked up the courage to come to see Olive, because of a mix-up Olive had already let the room to Dulcie. Olive had felt terrible when she had realised how vulnerable and alone Agnes was, and very proud of Tilly when she had in-sisted on sharing her room with the girl.

When Agnes had been taken under the wing of a young underground train driver, both she, and then romance, had bloomed, and the young couple were now going steady.

Olive smiled as she reflected on Agnes's quiet happiness now, compared with her despair the first time she had seen her.

'Agnes said this morning that she had volunteered to stay on at work this evening now that London Transport has agreed to open Charing Cross underground station as a shelter if there's an air raid.'

Tilly nodded. There had been a good deal of pressure from people, especially those who were suffering heavy bombing raids, to be allowed to take shelter in the underground where they felt they would be safer than in some of the other shelters. After initially refusing, the authorities had changed their mind when Winston Churchill had agreed with the public, and certain stations were to be opened for that purpose.

'What about Dulcie?' Tilly asked.

'She's been dreadfully worried about her family, especially with her sister being missing, and them living in Stepney, although she's pretended that she isn't. She went over to the East End this afternoon.'

'With that ankle of hers in plaster, and her on crutches?' Tilly protested, horrified. 'Especially now that she's been told she's got to keep the plaster on for an extra two weeks.'

Dulcie hadn't liked that at all, Olive acknowledged ruefully, although when the hospital doctor she had seen before she had been discharged into Olive's care had told them both that it was because Dulcie's ankles were so slender and fine-boned that they wanted to take extra care, Dulcie, being Dulcie and so inclined to vanity, had preened herself a little.

'It's all right,' Olive assured her daughter. 'She

39

hasn't gone on her own. Sergeant Dawson has gone with her. He's got a friend who's a policeman over there who he wanted to look up, so he said that he'd go with Dulcie and make sure that she can manage. She should be back soon, but you and I might as well go ahead and have our tea.'

As she spoke Olive glanced towards the clock, betraying to Tilly her concern for the lodger whom initially Olive had not been keen on at all.

'She'll be all right,' Tilly comforted her mother. Olive smiled and nodded in agreement.

What Tilly didn't know was that Olive's concern for Dulcie wasn't just because of the threat of the Luftwaffe's bombs, and her broken ankle. It had shocked and disconcerted Olive when she had visited the small untidy house in Stepney to tell Dulcie's mother that Dulcie had broken her ankle after being caught in a bomb blast, to recognise that Dulcie was not being sharp or mean when she had said that her mother preferred her younger sister, but that that was the truth. Olive knew that, as the mother of an only and beloved child, she wasn't in a position to sit in judgement on a mother of three, but she had understood in an instant, listening to Dulcie's mother, that the deep-rooted cause of Dulcie's chippiness and sometimes downright meanness to others was because she had grown up feeling unloved by her mother.

And yet despite that, since the bombing had started and in spite of Dulcie's attempts to conceal it, Olive had seen how anxious the girl secretly was about her family, living as they did near the docks,

40

which were the target of Hitler's bombing campaign.

Being the loving, kind-hearted person she was, Olive was now concerned that Dulcie might be hurt by her visit to her old home. Olive had seen for herself when she had gone there on Sunday that Dulcie's mother was beside herself with anxiety for her younger daughter, whilst in contrast she had hardly shown any concern at all for Dulcie.

Not that Olive would discuss any of this with Tilly. Dulcie's home situation was her private business until such time as she chose to air it with the other girls in the house. She hadn't said anything about her concern for Dulcie to Sergeant Dawson either, their neighbour at number 1 Article Row, though he would have understood that concern, Olive knew. He and his wife had, after all, had more than their fair share of personal unhappiness through the loss of the son who had died as a child. Mrs Dawson had never really recovered from the loss and was now something of a recluse. Olive felt rather sorry for Sergeant Dawson, who was by nature a friendly and sociable man – kind, as well, as his offer to escort Dulcie on her visit to see her mother had proved. Dulcie might insist that she could manage perfectly well on her crutches, but Olive had had awful mental images of the air-raid siren going off and Dulcie, all alone, being knocked over in the rush to reach the nearest shelter.

'I saw Sally just before I left work today,' Tilly informed her mother once they were seated at the kitchen table, with its fresh-looking duck-egg-blue, pale green and cream gingham table-cloth, trimmed with a border of daisies, eating the simple but nourishing meal of rissoles made from the leftovers of the special Sunday roast Olive had cooked in celebration of Tilly's birthday, and flavoured with some of the onions Sally had grown in their garden, served with boiled potatoes and the last of the summer's crop of beans.

'She said to tell you that she doesn't know when she'll be home as she's offered to sleep over at the hospital whilst they are so busy. They've had to bring back some of the staff who were evacuated to the temporary out-of-London hospital Barts organised when war was announced.'

Tilly put down her knife and fork, and told her mother quietly, 'Sally said to tell everyone that we should all sleep face down and with a pillow over our heads. That's what all the nurses are doing, because of the kind of injuries people have been brought in with.'

Olive could see that Tilly was reluctant to elaborate, but she didn't need to. Olive too had heard dreadful tales of the kind of injuries people had suffered.

Picking up her knife and fork again, Tilly wished that Sally's advice hadn't popped into her head whilst she was eating, stifling her appetite; no one with anything about them even thought of not clearing their plate of food, thanks to rationing.

As though she had read her thoughts Olive told her firmly, 'Come on, love, eat up. We can't afford to waste good food. There's plenty from the East

End right now that are homeless and with nothing but the clothes they're standing up in who would give an awful lot to be safe in their homes and eating a decent meal.'

Olive's familiar maternal firmness, reminiscent as it was of the days when Tilly had been much younger, made the girl smile, although the truth was that right now there wasn't very much to smile about for any of them.

TWO

'Suture, please, Nurse.'

The surgeon operating on the young child lying motionless on the operating table didn't need to tell Sally what he required. She already had everything ready for him to sew up the wounds to the little boy's body, from which he had just removed several pieces of shrapnel.

Having evacuated most of its staff out of London and closed down all but two operating theatres, which had been moved down to the basement for safety, Barts, like all London hospitals, was now having to cope with a huge influx of patients, many of whom, like this little boy, had very serious injuries indeed.

Those patients who could be moved were being sent out to Barts in the country for treatment, but those whose injuries were too severe, too life-threatening for treatment to be delayed or a long journey undertaken, were having to be operated

43

on here, despite the bombs falling all around.

Down here in the basement, in the focused quiet of the operating theatre, the sound of bombs and anti-aircraft guns had to be ignored.

The operation was over. The consultant surgeon had gone to scrub up for the next one. The young patient was being wheeled out of the operating theatre ready for the porters to take him back to the ward where he would be nursed until – and if – he recovered sufficiently to be transferred to the country.

Sister had disappeared – no doubt to make sure that someone brought a cup of tea for Mr Ward the surgeon.

Sally's boyfriend, George Laidlaw, was one of Mr Ward's housemen, as the junior doctors were called. George was currently on duty in Casualty, where the flood of patients arriving seemed to increase with every bombing raid.

'What have we got up next?' Johnny MacDonald, the anaesthetist, a Scot, asked Sally, tiredly pushing his hand through his thinning ginger hair. Johnny was only in his mid-thirties but tonight he looked closer to fifty, Sally thought, and no wonder. They had almost lost the little boy twice during the op, only Johnny's skill had kept him going.

'Amputation that needs cleaning up,' Sally answered without looking at him. No one liked amputations, and they liked them even less when someone or something else had done the amputating for them – in this case a falling roof slate that had sliced a fireman's leg off just above his knee as he fought to save a burning building down on the docks.

'I thought we were going to lose that wee laddie back there,' the anaesthetist told Sally without saying anything about the next patient.

Sally didn't reply. The reality was that they would probably lose the little boy anyway, and they all knew it. His little body had been pierced with so much shrapnel that it had left him, in the surgeon's own words, 'looking like a sieve'.

Somewhere in the hospital the boy's mother would be waiting and praying, but there was only so much that even the best surgeon could do, and they did have the best here at Barts, Sally thought proudly, as she made her way to the sluice room to scrub up ready for the next operation. However, no matter how hard she scrubbed her hands Sally couldn't rid her nostrils of the smell of blood, nor her mind of images of mangled, maimed bodies. The surgeons had been operating nonstop and suddenly, for no reason that she could think of, to her the smell of blood had become the stench of death. She leaned forward and closed her eyes as a surge of nausea gripped her.

The voice of one of the more senior theatre nurses who had already been in the sluice room, a short, stocky girl called Mavis Burton, reached her.

'Bear up, Johnson,' she said bracingly. 'The theatre porters will be bringing the next patient along any minute.'

Immediately Sally snapped out of her uncharacteristic weakness. 'Sorry about that,' she apologised. 'I don't know what came over me. I'm not

45

normally squeamish.'

The other nurse shook her head. 'It would be hard to be anything else, given what we've been seeing. We all know that nurses are supposed to keep their distance and remember that they've got a job to do, and that weeping and wailing over injured patients doesn't help anyone, but I've got to admit I've seen some things these last few days...' She paused before continuing, 'Mind you, with St Thomas' being bombed on the first night of the blitz and its doctors and nurses risking their own lives in the damage to save patients, they've rather stolen a march on us in terms of showing the Germans what British medical staff are made of.'

St Thomas' was the second oldest hospital in London, and there was a degree of professional rivalry between the two renowned establishments. On Sunday night a bomb had destroyed Medical Out Patients and most of college house, where the doctors were housed, killing two of them.

Only the bravery of three doctors, Mr Frewer, Dr Norman and Mr Maling, had saved two of their colleagues, who had been trapped by falling debris and ignited dispensary stores. Of course, no one working at Barts wanted their own hospital to be bombed, but Mavis was right: the bravery shown by St Thomas' staff had naturally made everyone at Barts feel they had something to live up to.

Two hours later, when Sister Theatre had dispatched her to get herself a cup of tea and have a short break, Sally made her way tiredly to the canteen, almost walking right past George, her boyfriend, who was striding purposefully the other way, his white coat flapping open and his stethoscope round his neck.

'Oh, George, I'm sorry.'

'No need to apologise.' His smile creased his kind face, but he looked as weary as she felt, Sally acknowledged, as he pushed his thick light brown hair back off his face.

George might not be movie-star handsome but there was something about him that was very attractive. He had a kindness and a concern for others, combined with his warm smile and the twinkle in his eyes, that made him popular. Tall and rangy, George had the kind of slight stoop that came from bending over patients' beds, but like all of those who worked with people whose health and lives had been blighted by the blitz of bombing on London, there were shadows at the backs of his eyes now from witnessing such suffering.

'Sister's just sent me to grab something to eat. We've got an impossibly full list. I've never seen anyone operate with the skill and the speed Mr Ward has shown these last few days. We had this little boy in earlier, peppered with shrapnel...'

'I know. I saw him when he was brought in to Casualty earlier.' George rubbed his face with both hands. In common with many of the other medics at the hospital, his jaw was showing the signs of stubble that came from working hours that were far too long and then falling into bed, only to be roused within a couple of hours to deal

47

with another crisis.

They exchanged tired smiles, then both of them stiffened in response to a particularly loud explosion.

George reached out to grab hold of Sally protectively, saying when the building didn't move, 'Not us this time.' But his words were inaudible above the pound of the ack-ack guns.

George was still holding onto her, and Sally looked up at him. She had seen those lean, long-fingered hands of his holding patients with such compassion and kindness. That thought brought a lump to her throat. George was such a good man.

'This so-and-so war,' he groaned. 'More than anything else I want to have the time to court you properly, Sally, as you deserve to be courted, but we haven't got that time. There isn't time to even kiss you any more never mind court you. I've got to get back: Casualty is bursting at the seams with patients we haven't got beds for already, and by the sound of what's going on we're going to have a hell of a lot more to deal with before tonight's over.'

He lifted one of her hands to his lips and kissed it gently.

Her skin should smell of roses, not carbolic soap, Sally thought sadly, but the look she could see in George's eyes said that he hadn't even noticed the carbolic.

'You'd better go and get your tea and I'd better get back to my patients,' he said, releasing her.

Sally nodded and hurried down the corridor, pausing to look back when she reached the end.

48

George was still standing where she had left him, watching her.

She was so lucky to have met him. He was kind and loving and fun to be with. He was also a good doctor who one day would be a first-rate doctor. And a first-rate husband?

It was far too soon to be thinking along those lines, Sally knew, even though she also knew that George himself would love to progress their relationship. There had, after all, been another man in her life she had once hoped to marry. Callum.

She was over Callum now. Callum's refusal to understand the hurt and sense of betrayal she had suffered on discovering that her supposed best friend and her father were involved with one another, had destroyed the feelings she had once had for him. He might have followed her to London after she had fled here, unable to bear to stay in Liverpool and witness the relationship between Morag and her father, but he had not sought her out to beg her forgiveness. No, he had sought her out to tell her that, following their marriage, Morag was expecting a child.

Would she have weakened if he hadn't told her that his sister and her father were expecting a child? No! She wouldn't.

She was happy now, Sally reminded herself. Far, far happier than she had ever expected to be when she had left Liverpool. Where she had had one best friend she now had three very good close friends. Where she had loved a man whose loyalty to her above all others she had not been able to rely on, she was now loved by a man who she knew instinctively would always put her first. There was no going back, nor did she want to do so.

THREE

'But, Mum, you can't just up and leave London.'

As she spoke Dulcie couldn't help looking at the firmly tied and bulging sacks of household goods in the middle of the floor of the main room of her family home, the bed linen tied up in a sheet. The family didn't possess the luxury of proper suitcases. Very few of those living in Stepney did, unless they were the sort that, for one reason or another were constantly on the move. The sort her own parents had always kept clear of and thought were beneath them. The sort that couldn't go to church unless they'd got enough money to get their good clothes out of hock at the pawnshop.

For Dulcie, seeing her parents' possessions gathered together came far too close for comfort to the images from the newspapers she had inside her head: the dispossessed of the East End wandering helplessly and hopelessly through the streets of London clutching their sad bundles of whatever they had managed to rescue from their bombed homes.

The last thing Dulcie had expected when Sergeant Dawson had delivered her to the door of her parents' home, before checking his watch and telling her that she'd got an hour before he came back for her, was that she would find her mother on the verge of leaving London. But her mother's nerves were so shattered by the relentless bombing that her hands had been shaking too much for her to fill the kettle and make them a cup of tea.

Having taken over that task for her, Dulcie had waited for her mother to say something about her accident and to express maternal concern, but she might as well have not bothered because, despite the fact that Dulcie was on crutches with her ankle in plaster, her mother hadn't said a word about her injury, merely greeting her with a blunt, 'Oh, it's you, is it?'

'You can't just leave,' Dulcie reiterated now.

'Oh, can't I? We'll just see about that. It's all right for you, Dulcie, living in Holborn. That hasn't been touched. You're safe. You should have tried living down here since Hitler started bombing us.'

Mary Simmonds' hand shook so much that she had to put her teacup back in its saucer, spilling some of the tea as she did so.

'I didn't get this running for a bus,' Dulcie felt justified in pointing out smartly as she held out her plastered leg, 'and I'm going to have to keep this ruddy plaster on for longer than normal on account of me having such delicate ankles.'

When her mother still didn't say anything Dulcie was unable to prevent herself from adding bitterly, 'Not that you seem to care that much.'

'Oh, that's typical of you, Dulcie. You've always been selfish and thinking only of yourself. Not one word have you said about poor Edith. I can't

51

sleep at night for thinking about what might have happened to your sister, and how she might have suffered. I can't stay here in London, knowing them Germans have taken her life.'

Tears filled Dulcie's mother's eyes, her hands now shaking so badly that she folded them together in her lap as she and Dulcie sat opposite one another on the two hard dining chairs either side of the battered oak table, which had to be pushed up against the wall to make space for people to walk past it. The fire that heated the room was, for once, unlit, the September sunshine cruelly bright on the faded striped wallpaper. The three plaster ducks, which had adorned the wall opposite the fireplace, and of which her mother had been so proud, had been removed, leaving brighter patches of paper. Even the curtains had been taken down, allowing the sunlight to highlight the shabbiness of the room.

It had been in here, on the rag rug in front of the fire, that Dulcie and Edith had squabbled and, indeed, fought, pulling one another's hair and screaming over the possession of some toy; fights that Edith had always won, of course, because she had had their mother to take her side. Now any sisterly sense of loss was stamped out by Dulcie's knowledge that her sister had always been their mother's favourite.

'You don't know that she is dead yet,' she reminded her mother.

Dulcie had never got on with her sister, but deep down, although she wasn't willing to admit it, there was a small scratchy sore place, an unhappy feeling, because several bombs had fallen

52

on the area where Edith had been.

'There's not been any official notice, or any-thing...' A body, Dulcie meant; concrete evidence that Edith was in fact dead, but she couldn't say that to her mother. 'She might just be missing.' But she offered these words more dismissively than comfortingly.

'Missing?' Mary retorted. 'Of course she isn't missing. Me and your dad have been to all the hospitals and all the rest centres. I know my Edith: the first thing she would have done once the air raid was over, if she'd been all right, was come home to let me know that she was safe.' Her voice shook, tears filling her already swollen eyes. 'No. She's gone. Killed by Hitler when she was singing her heart out trying to do her best for other people. The theatre she was in took a direct hit, after all. She didn't have a selfish bone in her body, Edith didn't. Always thinking of others, she was.'

Always thinking of herself, more like, Dulcie thought, but she knew there was no point in saying that to her mother, who had thought that the sun shone out of Edith's backside. It felt odd to think that Edith had gone, that they'd never quarrel with one another again, that she'd never see her sister again. Dulcie's heart started to beat faster, a lump of emotion clogging her throat as unexpected feelings gripped her. There had been no love lost between her and Edith, after all, so there was no cause for her to go all soft about her now. It was a shock, though, to think of her being dead.

Unsettled by her own emotions, Dulcie reached

for her mother's hand but immediately her mother shrugged her off, saying despairingly, 'I don't know how I'm supposed to go on without Edith. She was the best daughter any mother could want.'

A far better daughter than she was, Dulcie knew her mother meant, the brief moment of sadness and loss she had been feeling overtaken by the bitterness their mother's favouritism always aroused in her.

'There's nothing to keep me here now,' her mother continued bleakly.

'What about Dad?'

'Your dad's leaving as well. Dunham's that he works for had their yard bombed and everything in it destroyed, and so Paul Dunham has decided to get out of London and go into business with a cousin he's got who's a builder down in Kent. He's offered your dad a job with him, and there's a couple of rooms we can have with a chap who's already working for this cousin of his. We're going down in Dunham's lorry tomorrow morning.'

For once in her life Dulcie was silent, struggling to take in everything that her mother had told her and all that she hadn't said as well.

'And what about Rick and the Dunhams' son, John?' she finally demanded in a sharp voice. 'What about them when they get leave from the army and find that they haven't got a home to come to any more?'

'Your dad wrote to Rick last night to tell him about Edith and what we're doing.'

'And I suppose you were going to send me a letter as well, were you?' Dulcie asked sarcastic-

54

ally, causing a dull flush of colour to spread up under her mother's previously pale face.

'Don't you take that tone with me, my girl. You were the one who chose to move out and go and live somewhere else.'

'I only moved to Holborn, not Kent, and I came back every Sunday for church,' Dulcie pointed out, using her anger to conceal the pain burning inside her.

'Your dad was going to arrange to send a message round to Holborn to let you know that we're leaving.'

'But you weren't going to take the trouble to come and see me,' Dulcie accused her mother, 'even though you knew I'd got a broken ankle.'

'Trust you to make a fuss about yourself, Dulcie. Your dad and me knew that you were all right and, after all, a broken ankle's nothing compared with what's happened to your poor sister.'

Dulcie didn't know what she might have said to her mother if there hadn't been a knock on the door. She looked at her watch.

'That will be Sergeant Dawson, come to help me get back to Holborn. Luckily for me at least some folk think enough of me to worry about me,' was her parting accusation as she stood up and reached for her crutches, making her way along the narrow hallway to open the front door.

Despite the justification she felt for simply walking away with Sergeant Dawson and slamming the door behind her without another word, somehow Dulcie couldn't stop herself turning back into the house and hobbling down the hall.

'You'd better write and let me know where

you're staying,' she told her mother in a curt voice, 'just in case Rick doesn't get his letter from you and turns up in Holborn, wanting to know where you are.' She paused, whilst her mother wrote down their new address for her and then, against her will and awkwardly, Dulcie leaned forward and kissed her on the cheek. She smelled of dust and tiredness mingled with despair.

If she had hoped to feel her mother's arms coming round her in a maternal hug then Dulcie had hoped in vain because her mother sat rigidly, not kissing Dulcie back or even looking properly at her, staring straight ahead.

It was her mother's lookout if she was too wrapped up in ruddy Edith to remember that she had another daughter, Dulcie told herself fiercely as she rejoined Sergeant Dawson, pulling the door, with its peeling paint, sharply closed behind her, then carefully negotiating the front step. She certainly didn't care!

Wearing her London Transport uniform of grey worsted fabric piped in blue, and trying to look as official as she possibly could, Agnes stood at the top of the stairs leading down into Chancery Lane underground station where she worked, watching the crowd of people making their way down to take refuge in the underground in case the night brought yet another attack from the German Luftwaffe.

When Mr Smith, who managed the ticket office, had asked for volunteers to help organise and keep an eye on things in anticipation of the number of people who would want to use the underground to

56

shelter in, Agnes had been the first to shoot up her hand, but not just because she wanted to do her bit. Ted, the young underground train driver with whom she was walking out, and to whom she was going to become officially engaged at Christmas, had told her that he intended to bring his widowed mother and his two young sisters down to Chancery Lane for protection. This would be Agnes's first opportunity to meet them. Ted had hoped to arrange for them all to meet up at the small café close to the station where Ted and Agnes often went, as Ted had explained to her that his mother was reluctant to invite Agnes round to their home. They lived in a tiny two-roomed flat owned by the Guinness Trust, which provided rented accommodation to respectable but poor working-class families in London.

'The truth is that there isn't room for the four of us to sit down together at the table all at the same time, never mind five of us,' Ted had ex-plained to her, and Agnes had understood. She might have been abandoned at birth by her mother and raised in the orphanage attached to the Row's local church, but Agnes had seen how proud Olive, her landlady, was of her home and she had quickly grasped what Ted was not saying, which was that his mother felt embarrassed about inviting her to their small home. Or at least that was what Agnes hoped Ted had meant. She couldn't quite stop worrying that Ted's mother might think an orphaned girl who didn't know where she came from was not the kind she wanted her son to get involved with. Agnes didn't like thinking about the circumstances of her birth

57

and subsequent abandonment. Doing so made her feel all prickly and upset inside.

Now that the children and staff from the orphanage had been evacuated to the country, the building was used as a drill hall, and potential rest centre, should the unthinkable happen and the area be bombed, making people homeless.

Of course there was no question of her and Ted getting married any time soon. Not with Ted being the only breadwinner in the family and having his mother and two sisters to support. Ted had been honest with her about that, and Agnes fully understood what he had said to her. He wouldn't have been her good kind Ted if he hadn't looked after his family.

Ted was off duty at the moment and he'd told her that he would bring his family down early in the evening to make sure they got settled in a good spot before he went back to work, but the stream of people approaching the station was getting heavier now, and Agnes was worried that she might somehow miss them in the crush.

Predictably, of course, Mr Smith had initially thoroughly disapproved of and objected to the public more or less 'taking it upon themselves', as he had put it, to have the right to sleep in the underground. But once Winston Churchill himself, of whom Mr Smith was a great admirer, had sanctioned this, his objections had slowed to muttered grumbles about the mess people were making, especially those who had no homes to go to any more, and who brought with them what belongings they had been able to salvage.

Agnes, on the other hand, felt sorry for them.

She was so lucky to have her lovely room at number 13 Article Row, her kind landlady Mrs Robbins, and her wonderful friends there, especially Tilly. She didn't want to think of how it would make her feel if she were to lose any of that.

She scanned the growing crowd of people approaching the steps to the underground, searching for Ted's familiar face, feeling both excited and nervous at the prospect of meeting his family – and especially his mother – at last.

However, when they did arrive Agnes almost missed them. An elderly woman was so laden with the weight of her possessions that her slow progress was holding other people up. Some were losing patience and starting to mutter complaints so Agnes stepped in to help her.

Once she got her down the stairs, though, the woman refused to let go of her, and Agnes tried not to react to the musty smell of stale sweat and bad breath coming off her as she dragged the girl closer with one grimy hand to insist, 'I ain't done with you yet, missie. I want you to find me somewhere comfy to put me bed. I've got it rolled up in here.' She patted the bundle Agnes had taken from her. 'Sleep in 'yde Park normally, I do.' She tapped the side of her nose. 'I knows all the ways of avoiding the park keepers, an' all. They won't catch me, they won't, and neither will ruddy Hitler.'

As Agnes guided the woman along the platform one small boy protested to his mother, 'I don't want her near me, Ma. She stinks.'

It was true, and Agnes was glad to escape from her. She was almost at the top of the steps, strug-

59

gling to pick her way through the mass of people coming down, when she heard Ted's voice calling her name. He stood at the top, beaming her a smile.

To other people Ted might be a relatively ordinary-looking young man of middling height, with a wiry frame, mouse-brown hair and ears that stuck out, but to Agnes he was a hero and his bright blue eyes were the kindest she had ever seen.

Immediately she made her way towards him, until he could reach out, grab her hand and haul her onto the top step where he was standing.

'I was getting worried that I must have missed you,' Agnes said breathlessly.

'As if I'd let that happen,' Ted replied with a grin, giving her that special look that made her heart do a somersault.

'Come on, you two,' he called out, reaching into the shadows behind him. 'Come and say hello to Agnes.'

The two small girls who emerged to stand beside him had Ted's brown hair and blue eyes. Their hair was neatly plaited and their eyes filled with apprehension as they pressed closer to their brother, whilst staring saucer-eyed at the crowd which was now pouring down the stairs in front of them.

'Marie, Sonia, you hold tight to your brother's hand. Ted, you just make sure you don't let go of them.'

The small thin woman, who had now materialised on Ted's other side, and who it was obvious from her looks was Ted's mother, hadn't looked at Agnes yet, but Agnes could understand that her first concern must be for her younger children, just as she understood the bashful shyness that kept the two girls themselves silent as they looked swiftly at her, then away again.

'Don't fret, Mum, I've got them both safe.'

The sound of the calm loving reassurance in Ted's voice made Agnes's heart swell with pride. He was so very much the man of the family, the one they all relied on, just as she had known he must be.

'This is Agnes, Mum,' Ted was saying, putting an arm protectively round his sisters' shoulders as he reached for Agnes's hand to pull her gently closer.

But although Ted had drawn them altogether like a proper family, and although he was saying with pride in his voice, 'Come on, girls, give Agnes a smile. After all, she's going to be your sister,' neither of the girls would look at her, and Ted's mother didn't speak to her at all.

Agnes had been used to dealing with girls younger than she was at the orphanage, and she guessed that the girls' reluctance to look at her sprang mainly from shyness, but Ted's mother's refusal to smile or extend her hand to her was another matter.

Instead of responding welcomingly to her, there was coldness and disapproval in Ted's mother's eyes when she looked at her, and hostility too, Agnes feared. But now wasn't the time to do anything about that because suddenly the air was filled with the shrieking rise and fall of the air-raid siren, causing panic to descend on those still at the top of the steps.

'Come on,' Ted instructed his sisters, grabbing each of them by the hand. 'Mum, you take Sonia's hand, and, Agnes, you take Marie's. Don't let go, either of you,' he warned his sisters as he hurried them down the steps. 'Stay close to me, all of you.'

The crowd pressed in on them from all sides, and Agnes felt it was more by good luck than anything else that she managed to keep her feet on the steps. She was sure that she would have panicked herself, worried that she'd fall and be trampled underfoot, if she hadn't had the role of looking after the elder of Ted's two sisters. But she kept hold of the little girl's hand and tried to protect her by keeping as close to her as she could.

They could already hear the planes and they weren't even down at the bottom of the stairs. The dull menacing thrum of their engines became louder with every breath Agnes took, and she tried to ignore the sounds of panic behind her from those who had yet to make it inside, and the angry protests from those already safely installed, objecting to having to make room for more people.

'Come on, this way,' Ted urged his family and Agnes, hurrying them towards a doorway in the wall that led, Agnes knew, to a small storeroom.

'It will be locked,' Agnes told him, breathless with anxiety.

'I've got the key,' Ted responded with a grin. 'Got it off Smithy this morning, only you'd better not let on to anyone else, otherwise we'll be crammed in here like sardines in a tin. Do you fancy that, girls,' he teased his sisters, keeping them in front of him as he let go of their hands to remove the key from his pocket, 'being squashed like sardines?'

Agnes was very conscious of the fact that right now she was squashed up very close to Ted. It made her feel warm and safe and somehow very grown up to be this close to him in this kind of situation. The intimacy between their bodies was that of a couple bonded together by their need to protect the young lives of Ted's sisters, just as one day they would protect their own children.

'In you go, all of you,' Ted told them once he'd got the door open just enough for them to slip in.

'It's dark inside, and I don't like the dark,' little Sonia piped up unhappily.

'There's a light inside, love, but I don't want to switch it on until you're all safely in there,' Ted tried to reassure her.

Agnes guessed that he didn't want to put the light on straight away and alert others to the existence of the small hideaway, so she smiled at the little girl and told her, 'I've got my torch, look...' She flashed it briefly ahead of her so that she could see inside what was little more than a large cupboard. About six feet square, with a washbasin inside, it had some hooks on the wall and three battered-looking bentwood chairs.

'Come on, you two.' Taking charge, Ted's mother went into the storeroom, dragging her daughters with her, but still ignoring Agnes.

'I'd better get back to the office,' Agnes told Ted. 'They'll be expecting me there, seeing as I'm supposed to be volunteering to help out.'

'I'll walk you back there,' Ted told her.

But as he reached for her hand his mother said sharply, 'Ted, the girls are getting upset. You'd better get in here and help me calm them down.'

Agnes could see how torn he was, so she touched his arm and smiled reassuringly. 'I'll be all right. You stay here.'

She could tell that he didn't like letting her go on her own, so she added firmly, 'When people see that I'm in uniform they'll let me through.'

'Ted, your sisters need you,' Mrs Jackson announced in an even sharper tone.

'Mum's a bit on edge and not herself with all this bombing going on,' Ted whispered apologetically to Agnes, giving her hand a little squeeze.

Agnes nodded. She hoped so much that he was right, she thought, as she made her way slowly and with great difficulty through the mass of people filling the platform and back towards the ticket office. She hoped so much that it was only because Ted's mother was worried for her children that she had been so off with her, and not because she didn't like her.

Sergeant Dawson and Dulcie were four houses away from number 13 when they heard the air-raid siren. Without a word the policeman took Dulcie's crutches from her and, wrapping one strong arm around her waist half carried and half dragged her as he ran with her in the direction of her landlady's front door.

Dulcie wasn't the sort to show fear – of anything or anyone – not even to herself. It was a matter of pride, something she had set out to teach herself from the very first minute she had seen her mother gazing into the basket that contained her new baby sister, Edith, with a look of such love in her eyes. So she told herself now that the hammering of her heart was caused by her exertion and not by anything else.

'I hope that they aren't in their Anderson already,' Sergeant Dawson muttered half under his breath as he made to knock on the door, but Dulcie shook her head.

'It's all right, I've got a key.'

However, the door was already being opened by Olive, who exclaimed, 'Thank heavens! I was beginning to worry that you'd be caught out in the open somewhere.'

'Not twice in less than seven days I'm not going to be,' Dulcie grimaced as she took her crutches from Sergeant Dawson, thanked him and hobbled inside. She had to raise her voice to make herself heard over the sound of the sirens, yelling as though in warning to the oncoming bombers: 'You aren't getting a second chance to get me.'

'Come on. I'll help you both down to the Anderson,' Sergeant Dawson told them, also raising his voice, as the noise of the planes' engines vied for dominance with that of the siren.

'You should be getting yourself to safety,' Olive, who had her arm around Dulcie and was guiding her down the hall, protested as he stepped inside and closed the door behind him.

'I'm on ARP duty. I'll have to check the street and make sure that everyone's left their houses, so I may as well start here.'

'Where's Tilly?' Dulcie demanded when they

65

reached the empty kitchen; the anxiety sharpening her voice touched Olive's heart and reminded her of just how much her opinion of this young woman had changed in a year.

'I sent her to the Anderson the minute we heard the siren,' Olive told her.

Meaning that Olive had waited for her, Dulcie recognised. The tears she hadn't allowed herself to cry with her mother now filled her eyes and made her blink determinedly to hide her emotion. Dulcie didn't believe in having emotions, never mind giving in to them. Or at least she hadn't done until the other girls living at number 13 had risked their lives to save hers when they had been caught in the open in the city's first big bombing raid.

That night had bonded them together for ever and had completely changed how Dulcie felt about them and about living at number 13. But most especially it had changed how Dulcie felt about Olive.

Olive was glad of the carefully shielded beam of Sergeant Dawson's torch after they had left the blacked-out house behind and were making their way down the unlit garden path to the Anderson, where, against all the rules, Tilly had the door open, the lit oil lamp glowing out from inside.

There was just time for her to thank Sergeant Dawson yet again before the sound of their voices was drowned out by the incoming bombers, so close now, surely, that Olive didn't dare risk glancing up at the sky as she shooed Dulcie into the shelter ahead of her and then pulled the door closed behind herself.

'Mum said that you'd make it back,' Tilly greeted their lodger. 'She's made you some sandwiches in case you didn't get round to having your tea, and there's a flask here as well.' She held up the flask to show Dulcie, who nodded her head.

It was not in Dulcie's nature to thank others effusively for anything, but there was something in the smile she gave Olive that sent its own special message of all that she now felt for her landlady and her kindness.

'How was your mother, Dulcie?' Olive asked as they all settled themselves on the three bottom bunk beds that formed a U shape at the far end of the shelter. 'Has there been any news about your sister?'

'No. Mum's convinced that Edith's dead, though, and I suppose she must be. She and Dad have been round all the hospitals and the rest centres, and Mum reckons that as Edith would have let her know if she's all right, she must be dead. She says she doesn't want to stay in London any longer. Her and Dad are off to Kent in the morning. Dad's got the promise of a job and somewhere to stay from Paul Dunham. He's the builder Dad already works for, and he's got contacts in Kent. We all used to go to Kent hop picking when I was a kid. Hard work it was as well.'

There was a wealth of bitterness in Dulcie's voice when she talked about her mother that gave away her real feelings, but Olive felt it tactful not to say anything.

The increasing noise of the incoming bombers was now making conversation all but impossible.

Tilly covered her ears, and they all looked upwards at the dark roof of the shelter.

'It will be the docks they'll be after again, not us,' Dulcie mouthed.

'At least we've got the ack-ack guns defending us now,' Tilly mouthed back against the fierce pounding noise from the British gun batteries.

Of course, it was impossible for them to see what was happening as they daren't risk breaking the blackout by opening the door, but they could hear a second wave of bombers directly overhead, whilst the shrill whistle of bombs falling from the first wave could be heard mingled with the dull heavy 'whoomf' sound of the explosions.

'They were saying at work this morning that the docks were burning so fiercely the other night, the wood was reigniting even though the firemen had soaked it and put the fire out once,' Tilly said. 'I never thought before of fire being so dangerous. A fire used to be something I'd look forward to coming home to on a cold winter's day, something that warmed you, not killed you, but now...'

'At least the RAF are giving the Germans a taste of their own medicine,' Dulcie replied, trying to lift Tilly's spirits by reminding her of what they'd heard on the wireless of a night time raid Bomber Command had made on German cities earlier in the week in retaliation for the Luftwaffe's attack on London.

'Time we had those sandwiches, I think,' Olive decided when a fresh crescendo of explosions had both girls looking noticeably pale-faced in the glow of the oil lamp. Olive couldn't forget the danger they had already faced and from which, miraculously, they had escaped safely. They had made light of the experience since, but Olive wouldn't have blamed them if they had shown far more fear now than they were doing.

'Some East Enders we've had at the hospital have been saying that Hitler is only bombing the East End because he wants to get rid of it before he sets himself up in London,' Tilly told her mother. 'He doesn't care how many people he kills and hurts.'

'It's the docks the Germans have been aiming for,' Olive pointed out, 'because they know how important they are for bringing in supplies to keep the country running.'

'They're bombing more than just the docks and the East End now,' said Dulcie 'although it's true that the East End has been the worst hit. There's whole streets gone; nothing left at all except half a house here and there. I saw one when I went to see my mother, where the whole side of the house had been taken off and you could see right into every room. Of course, the downstairs rooms had been cleared. There's looters everywhere, Sergeant Dawson said, nabbing everything they can. But upstairs you could see the bed and all the furniture with a rag rug half hanging off the floor where the wall had gone. I'm glad it wasn't my bedroom. Horrible, it was, with a really nasty green bedspread on the bed. I'd have been ashamed to call it mine.'

Olive reached for the sandwiches, carefully wrapped in a piece of precious greaseproof paper – precious because it was virtually impossible to buy it any more, thanks to the war – and then almost dropped them when the sound of a bomb exploding somewhere close at hand was so loud that both girls immediately clapped their hands over their ears. Putting the sandwiches aside, Olive opened her arms and immediately the girls came to sit one on either side of her so that she could hold them both close. The warmth of them nestling close to her reminded her of something she needed to say to Dulcie.

Olive placed her lips close to Dulcie's ear and told her, 'Dulcie, I've decided that whilst you're off work with your ankle, you don't have to pay me any rent.'

Dulcie opened her mouth and then closed it again. She had been worrying about paying her rent whilst she was off sick and on short wages, but she was a thrifty young woman and she'd worked out that if she was careful she'd got enough in her Post Office book to pay her rent for the six weeks she'd be in plaster. To have Olive tell her that she didn't need to pay her anything for those six weeks wasn't just kind, it was generosity the like of which Dulcie had never previously known.

For a few seconds she was too surprised to say anything, able only to stare at Olive with wide disbelieving eyes, before replying, 'That's ever so good of you, but I'd like to pay half of my rent. I can afford to, and it doesn't seem right you letting me stay for nothing.'

Her offer touched Olive's heart. She knew how difficult it was for Dulcie to be gracious and grateful to anyone, but especially to her own sex,

70

so she gave her an extra hug and shook her head.

'No, Dulcie. I've made up my mind.'

To Dulcie's horror her eyes had filled with tears and now one rolled down her cheek to splash on Olive's hand.

'I've never known anyone as kind as you...' Dulcie began, but what she wanted to say was silenced by the sound of more planes overhead.

There was no need for any of them to speak. They all knew what they were feeling. There were bombs dropping all around them, even though the docks, and not Holborn, were the bombers' targets. Everyone knew that the planes dropped whatever they had left before turning homewards, and if you just happened to be underneath that bomb then too bad.

The night stretched ahead of them, filled with danger and the prospect of death. There was nothing they could do, certainly nowhere for them to run to. They could only sit it out together, wait and pray.

FOUR

When the sound of the all clear brought the three occupants of number 13's Anderson shelter out of their fitful light sleep and Olive opened the door, the sight of the house still standing – and with it, as far as they could see, the rest of Article Row – was a huge relief. They trooped wearily and thankfully back indoors, ignoring the smell of burning in the air, the taste of brick dust, and the sight of the red glare lighting up the sky to the east.

'Nearly four o'clock,' Olive commented, seeing Tilly stifle a yawn. 'That means we can have three hours' decent sleep before we need to get up again.'

Olive had been intending to have a bed put up in the front room for Dulcie because of her broken ankle, but her lodger had insisted that she could and would manage the stairs, and she had been as good as her word. Secretly Olive had been relieved by Dulcie's insistence about this. Olive was very proud of her front room. Upstairs in the bedrooms she still had the dark wood furniture she had inherited, with the house, from her in-laws, but in the front room she had replaced everything.

Olive had redecorated the room herself, painting the walls cream, and the picture rail green to match the smart, shaped plain pelmet, and curtains in a lighter green pattern of fern leaves. During the winter months, drawn over the blackout fabric, the curtains gave the room an air of cosy warmth, whilst in the summer they let in the light. Olive had made the curtains herself using a sewing machine borrowed from the vicar's wife.

A stylish stepped mirror hung over the gas fire. The linoleum was patterned to look like parquet flooring, and over it was a patterned carpet in green, dark red and cream to match the dark green damask-covered three-piece suite. On the glass and light wood coffee table, which was Olive's pride and joy, stood a pretty crystal bowl, which she'd bought in an antique shop just off the Strand. Against the back wall, behind the sofa, was a radiogram in the same light wood as the coffee table.

Olive had been perfectly prepared to push her precious furniture to one side to put a bed up in the room for Dulcie, but Dulcie had gone up in her esteem for insisting on not 'putting her out', as she had called it.

In the ticket office Agnes heard the all clear with great relief. She hadn't really slept at all, partly because of the bombs and partly because of her anxiety about Ted's mother. Now she had to get up and get back to her voluntary duties. Not that she minded. Her truckle bed wasn't very comfortable, and Miss Wood, who also worked in the office and had volunteered to come in overnight, had snored dreadfully.

People were already starting to make their way out of the underground, a small stream of yawning, tired-looking humanity: mothers carrying babies, fathers with children, on their shoulders, families with older children, their silence punctuated by the laughing and whistling of several men who staggered past the ticket office carrying bottles of beer.

Mr Smith, who had emerged from his office looking, Agnes noticed, every bit as spruce as though he had only just arrived at work and not spent the night there, glared after them disapprovingly.

'Disgraceful, carrying on like that. And at a time like this,' he told Agnes.

73

'Perhaps they were trying to cheer themselves up,' she replied.

'Make a nuisance of themselves, more like.'

'I've heard that at some of the undergrounds they've had people organising singsongs,' Miss Wood confided to Agnes, when Mr Smith had gone 'up top' to see 'what was what'. 'I can't see Mr Smith encouraging that here.'

Agnes didn't like to think of how much more damage the bombs must have done overnight. The noise had been dreadful.

Would Ted have time to come into the office to see her? He'd want to see his family safely home, of course, and then he'd have to come back to work himself. She wasn't going to think about Ted's mother not speaking to her. Agnes swallowed hard against the lump in her throat. Ted was her hero and she wanted so very much for his family to like her. There was no getting away from her shaming background, though. As one of the other children at the orphanage had told her, 'If your ma leaves you outside the orphanage and then scarpers, that means that you're a bastard and that you've got bad blood in you 'cos your pa didn't want to marry your ma.'

Agnes had known from the way that Ted talked about his mother and their family life that being respectable was important to her. This thought brought another lump to Agnes's throat, and her eyes began to sting.

It was daylight when Sally left the hospital, with the kind of misty smoke haze hanging over the city that September mornings could bring. But

74

this was a different kind of haze: small black smuts and even hot cinders were floating down from the sky. She could smell burning in the air, a smell with which all Londoners were becoming familiar. This morning's smoky haze smelled unpleasantly of tallow fat. In the direction of the docks a red glow lay on the sky like a painful raised weal on a patient's flesh, betraying the savagery of the wound they had suffered.

Just as Sally had left, one of the theatre porters, also going off duty, had told her with real shock in his voice, 'St Paul's nearly got it last night. Dropped an eight-hundred-pound bomb on it, Jerry did. Landed right in front of the steps and would have blown the whole front to bits, but someone up there,' he had gestured towards the heavens, 'wasn't going to let Hitler get away with that.'

Now Sally felt impelled to go and view the cathedral herself – just to make sure it wasn't damaged.

Of course, the area around it had been cordoned off, and a crowd had gathered at a safe distance. From what she could see, soldiers, the Home Guard, policemen and fire fighters were all busy working by the steps.

'Got to dig the bomb out, and that will take some doing,' a man standing next to Sally informed her.

'They'll have the bomb disposal lot in, of course,' another man put in, older and possibly ex-military himself, from his upright bearing.

As comments and opinions flew back and forth – East End accents mingling with upper class and

75

the falsely 'refined' tones adopted by those who wanted to 'better themselves' – the fate of Sir Christopher Wren's cathedral drew the people of the city together in a common cause.

Once she had assured herself that St Paul's was undamaged, Sally started to make her way back to Article Row. At least working nights meant that she was avoiding the sleeplessness of night raids. She'd never thought it lucky to be doing night shifts before, she smiled to herself ruefully, acknowledging the shouted, 'Watch out for the hoses,' from a fireman with a nod of her head, as she stepped carefully over them.

From the evidence of the large basket on the other side of the street, incendiaries had obviously been dropped. These bombs were easy enough to put out if one was swift to collect them on a shovel and douse them in water or sand before the chemicals inside them exploded, but the baskets in which they were dropped contained hundreds, and even the most fleet-footed fire watcher couldn't possibly extinguish them all. Once the fires took hold, no building was safe. Apart from shattered windows, the buildings either side of the road seemed to be intact, although from the evidence of so many hoses, their interiors would now be soaked and damaged, Sally thought sympathetically.

A flat-bed lorry was parked at the end of the street, a salvage team working busily to clear up the mess of roof slates, and broken glass. Sally could see two men removing broken glass from one of the windows, one of them giving a warning shout to the other as a large piece from higher up fell towards him.

As though she was watching it in horrific slow motion Sally saw the man giving the warning putting out his hand towards his workmate; saw this man looking up and then stepping back and stumbling; the glass catching the morning light; the sticky tape that had once secured the edges rolled back in pale brown ringlets. She saw the glass slicing into the first man's arm; the bright plume of arterial blood shooting upwards; the silence and then the frantic surge of men towards their injured comrade.

Sally ran to the men. 'Don't try to remove the glass,' she said quickly. 'I'm a nurse. Barts.'

The men immediately fell back respectfully, except the one supporting the injured man.

'He needs to get to hospital,' he told her unnecessarily, his voice gruff with shock.

'Yes,' Sally agreed, kneeling down beside the injured man, who was now looking, to her, that familiar shade of grey-green white that came with shock and loss of blood. 'But first we need to tourniquet his arm.' Because if they didn't he wouldn't get there at all, at least not alive, Sally recognised, although she didn't say that to the men.

'There's a first-aid kit in the cab of the fire engine,' a fireman who had come to offer help told her. 'Do you want it?'

'Yes, please.' Sally gave a small silent prayer of thanks for the insistence of the powers that be that first-aid kits were carried, whilst she applied what pressure she could to the artery still pumping out blood.

'Pity we can't get the Thames to give us that kind of pressure for our pumps,' another of the firemen who had now gathered around joked in that way that men do when they are desperately concerned.

'I'll be all right, Nurse, if you can just take this glass out of me arm,' the injured man assured her in a thready thin voice.

'I'm sorry, I'm not allowed to do that. Doctors all over London will go on strike if a mere nurse takes over their duties,' Sally responded. 'We need an ambulance or, failing that, stretcher,' she told the other men without turning her head.

She was already concerned that her patient might lose his arm, and she dare not risk trying to remove the glass in case she caused even more damage. Her comment about doctors, though, seemed to reassure them because they started telling her that they'd rather have a nurse treating them than a doctor any day. Meanwhile Sally had seen some men hurrying away in search of an ambulance, and the nearest ARP post.

Two of the firemen were back, one carrying the fire engine's first-aid kit, which was placed on the ground and opened for her.

'I'll need a nice short straight piece of wood for the tourniquet,' she told them, and almost before she had got the tourniquet bandage in place, exactly what she needed had been produced.

It was a relief to get the tourniquet on. The man had already lost a serious amount of blood, and was now unconscious. Sally didn't like the colour of him, or the weakness of his pulse, now that his body had gone into shock from the accident. She hoped that an ambulance turned up soon, because she didn't hold out much hope of his surviving for very much longer without proper medical attention.

'Here comes the stretcher.'

Sally turned to see two ARP wardens hurrying towards her with it.

'It's going to be a while before we can get an ambulance to you. The ambulance service has been overwhelmed with calls,' one of the wardens told her.

How long was 'a while'? The man desperately needed hospital attention. Sally looked towards the empty flatbed lorry belonging to the salvage crew and made up her mind.

'We can get him onto the stretcher and then, provided he wasn't the driver of the lorry...?' She paused.

'He wasn't, miss, I mean, Nurse,' one of the men told her. 'John here is the driver.'

John, bashful and very young, removed his cloth cap as he was pushed forward by the others, and rubbed a hand over his dust-covered face before confirming that he was indeed the driver.

The main problem, as far as Sally could see, was going to be the piece of glass firmly embedded in her 'patient's' arm and which must stay there.

'I'll need enough men to get...' she paused and John the driver supplied her patient's name, as 'Eric', revealing two missing teeth as he did so.

'...We need to get Eric onto the stretcher and then into the lorry as carefully as possible. I'll stay with him and hold onto his arm and the glass. We need to keep both as still as we can,' she explained to the men.

If one of the many newspaper photographers recording the devastation left by the bombs had been around, he would have got a photograph like no other, Sally thought ruefully when, in order to carry out her instructions, the salvage men, along with the firemen, formed a group to lift not only their workmate, but Sally herself, bodily into the back of the flat-bed truck.

Not that any of the men took advantage of that intimacy – far from it; their reluctance to look at Sally as they lifted her assured her of their respect.

Instead of an ambulance siren to speed their progress, an ARP warden rode with Sally and the four men who were holding down the stretcher, and the warden blew his regulation whistle to clear the way.

The only time they were stopped was when a policeman stepped out into the road in front of them, tilting back his helmet as he demanded to know why the warden was blowing his whistle when there wasn't an air raid on. However, as soon as the situation was explained to him they were waved on their way with great alacrity.

Although Sally's amateur stretcher-bearers had made a Herculean effort to keep the stretcher steady, when she could see the entrance to Bart's casualty department ahead of them Sally felt very relieved. Eric was still unconscious and his breathing had become worryingly shallow and fast. Her own fingers were practically numb from holding his arm with one hand and the glass with the other, and she was praying that she could continue to keep hold. At least he wasn't losing blood any more, thanks to the tourniquet.

The very moment they came to a halt an indignant ambulance driver came rushing over to the lorry.

'You can't park here, mate. This is for ambulances only.'

'This is an emergency,' Sally could hear the ARP warden telling him from the passenger window of the driver's cab. 'Take a look in the back and see for yourself.'

The next minute an ambulance driver's head appeared over the side of the lorry, his eyes widening as he took in the scene at a glance.

'Cor blimey,' he exclaimed, then called out to his partner, 'Frank, get some porters here, will you, mate?'

Once again all the men studiously avoided looking at Sally as she was lifted out of the lorry along with her patient, and it was with great relief that she found Sister Casualty waiting to take over the minute they got inside the hospital.

Sister Casualty's sharp knowledgeable eyes took in the situation at a glance, her voice calm and modulated into the tone that Sally remembered being taught to use in extreme emergencies so as not to frighten the patients, as she instructed the porters, 'Straight to the top of the queue for this one, I think, please,' before giving Sally a brisk nod of her head and asking almost casually, 'Would you like someone else to take over there for you, Nurse?'

'I'll hang on, if that's all right, Sister. Might as well see it through,' Sally responded in the same almost offhand tone, as though there were no emergency at all.

Despite the heaviness of the Casualty staff's workload, within seconds – or so it seemed to Sally, who was beginning to feel slightly light-headed – Eric was in a hospital bed with her still holding both his arm and the piece of glass, the curtains had been pulled round the bed and the senior registrar was bending over Eric's arm.

'Did you see what happened, and if so, any idea how deep it's gone in, Nurse?' he asked her.

'At least as far as the bone, I think,' Sally responded. 'Definitely deep enough to cut an arterial vein.'

'Mmm. If you can hang on we'll give him a shot of morphine and then take a proper look.'

Sally nodded.

'Not one of these nurses that is likely to faint on me are you?'

'Nurse Johnson is a theatre nurse, Mr Pargiter. I doubt anything is likely to make her faint,' Sister Casualty's voice came to Sally's rescue, leaving Sally to marvel at Sister Casualty's knowledge – until she caught a glimpse of George standing behind her.

'Come and have a look at this, Laidlaw,' the senior registrar told George. 'Damn near sliced the whole arm off, by the looks of it. But for the quick thinking of this nurse, the chap wouldn't be here now.'

'It was nothing. I just happened to be passing when the glass fell. He and some other men were

82

demolishing a burned-out building.'

Sister Casualty herself administered the morphine. She had arrived accompanied by a slightly green and very round-eyed nurse – still a probationer, Sally saw from her uniform – and a more senior nurse pushing an instrument trolley.

'Heart's beating a bit too fast for my liking,' the senior registrar told George. 'What we've got to hope is that we can get the glass out without it breaking. Didn't happen to see what it looked like before it went in, did you, Nurse?'

'Long and sharply pointed V-shape,' Sally responded.

'Mmm, well, at least that means that it isn't likely to have splintered already on impact with the bone, but we'll be lucky if the tip doesn't break off when we remove it. What I want you to do, Nurse, is to keep holding the glass steady but move your hands up a little so that I can get hold of it.'

Sally could see the look Sister Casualty was giving her. A look that said she would be letting all Barts' nurses down if she misjudged things. George, on the other hand, was giving her a look of total reassurance. She just hoped his faith in her was justified. She could almost feel the silence in the small curtain-enclosed area as she very slowly and carefully moved one hand and then the other further up the glass. Her whole body felt as though it were trembling inside, but she knew she must not allow that tremor to get into her hands.

Even when Mr Pargiter had placed his hands on the glass below her own, Sally hardly dare so much as exhale in case she jarred the glass.

'Come over here, Laidlaw, and see if you can tell just what we're dealing with,' the senior registrar instructed George.

Watching her boyfriend carefully exploring the site of the wound with one of the instruments from the trolley, his whole concentration on his task and the patient, Sally was filled with fresh admiration and respect, not just for George but for the hospital that had trained him.

'One side's pressed up close to the bone. Hitting it must have deflected the glass.'

'What I want you to do now is get under the tip of the glass and support it, but first we'll need you and Nurse Johnson to hold his forearms steady, if you please, Sister.'

At a brief nod from Sister Casualty, Sally went to Eric's injured arm whilst Sister Casualty took the other arm.

Now Sally really was holding her breath. Eric was still unconscious, now thanks to the morphine, but it was still possible that he might jerk his body – with potentially fatal consequences – under the exploration George had to carry out unless they held him still.

George leaned over the patient. Sally clenched her teeth when she heard the sound of the metal instrument grating against the glass.

'Got it?' Mr Pargiter asked.

'Yes,' George confirmed.

'Right.'

Slowly and carefully the senior registrar started to lift the glass from Eric's arm, the involuntary flinch Sally could feel gripping the muscles of his upper arm automatically causing her to press down on it more firmly.

'Got it.'

There was a note of quiet satisfaction in the senior registrar's voice, and a good deal of pride in Sally's heart when he added, 'Nice work, Laidlaw. Now we need to get him cleaned up. Not sure whether or not he'll be able to keep his arm, mind you. Still, he's a lucky blighter that you were around, Nurse.'

A little later, setting off for the second time in one morning for number 13 and her bed, Sally promised herself that this time she would go straight back without taking any diversions. She was so tired that she dare not even blink in case she fell asleep.

FIVE

'Hello, Kit. I haven't seen you all week. Are you going to St John Ambulance tonight?' Tilly asked Christopher Long, catching up with him when she saw him walking down the Row in front of her, no doubt making his way to work.

Kit, who lived with his recently widowed mother at number 49, was in the civil service. He was also a conscientious objector, something that Nancy in particular was inclined to make disparaging remarks about. Tilly felt sorry for Mrs Long, but more so for Kit, with his awkward uncoordinated walk, and his introverted nature.

'I won't be there tonight,' he answered her. 'I won't be able to make it.'

'You aren't not, not coming because one of the girls was so silly and mean the other week, are you?' Tilly asked, remembering how unkind another member of their group had been to Kit when he had first joined.

'No,' he answered her shortly, increasing his pace.

'Then why aren't you coming?' Tilly persisted, hurrying to keep up with him. 'I wanted to practise my bandaging on you,' she teased him, hoping to bring a smile to his face, but, if anything, he looked even more miserable.

'If you must know, I can't come. You'll have to find someone else to bandage, because I've got to go to enlist for bomb disposal training.'

Tilly couldn't contain either her gasp of shock or her disbelief. 'But you're a conscientious objector,' she protested.

'That means I don't believe in wounding or killing other people. According to the Government, that doesn't include not wanting to be wounded or killed myself,' he informed her bitterly, 'which is why I have to report tonight to enlist. Enlistment, medical check, uniform collection...' he ticked them off on thin trembling fingers, '...and then I'll be off somewhere to be trained in how ultimately to kill myself, seeing as that's what seems to happen to bomb disposal men.'

He was right, Tilly knew. It had been in the papers how many men were killed when the bombs they were trying to make safe exploded.

'I don't understand. Why are you doing it if you

don't want to? You're in a reserved occupation,' Tilly pointed out.

'You mean I was. We've got a new boss in our department. He doesn't like me and he's moved me to a non-reserved job, just because his own son has joined up and he thinks everyone else should do the same.'

Tilly didn't know what to say. It was plain to her that Kit was very upset. His Adam's apple wobbled when he spoke and his naturally pale face looked whiter than ever.

'It might be better than you think,' she tried to console him, biting her lip when he turned to her with a burning look in his eyes and demanded, 'How?' before walking away at a speed that told her that he didn't want her to catch up with him.

'Dulcie, you've got a visitor,' Olive told her lodger. 'A Lizzie Walters. She said she's come from Selfridges to see how you are. I've put her in the front room. You go in and I'll bring you each a cup of tea.'

It was half-past two, just about an hour since the all clear had sounded after a daylight air raid, during which Olive, Dulcie and Sally had all had to take refuge in the garden shelter.

'Another blinking raid, that's all we need,' Dulcie had huffed in complaint, before adding darkly, 'Mind you, it is Friday the thirteenth.'

'I didn't have you down as superstitious, Dulcie,' Sally laughed.

'I'm not,' Dulcie defended herself with her customary smartness, pointing out, ''Cos if I was I wouldn't be living here at number thirteen would I?'

Now they were back in the house, Sally had returned to bed, after the quick soup lunch. Olive was a firm believer in the efficacious effect of a warming bowl of soup, as comforting as it was nutritious. Her soup had been made from the last of the summer's home-grown tomatoes. Dulcie had been reading *Picture Post* when she and Olive had heard the knock on the front door.

Putting down the copy of *Picture Post*, Dulcie now stood up and leaned against the kitchen table to reach for her crutches.

Olive had gone to Selfridges to tell Dulcie's manager what had happened, and had come back with a message that Dulcie was to stay off work until she could walk properly, so that was exactly what Dulcie intended to do. She hadn't really been expecting a visit from any of her work colleagues, even Lizzie, who worked on the counter closest to her own, Lizzie being on bath salts and the like, and Dulcie being on a much more glamorous makeup and scent counter.

Small, homely-looking and now engaged to her long-term boyfriend, who was in the army, Lizzie was kind-hearted enough – not like Dulcie's arch enemies at Selfridges, Arlene on one of the other makeup counters, and Lydia, the ultra-snooty daughter of one of the store's directors. Not that they saw much of Lydia in the store since she had married her barrister and now RAF fiancé, David. Even so, Dulcie didn't want Lizzie getting the impression that she was not suffering with her broken ankle, so she wasn't at all pleased when the first thing Lizzie said to her when Dulcie hobbled into Olive's front room was an envious, 'Well, aren't you the lucky one?'

'Lucky? With me ankle in plaster and being on crutches?' Dulcie scoffed. 'I don't think so.'

'I certainly wouldn't mind a bit of time off work right now, with all these bombs falling,' Lizzie told her. 'It took me nearly two hours to get into work this morning, the trains were running that slow, and there's me worrying myself sick about the bombs.'

'Never mind being off work,' Dulcie retorted in typical fashion, 'what about not getting my wages, and ruining my best shoes? I suppose Selfridges have sent you to spy on me, have they, to make sure that I'm not swinging the lead?'

'Of course they haven't, and if they had asked me to I wouldn't,' Lizzie responded indignantly. 'I was worried about you. Mind you, it looks as though you've got yourself a really nice billet here.'

'Of course it's nice. You don't think I'd stay anywhere that wasn't, do you?'

Dulcie had never told anyone at work that she came from the East End. Some of the girls were so snooty they'd have refused to have anything to do with her or, worse, made fun of her, and now she was glad that it was here in Olive's house that Lizzie had come to see her.

'Everyone was really shocked when they heard what happened.'

'Everyone?' Dulcie raised an eyebrow. 'What, you mean including Arlene?'

'She's leaving. She said so this morning. She

89

said that her parents don't think it's safe for her to come in to London to work any more and they certainly don't approve of her having to do fire duty up on the roof, like Mr Selfridge had us all trained to do, before he stepped down and retired.'

'That's typical of Arlene, running home to her mum and dad. Not that I'm going to miss her. Got right up my nose, she did, always making out she was something special.'

'She's not the only one who's left.' Lizzie stopped speaking when Olive opened the door and came in with cups of tea on a tray for them both.

'I'm just off out now to the WVS, I don't know when I'll be back,' she told Dulcie.

'None of us know if we're even going to get back at all these days,' Dulcie pointed out truthfully, which made Lizzie shiver slightly.

'I wish you hadn't said that,' she complained, as the door closed behind Olive. 'It's made me start worrying about my Ralph all over again. I still can't believe I'm actually going to be marrying him in three weeks' time.'

A dreamy look came over her face and Dulcie eyed her with irritation. Lizzie was supposed to be here asking after her, not mooning over her fiancé and their wedding.

'Of course, I'll be staying at home with my parents, with him being in the army, but like he says, it will be company for me. Oh, I nearly forgot! Arlene said this morning that she'd heard that Lydia's husband, who joined the RAF, has been shot down and is in hospital, badly injured.

I know you never liked Lydia, Dulcie, but you can't help feeling sorry for her.'

Dulcie, who had just picked up her teacup, put it down again abruptly, keeping her face averted from Lizzie as she told her in a sharp voice, 'If I were to feel sorry for anyone it would be for him, for being married to her.'

'That's typical of you, Dulcie, it really is, making a remark like that. Of course you always did have a bit of a soft spot for him, I seem to remember,' Lizzie scolded her good-naturedly.

'Well, you remember wrong,' Dulcie snapped rudely.

'You wanted him to take you out dancing,' Lizzie reminded her, holding her ground.

'Only because of her – Miss Smarty Pants – and the way she carried on like we were all beneath her and she was something special, that was all. It had nothing to do with him,' Dulcie retaliated swiftly.

David – shot down and badly injured. David, with his thick well-groomed head of hair, his knowing and amused hazel eyes. Somehow it didn't seem possible. That was the kind of thing that happened to ordinary men, not posh men with double-barrelled names and a title to look forward to, like handsome, charming David James-Thompson, whose sense of entitlement to be what he was through birth and upbringing had secretly been one of the things that had attracted Dulcie to him.

Attracted her to him? He had meant nothing like that to her, she reminded herself. She had just flirted with him, that was all, and only then

91

to annoy Lydia. After all, she had turned him down when he had offered her a bit of fun on the side, hadn't she? Sent him packing straight off! David... Dulcie could see him now striding in through the doors of Selfridges and smiling at *her*, even though it had been Lydia he had been walking out with. Dulcie had known then from the look in his eye that he liked her. She could have taken him off Lydia good and proper if she had really wanted him.

'What do you mean, badly injured. How badly injured?' Somehow the words had been uttered through her dry lips and throat without her being able to stop them.

Lizzie gave her a shrewd look.

'I'm only asking,' Dulcie defended herself, shrugging angrily. 'Can't a girl ask? Only a couple of minutes ago you were accusing me of being unfeeling and now when I show some feelings you're giving me that kind of look.'

'I don't know how bad his injuries are,' Lizzie answered, her expression softening.

Lizzie liked Dulcie even though she knew that she wasn't very popular with some of the other girls. That was because Dulcie, with her long blonde hair, her big brown eyes and her curvaceous figure was so very, very pretty. Dulcie being so very pretty and so very forward and flirtatious didn't worry Lizzie. Her husband-to-be was the steady, serious type who would run a mile from a girl like Dulcie, but some of the girls they both worked with excluded Dulcie because, Lizzie suspected, they felt that if they welcomed her into their groups she would cast them into the shade. And knowing Dulcie, she probably would, Lizzie thought ruefully. She had certainly made it plain when she had first seen David James-Thompson that she wasn't going to let the fact that he was virtually engaged to Lydia Whittingham stop her from flirting with him.

Remembering that, Lizzie felt bound to remind Dulcie warningly, 'It's Lydia, his wife, who'll be most concerned about that and about him, especially with them not being married all that long.'

'She certainly won't be pleased if it means there's not going to be any little James-Thompson heirs coming along,' Dulcie said frankly. 'And neither will that snobby mother of his. She was the one who was desperate for him to marry Lydia, not David himself.'

Lizzie was scandalised. 'You can't know that, Dulcie, and it's a mean thing to say.'

'It's the truth and I do know it,' Dulcie retaliated. 'David told me himself that his mother is a snob.'

'I thought you said you barely knew him. Him telling you things like that doesn't sound much like you barely knew him to me.'

Lizzie had caught her out and Dulcie knew it. But Dulcie wasn't the kind to give in – over anything.

'So him and me just got talking to one another – that doesn't mean anything.'

Only, of course, they had done far more than just talk. David had kissed her and she had let him. Dulcie would never let her heart rule her head, but there had been something in that kiss that had left her feeling unexpectedly vulnerable.

'Not to you, perhaps,' Lizzie agreed, 'but I dare say that Lydia wouldn't like it very much if she knew that her husband had been exchanging confidences with you. I wouldn't like it myself...

'Oh, did I tell you that we've managed to book an hotel for our honeymoon?' she demanded, her own upcoming marriage pushing everything else out of the way. 'It's only for the one night, 'cos my Ralph can only get a forty-eight-hour pass, but we've managed to get booked in at this hotel in Southend, although heaven knows how long it will take us to get there, the trains being as slow as they are right now and filled with troops. I can't wait...' she sighed, that dreamy look on her face again.

'What for?' Dulcie said scathingly. 'To start slaving away for a man? You'd never catch me doing that. And that's what men expect once you marry them. A girl's better off single, and being treated like she's special.'

SIX

'I heard that Buckingham Palace was bombed this morning in that raid we had, and that the King and Queen only just escaped being hit,' Mrs Windle told Olive as she sat next to her in the front passenger seat of Gerry Lord's van. Gerry's parents, who owned a local grocery shop, had loaned the van to the WVS whilst Gerry was in the army. Olive and Mrs Morrison, another

94

WVS member had been taught to drive it by Sergeant Dawson. Now Olive was driving as many of their group as had been able to cram into the small van towards the rest centre where they were to be on duty that afternoon to help those who had lost their homes and their possessions in the bombings.

It wasn't easy driving through London with so many streets blocked off because of damaged buildings and unexploded bombs, but Sergeant Dawson had taught Olive well.

'But the King and Queen are all right, aren't they?' Olive asked Mrs Windle anxiously.

'Yes, thank goodness. I do admire them for insisting on staying in London. It sets us all such a good example.'

'It's no picnic, though, is it?' Nancy Black, Olive's next-door neighbour complained.

'No, it isn't,' someone agreed. 'We were without electricity, gas and water on Sunday.'

'Do you think it's really true that Hitler is about to invade?' Mrs Morrison asked from the back of the van, whilst Olive drove carefully round a bomb crater in the road, and then equally carefully over the fire hoses that lay beyond it. Blackened buildings still smoked and Olive glimpsed a small party of people, white-faced with plaster dust, being escorted away from a half-collapsed house by two rescue workers.

'Well, Mr Churchill seems to think so, since he warned us all about it last Wednesday on the wireless,' another member of the group answered.

Olive's hands tightened on the steering wheel of the Austin van. She tried not to think about what

95

would happen if Hitler did invade. To do so would be to add another layer of fear to those the war had already brought. No woman with a young daughter who had just entered womanhood could help but be fearful of what an invasion would mean for that daughter, never mind for the country itself.

'The RAF will never let Hitler invade, and neither will Mr Churchill.' Mrs Windle spoke up firmly. 'I've heard that with every raid the Germans make, our boys are shooting down more of their planes.'

That was the kind of stirring talk they all needed to hear, Olive acknowledged gratefully.

'Well, of course you're bound to say that, Mrs Windle, with your nephew being in the RAF,' Nancy replied, 'but if you don't mind me saying so, I think the RAF have been a bit slow off the mark. Where were they on Saturday night when the raids first started? That's what I want to know.'

It was typical of Nancy that she should find fault, Olive thought, as she started to turn into a street and then had to reverse when she saw it was blocked halfway down by a fire engine.

She felt rather sorry for Mrs Windle, and cross with Nancy when the vicar's wife leaned close and whispered to Olive, 'I can't say so publicly, of course, Olive, but my nephew hinted to us that the reason the RAF didn't appear the first night of the bombs was because they'd been ordered not to. Apparently the authorities wanted the Germans to think that they'd done for the RAF so as to give our boys a better chance of getting more of them now. The Battle of Britain lost us so many planes and pilots that they needed to build up the numbers again. Not that I'd want to say anything about this to Mrs Black.'

Olive nodded, knowing what a gossip Nancy could be.

'I dare say there's a lot goes on that we don't know about,' she said to Nancy, in support of Mrs Windle.

Olive felt that that was the truth, but she was glad that she wasn't the one who had to make what must be very difficult decisions, putting the future of the country in the long term above the safety of some of its people in the short term.

The next street was passable and within a few minutes she was able to park the van outside the school that had been taken over as a rest centre.

'Just look at that queue, poor souls,' said Mrs Morrison, as they passed the long straggling line made up mainly of worn-down-looking women and grubby children, some of the women clutched bundles of possessions, others tightly gripped the hands of their pale-faced, undernourished-looking children.

Poor souls indeed, Olive thought compassionately. The East End wasn't that far, as the crow flew, from Article Row but, in terms of how so many of its people lived, it was almost another world.

'I hope you've remembered to bring that disinfectant spray, Olive,' Nancy warned, running true to form as she gave a dark look in the direction of the queue.

Olive exchanged a rueful look with the vicar's

wife. It was true that the smell from some of the really poor people from the East End was very pungent and unpleasant, but one had to be charitable and do the best one could to ignore it, and to think how lucky one was to have the life one did.

'A cousin of mine who works as a social worker told me yesterday that she'd had to cover her nose with a handkerchief soaked in eau-de-Cologne when she went with a group of dignitaries to inspect one of the public shelters. No toilet facilities,' Mrs Morrison explained succinctly. 'Apparently the council had simply not thought to provide anything more than a couple of buckets and a curtain. They'd had over four hundred people crammed into the shelter, so you can imagine the result.'

'Some councils have been very lax about providing adequate resources in the shelters,' Mrs Windle agreed.

Their WVS uniforms proclaimed their status and their purpose, allowing them to go ahead of the queue into the school, where they were welcomed with relief by the hard-pressed volunteers.

In a cloakroom to the rear of the main school hall, with its green paint and wooden floors, Olive removed her smart WVS jacket and hung it on a peg. The smell of chalk, damp woollen coats, and cabbage, which hung in the air, took her back to her own schooldays. She took an apron from her basket and put it on to protect her uniform blouse and skirt, whilst a weary-looking fellow WVS volunteer waited for her.

'As people come in we try to find out their

98

situation and then we divide them into three different queues,' she explained to Olive. 'One for people who have lost everything – that's the hardest queue to deal with, and the longest I'm afraid. Some of them are in such a state that they can barely comprehend what's happened to them. They need everything: new ration books and papers, somewhere to sleep; food, clothes... We explain to them where to go to get their replacement papers, give them a cup of tea and something to eat here, and some clothes. We're using one of the classrooms to store all our second-hand clothes in. They can go there and be issued with whatever they need, and then we hand them over to the billeting officers at the other end of the hall. We've got a fully operational canteen here, with it being a school, so they can get a proper meal, but what we could do with is better washing facilities.' She pulled a tired face. 'The local public baths are still operational so we're sending people down there. It's all a bit of a muddle, really, but we're doing our best.

'Some of them come in with the most pitiful stories. There was a woman this morning who never spoke, she simply stared at me, and then another woman who was her neighbour told me that her little girl had run back into the house for her doll just as a bomb struck it. All they found of her was one of her shoes. It really makes you think, doesn't it?'

'It certainly does,' Olive agreed quietly as she followed her guide towards the long row of trestle tables behind which the WVS volunteers were seated to deal with the queue as it filed into the building.

Olive sighed a little when she realised that Nancy had taken the seat next to her. Olive was a peaceable person but Nancy's acerbic tongue and lack of compassion for others could be a trial at times. They had had words over Olive learning to drive. Nancy hadn't approved at all, but Olive had stuck to her guns and now she was glad that she had done so.

The first person Olive dealt with was a young mother with two children clinging to her legs.

Tired and unkempt-looking, with a thin face and wary eyes, the woman announced immediately, 'I'm not having you taking the kiddies from me. Not for anything, I'm not. We might have been bombed out but that doesn't give no one the right to take my kiddies.' Her voice was high and strained, rising in volume as she spoke.

'Of course you want them to be with you,' Olive agreed gently. Like their mother, the children looked underfed. Gently she coaxed the mother to give her her name and those of her children.

'And your address?' she asked patiently.

'We haven't got no address, not any more. Blown up, it was.' The woman started to shake.

'You stay here,' Olive told her. 'I'm going to go and get you a nice hot cup of tea and some biscuits for the children. And don't worry, we'll get everything sorted out for you.'

'You're too soft by half that's what you are,' Nancy chided Olive later when they were having their break.

'I can't help thinking how I'd feel if I were in

their shoes, Nancy,' Olive replied.

'Well, for all you know we may be soon, if Hitler keeps up this bombing. Not that you'd ever get me coming in somewhere like this, all covered in dust and looking like a scarecrow. Mrs Dawson wasn't at church again on Sunday,' she told Olive as they queued together to get tea from the large urn standing on the table in the classroom that had been designated for the volunteers' tea breaks.

Automatically Olive delved into her bag for her mug – one soon learned that it helped others if you were as organised as possible – putting it under the tap on the urn to fill it with strong hot tea.

'She's always kept herself very much to herself,' Olive reminded her neighbour as she added a dash of milk and then wrapped her hands round the hot mug. It was only September and warm outside – the burning buildings had seen to that – but inside the school there was that lack of warmth that Olive remembered from her own schooldays.

'And who can blame her, with that husband of hers carrying on the way he does with other women?' Nancy pursed her lips in a disapproving manner whilst Olive gazed at her in astonishment.

'Nancy, what on earth are you saying? Sergeant Dawson is a good husband, and a good man.'

'Well, you would say that, you being taken in by him, but I've got eyes in my head. I saw him going into Mrs Long's house this morning and he didn't come out again until after the all clear

101

went. What was he doing there all that time, I'd like to know?'

Olive frowned. She didn't like argument or quarrels, and she had no idea just why Nancy seemed to have taken so against Sergeant Dawson, but she couldn't allow her to talk about him in that way.

'That's a terrible thing to say,' she told her quietly but firmly. 'I'm surprised at you, Nancy, making such suggestions against Sergeant Dawson. I dare say the reason he was at Mrs Long's was to make sure she was safely in her Anderson shelter. He probably stayed with her until the all clear had gone out of kindness. You know how nervous Mrs Long is now that she's widowed, and Christopher's not always there.'

'Oh yes, we all know about the kind of men who have wives of their own but go round preying on lonely women. Look at the way Sergeant Dawson's been buttering you up, Olive. I'm surprised at you being taken in by him, I really am. Not that I'm saying that you'd do anything wrong, but like I've warned you before, people notice these things and you did spend a lot of time with him when he was giving you those driving lessons. Always up and down the Row, he is, when there's a pretty girl walking along it.'

'He's a policeman and our ARP warden,' Olive pointed out. She was horrified and angry but she had no wish to feed the flames of Nancy's unkind gossip by seeming to be overprotective of the sergeant. Not for a minute did she believe a word of what Nancy was implying. She'd seen and heard in his expression and his voice Sergeant

Dawson's concern for and loyalty to his wife. He had certainly never once given her any cause to feel uncomfortable in his company.

The trouble was that in her widowed state, and given Nancy's turn of mind, she could hardly leap to his defence without potentially making matters worse.

'Of course, it's up to a wife to make sure her husband doesn't stray, and that he gets all he needs at home, if you take my meaning, and from what I've seen of her, Mrs Dawson doesn't have much about her.'

'She's never got over them losing their boy, Nancy. You know that,' Olive felt obliged to remind the other woman.

'Well, that shouldn't stop her coming to church, should it? Many a time I've been round there to knock on the door and do my Christian duty by her, but never once has she asked me in. And as for him asking me not to call round any more! I'd give a pound to a penny that's because he doesn't want her being put to the wise about what he's up to.'

So that was it, Olive thought. Nancy was offended because Sergeant Dawson had stepped in to protect his wife from her nosiness and she was now trying to get her revenge.

Olive was glad when they had finished their tea and it was time to return to their work. She just wished she had someone other than Nancy and her spiteful tongue sitting next to her.

David shot down and injured. Dulcie put down the copy of *Picture Post* she had gone back to reading, as she stared round Olive's pretty kitchen without really seeing it. She had meant what she had said to Lizzie about being better off single, Dulcie assured herself. She certainly wasn't mooning around over David James-Thompson. She had known right from the start that there could never be anything between them, even without David telling her about his snooty mother. And Dulcie hadn't wanted there to be anything between them. Why should she? She could take her pick of lads, and that was how she liked it. All she'd wanted to do was get her own back on Lydia for being so stuck up about her, by flirting with David, who she'd known immediately found her attractive. Well, she'd done that all right, what with him waiting for her when she'd finished work, and then giving her that expensive vanity case she'd fallen in love with. Of course, she'd made it plain to him that she wasn't the sort to do what she shouldn't with any man, never mind one who was married, but that hadn't stopped him trying to persuade her – or kiss her.

Dulcie got to her feet, only to sit down again. She kept forgetting she wasn't really mobile. What she needed was a good night out at the Hammersmith Palais, where she could dance and flirt and have a bit of a laugh. Dulcie wasn't given to introspection or examining her own thoughts or feelings. Her confidence in herself was absolute and inviolate, because it had to be if she was to armour herself against her mother's preference for her sister, so it was easy as well as necessary for her to put the sudden feeling of being helpless to do anything down to her broken ankle, and the way it restricted her movements, and to blame that for those feelings rather than the news about David's accident. The plain fact was that this war was a ruddy nuisance, Dulcie thought to herself, and they could well do without it.

'I just hope we don't have another air-raid warning before we finish work this afternoon,' Clara, who worked with Tilly in the Lady Almoner's office, sighed to Tilly as they sat side by side filling in forms for the influx of patients the bombings had brought. 'It was all stop and start on the train getting to work this morning, and my mum will be thinking the worst if I'm late home. She was going to help me re-do my perm tonight. My hair is as straight as a die without it. You don't know how lucky you are to have them curls of yours, Tilly.'

'You wouldn't think that if you had to brush them,' Tilly assured her fellow worker. Then both of them were grimacing as the wail of the air-raid siren began, quickly reaching for their bags before hurrying to join the trudge down to the basement hospital shelters.

Tilly was still thinking about what Kit had told her that morning, as they made their way along the corridor, and then down the stairs – it was forbidden to use the lift during an air raid – and feeling sorry for him. Secretly she would have liked to have played a more exciting role in the war herself, but dealing with unexploded bombs was more than exciting it was dangerous and surely the very last occupation suitable for someone of Kit's slightly nervous and defensive temperament.

'Three more warnings we've had today, and one of them was a false alarm,' Dulcie complained to Olive and Sally as the three of them sat round the kitchen table drinking the tea Sally had made before she left for her night shift at the hospital.

'At least we've got gas, electricity and water here. There was chaos at the rest centre this afternoon when the water went off. Oh, and I heard that Buckingham Palace was bombed today, twice,' Olive told them, 'but the King and Queen are all right. How does your ankle feel, Dulcie?'

'I'm all itchy,' Dulcie told her.

'That's the plaster,' Sally told her knowledgably, adding in a no-nonsense voice, 'I hope you're still wiggling your toes every hour or so, like I told you to do.'

'Yes, Nurse,' Dulcie responded with a grin and a cheeky look, before sighing, 'I'd give anything for a proper bath.' She'd been told not to get the plaster wet under any circumstances and was having to make do with a soaped flannel and a good scrub.

Itchy *and* bored, by the look of her, Olive thought sympathetically, Dulcie wasn't the stay-at-home sort.

'Tilly and Agnes will be going to their St John Ambulance class tonight – why don't you go with them? There'll be a lot of young people there and it will be more fun for you than staying here,' Olive suggested.

Dulcie opened her mouth to tell her that atten-

106

ding a St John Ambulance class was not her idea of fun, and then closed it again. Olive meant well, she admitted, and at least it would get her out.

There was a large public shelter not far from the hall where the classes were held, so Olive had no fears about the girls going.

'I'd better get on with tea. Agnes and Tilly will be back soon. It will have to be fried Spam fritters tonight with cold boiled potatoes, just in case we get an air-raid alert before I've managed to get it ready.'

'I'd better go,' Sally announced. 'I want to leave a bit of extra time so that I'm not late going on duty.'

Sally had always taken her work seriously, but since Matron had told her that she was planning to promote her to the rank of Sister Theatre Sally had been determined to repay Matron's faith in her. She wanted to succeed for herself, but most of all because she felt that it was something she could do for her late mother: a way of repaying all the love her mother had given her, and of showing the world the gifts her mother had passed on to her. Not that Sally would ever have voiced those emotions and thoughts to anyone – that just wasn't her way.

'I don't blame you,' Olive agreed as she opened her store cupboard to remove a tin of Spam. 'There were yellow "diversion" notices on so many roads today that I thought I'd never get us back from the rest centre.' She paused. 'Those poor people queuing there, I felt so sorry for them. Some of them were saying that they'd rather trek out to Epsom Forest every night than stay in the city, and others are talking about going down to Kent, to the accommodation they use when they go hop picking.'

Pulling on her cloak, Sally headed for the front door, calling out from the hall as she did so, 'Don't worry if I'm late back in the morning. If there's a raid overnight I may end up having to stay over.'

'Good luck,' Olive called back, slicing the Spam, ready to fry it up, her face breaking into a relieved smile as she heard Tilly exchanging greetings with Sally in the hall.

'It's me, Mum,' Tilly called, coming into the kitchen. 'We were given permission to leave early because of the bomb damage making it difficult for people to get trains and buses,' she explained. She kissed Olive's cheek before removing her outdoor clothes, taking her hat and coat back into the hallway to hang up.

'Dulcie's feeling bored, cooped up here all day so I suggested that she goes to St John Ambulance with you tonight,' Olive told her daughter as she removed a bowl of cold boiled potatoes from one of the shelves in her small narrow larder.

'Oh, yes,' Tilly agreed, smiling at Dulcie, 'although we'll have to make sure that everyone knows you've got a real plaster on your ankle so that no one tries to take it off.'

'Get that jar of relish out of the cupboard for me, will you, please, Tilly? Agnes shouldn't be long now,' Olive said, putting the bowl of potatoes on the oilcloth-covered table.

'I saw Kit this morning, Mum,' said Tilly, doing as she was asked. 'And guess what? He's joining the bomb disposal lot.'

'What, him? He'd run a mile if he heard a firework go off,' Dulcie scoffed.

'Oh dear, his mother will be distraught,' Olive sighed sympathetically, ignoring Dulcie's unkind comment. 'I must go round and see her. It can't be easy for her, now she's by herself. Oh, good, that will be Agnes now,' she announced as she heard the front door open.

Agnes forced a smile as she walked into the kitchen. She'd seen Ted very briefly for only a few snatched minutes when he'd arrived at work, but he hadn't said anything to her about his mother other than that she hadn't liked sleeping in the underground, but that he was trying to persuade her to come back because he felt it was safer for them. Agnes hadn't mentioned her fears that his mother might not have liked her because that seemed selfish when Ted already had so much to worry about, but she couldn't help worrying, all the same.

Within fifteen minutes of Agnes's arrival they were all sitting down to their evening meal of Spam fritters, their hotness making up for the coldness of the potatoes, and Olive's home-made relish adding some flavour to the blandness.

For pudding there were stewed apples from the apple tree in the garden, and custard followed by a fresh pot of tea, whilst they listened to the news on the wireless. Then it was time for the girls to clear the table and wash up before Tilly and Agnes went upstairs to change into their St John Ambulance uniforms.

Knowing the girls would be out, Olive had

volunteered to be on WVS duty herself during the evening, at their own local church hall, manning the tea urn, which provided welcome refreshment for all those in the area who worked in the emergency services.

By Sunday morning after church, after a Saturday of almost nonstop day-and-night bombing, people's sombre and often exhausted expressions showed what they had been through.

Even so, Tilly was making an effort, wearing her best coat, with its pretty velvet collar and cuffs, the rich darkness of the fabric setting off the equally rich darkness of the curls escaping from her hat – trimmed up with a new ribbon and a flower Olive had made from some spare scraps of fabric from her last year's new coat.

While Tilly looked like a young girl on the brink of womanhood, Dulcie was wearing a far more 'grown-up' outfit. Her coat was 'pretend' Persian lamb cut in a dashing A-line, the dark grey fabric complimented by a small stand-up black collar and deep turned-back black cuffs. The coat had pockets concealed in its seams, which allowed Dulcie to slip her hands into them to keep them warm, but she had already told the other girls that she had her heart set on a black muff to finish off her outfit, if she could pick one up cheaply somewhere. Where Tilly's hat was neat and pretty, Dulcie's, in the same fabric as her coat, was set on her blonde curls at a rakish angle.

The leaves on the trees close to the vicarage and the church hall were starting to fall, but their rich colours had been lost, dulled by the ever-present brick dust and ash in the air.

Tilly had just been trying to cheer up Christopher Long, without any success, and was on her way back to join her mother, Agnes and Dulcie when someone tapped her on the arm.

Swinging round, she saw the young American reporter who was staying with Ian Simpson.

'Hi there, remember me?' he smiled.

'Of course,' Tilly responded promptly. 'You're Mr Simpson's lodger, Drew Coleman.'

'That's right.'

Dulcie, who had seen the good-looking young man stop Tilly, quickly and determinedly made her way over to them, interrupting Drew's description of an article he had written for his home-town newspaper, to say archly, 'I hope you're going to introduce me, Tilly, and not keep this handsome man all to yourself.'

As she spoke Dulcie managed to position herself so that she was standing directly in front of Drew, whilst Tilly was now to one side of him. It wasn't that she really wanted to oust Tilly from his attention; it was just that Dulcie couldn't help herself when it came to claiming the limelight.

'Dulcie, this is Drew Coleman,' Tilly obligingly made the introduction. 'He's lodging with Ian. He's a reporter and he's American. Drew, this is Dulcie Simmonds. I told you about her when Ian Simpson introduced us.'

'Of course. Delighted to meet you, Dulcie.'

'That's a fancy ring you're wearing,' Dulcie announced, never backward about coming forward when she wanted to know something.

'It's my graduation ring – from Harvard,' Drew

informed her with a smile. 'It's an American tradition for successful graduates to wear a ring from their college.'

'So it doesn't mean that you're involved with a girl then?' Dulcie probed.

'No, it doesn't, and I'm not.'

There was no reason for her to feel pleased that Drew wasn't involved with anyone Tilly told herself, and yet she knew that she was.

Olive, who had been watching the trio, brought her conversation with Mrs Windle to an end and shepherded Agnes over to join them.

'Mum, this is Drew Coleman,' Tilly explained. 'Remember I told you about him?'

'Yes, of course.' Olive smiled, extending her hand. 'Olive Robbins. Welcome to Article Row, Drew.'

'Pleased to meet you, Mrs Robbins.' The young American smiled politely back.

'Drew writes about the war for a newspaper in his home town in America, Mum,' Tilly reminded her mother.

'Well, you'll certainly have had plenty to write about these last few days,' Olive told him sadly.

'Yes, ma'am. It surely takes some getting used to, seeing what's happening to you folks over here. The folks back home don't realise...'

'Which is why reporters like you are doing such a good job on our behalf, in telling them,' Olive praised him with a smile.

He seemed a very pleasant young man, – good-looking, certainly – but as a mother Olive looked well beyond a young man's looks, and what she could see in the young American's gaze and his

112

manner went a long way to reassuring her about his character.

'If you're going to attend church here regularly then perhaps you'd like to join us for lunch afterwards one Sunday?' she suggested, pleased when she saw how genuinely eager he was to accept her invitation.

'Yes, ma'am, I sure would appreciate that.'

'And we'll have to take him dancing at the Hammersmith Palais once I've had my plaster cast removed, won't we, Tilly?' Dulcie put in, giving the young American a distinctly saucy smile, whilst Olive looked on ruefully, her opinion of him rising still further when he looked more abashed than entranced by Dulcie's wiles. If anything, it was Tilly he seemed to admire, rather than Dulcie, Olive noticed, although that admiration was mannerly and respectful.

'I hear that the dear King and Queen have flatly refused to leave the Palace, even though Mr Churchill has pleaded with them to do so,' the vicar's wife, an ardent royalist, told Olive as Olive gathered the girls together ready for the walk back to number 13. 'So very brave and loyal of them.'

'I dare say that they didn't want the people of London to feel that they were being deserted,' Olive answered her quietly, 'especially when so many of them are having such a dreadful time.'

'Oh, indeed, yes,' Mrs Windle agreed. She had only to look at her husband's congregation to know that, never mind what she'd seen at the rest centre.

113

'Perhaps Ted would like to come and join us for Sunday lunch at the same time as Drew comes?' Olive suggested to Agnes as the four of them made their way home together. Sally hadn't joined them for church because she was on duty.

The wan smile Agnes gave her in return made Olive feel concerned, as did her low voice when she responded, 'That's ever so kind of you, but I don't think he'll be able to come. I reckon his mum wouldn't like it if he wasn't there on a Sunday to go to church with them.' Agnes's voice trembled slightly.

Now that Olive thought about it, Agnes had been very quiet since the bombing had started, but Olive had put that down to the natural dread and horror they were all feeling. Now, though, she wondered if something other than that was bothering her. Olive knew that there had been an upset between the young couple earlier in the year when Ted had backed off from their relationship, thinking he was doing the right thing for Agnes because he wouldn't be in a position to marry her until his sisters had grown up, but that was all sorted out now, or so Olive had thought. Something was definitely bothering her young lodger, though, and she'd have to try to find out just what it was. Olive's maternal heart was just as sensitive to hurt when she sensed it in the young lives of her lodgers as it was to any hurt in her daughter, and Agnes was an orphan, after all, and a gentle, vulnerable type of girl.

For her part Agnes felt thoroughly miserable. There was nothing she'd like more than for Ted to come and share their Sunday lunch, but she

114

suspected that his mother wouldn't approve. Because she loved him Agnes didn't want to put Ted in any kind of difficult position. All she could do was hope that somehow Ted's mother would get used to her being around and come to like her. Somehow.

'We'd better not dawdle, you never know when there's going to be another air raid,' Olive told them all, increasing her pace.

'The bombing can't go on much longer, surely,' Tilly protested optimistically. 'The Germans can't have many bombs left, having dropped so many on us.'

All of them automatically stopped walking to look up into the sky. The air still smelled of burning buildings – and of death and destruction.

'In church this morning I couldn't help thinking of all those people who couldn't ... who wouldn't be *there*.' Tilly almost choked on her last shakily whispered word.

Olive reached for her daughter's hand, holding it tight. 'We are here,' she reminded her, but even as she spoke Olive wondered for how long those words would hold good.

At Barts Sally emerged from the over-crowded hospital chapel where she had gone during her dinner break, readjusting her cap as she did so. She had been lucky enough to manage to squeeze inside the tiny chapel itself.

As always, since the war had started, it had been packed with those who, like her, had felt the need to draw close to a source of comfort that had sustained so many generations.

115

In the chapel's dimly lit mustiness, its silence broken only by the odd cough, the sound of shoes on its stone floor and the occasional heart-rending scrape of a single limb or a crutch dragged against it, Sally had offered up her own heartfelt prayers for those close to her, including everyone at number 13 and, of course, George. It wasn't, though, the sombre solemnity nor the timeless awareness of the fragility of human life that was causing her to frown now. She paused mid-step, for once oblivious to the busyness of the hospital all around her, as she remembered that moment in the chapel when, inside her head, she had had such a sharp mental vision of her father and Morag holding their child.

SEVEN

Sally was one of the first to admit, as the days grew shorter, that any hopes the country might have had back in September that the Germans had stopped bombing them were false. As the weeks went by the Luftwaffe proved that they had plenty more bombs to drop on Britain's towns and cities. Many of the stores on Oxford Street had suffered bomb damage, including Selfridges, and its rooftop restaurant was now permanently closed. But no matter how many times German bombers returned to attack, Londoners refused to be daunted. The theatres were open, and so were the cinemas and dance halls. Londoners shrugged and said that if your name was on a bomb then it was on it, so you might just as well get on with your life as best you could.

And that was exactly what everyone was attempting to do, especially the women of London. From the office girls who picked their way to their places of work through the rubble of newly demolished buildings every morning, to the housewives who queued resolutely for the food to feed their families, they were determined not to let Hitler get the better of them.

'At long last. I've bin waiting here for blumming ages,' Dulcie greeted Sally from her bed in Out Patients, where she was waiting to have the plaster removed from her ankle.

Guessing that, despite the fact that she had pretended not to be concerned about the procedure, Dulcie was in reality rather apprehensive, Sally had offered to stay on at the hospital after her shift ended to remove Dulcie's plaster cast for her.

Knowing Dulcie as she did, Sally didn't take offence at her manner. It was just Dulcie being Dulcie, determined not to let the outside world see her as vulnerable.

'Dr Tomkins will be seeing her next, and he'll want that cast off ready for him to look at her ankle, so I'll leave you to deal with her,' the nurse who had been standing beside Dulcie's bed told Sally with a cross look over her shoulder at Dulcie. 'She's done nothing but complain from the minute she arrived. She says she knows you...'

'Yes, we lodge at the same house,' Sally explained, rolling up her sleeves as the other nurse

117

disappeared in the direction of patients several beds away, leaving Sally to slip protective cuffs over her rolled-up sleeves and then reach for a pair of plaster shears from the waiting trolley.

She could see the way in which Dulcie's eyes widened when she saw the shears, and she wasn't surprised. Most patients reacted in the same way.

'It's all right,' she assured her friend. 'You'll be safe, just as long as you keep still, of course.'

'What are they for?' Dulcie demanded, ignoring Sally's reassurance, her expression distinctly wary.

'They're for removing the plaster cast. We have to cut through it. It's easier and faster than trying to soak it off. Now just lie still, Dulcie.'

'Are you sure you're qualified to do this?' Dulcie asked her, sitting up and clutching the plaster cast on her ankle protectively with both hands. There was a noticeable quaver in the expression on Dulcie's face, making Sally laugh, although she quickly straightened her face. As a nurse she knew how worrying and, indeed, frightening quite simple medical procedures could seem to patients who were not familiar with them. For that reason she did not tell Dulcie, as she could have done, that she had spent the last few hours in an operating theatre assisting a consultant surgeon in her capacity as a senior nurse and stand-in sister with several operations of great complexity, all dealing with injuries so severe that it had only been the dedication and the skill of the medical professionals working on them that had brought those patients through successfully.

Instead she teased Dulcie, 'You're not trying to

118

tell me you want to keep it on, are you, after all the complaining you've done about it?'

'Course I'm not,' Dulcie agreed. 'I just want to make sure that you know what you're doing, that's all.'

'I do,' Sally assured her, before adding in a deliberately kind voice, 'but if you'd like me to ask Nurse Fletcher to come back instead...'

Dulcie shuddered. 'What, that nurse with the thick ankles, who looked as though she'd be at home with a meat cleaver in her hands? No thanks.'

'Just keep still then,' Sally said briskly, putting her left hand on Dulcie's leg and leaning over so that Dulcie couldn't see what she was doing. 'I'll have this off in a couple of ticks, because if I don't, and it's still on when Dr Tomkins gets here, we're both going to be in trouble.'

Swiftly and expertly Sally proceeded to cut through the plaster, within which Dulcie's leg had shrunk a little, allowing good purchase for the plaster shears. Within a very short space of time indeed Sally had removed the cast, revealing Dulcie's pale-fleshed and very slender-looking ankle to be revealed to the light of day for the first time in many weeks.

After a brief moment of relief, and something that for Dulcie could have been a look of gratitude, Sally could see that Dulcie was back on form again.

'Now what?' Dulcie demanded warily.

'Now the doctor will come and look at your ankle to check that everything is as it should be,' Sally answered her.

'To make sure you've taken that cast off properly, you mean?'

'No,' Sally corrected her, 'to make sure that the bone has set properly, 'cos if it hasn't then you'll have to have the ankle rebroken and set again.'

It was unkind of her to say that, Sally knew, but sometimes Dulcie needed a bit of firm handling and putting in her place, and this, in Sally's opinion, was definitely one of those times.

Whilst Dulcie was grappling with this piece of information Sally took advantage of her uncharacteristic silence swiftly to remove the remainder of the plaster, unable to resist a grin of pure mischief when Dulcie realised too late that she had missed an opportunity to register her disapproval by giving a rather too belated 'ouch'.

'Ouch nothing,' Sally laughed. 'You never felt a thing.'

'Yes I did,' Dulcie protested.

Sally laughed again and warned her, 'I'd save your ouches, if I were you, for when the doctor arrives.'

'Why? What is he going to do? Will it hurt?' Dulcie demanded, looking so genuinely apprehensive for the first time that Sally's desire to tease her was banished by her training, and her natural instinct to protect her patients.

'No, not at all,' she reassured her. 'Ah, here he is now.'

Unexpectedly Dulcie reached for her hand and held it tightly. Sally was used to patients needing this comfort and support, but she wasn't used to seeing such vulnerability in Dulcie. It touched her heart in a way that she hadn't expected. She gave Dulcie's tense fingers a reciprocal squeeze and assured her, 'Honestly, there's nothing for you to worry about.'

No, it was the young house doctor attending to Dulcie who needed to worry, Sally thought ruefully a couple of minutes later as she watched the effect of Dulcie's smiles and pouts as she tossed her blonde hair and batted her mascared lashes in the doctor's direction. No wonder he seemed all fingers and thumbs. But Sally gave Dulcie a cool look that warned her that she was going too far, when Dulcie told him admiringly, 'Oooh, you've got ever such nice warm hands. Not like Sally's, but then of course she's only a nurse.'

The young doctor was putty in Dulcie's skilled hands, Sally could see, his face so flushed that she was tempted to suggest she should take his temperature. Dulcie, of course, was thoroughly enjoying herself, wringing out every last drop of drama from having her ankle checked.

And then, when he was very gently rotating her ankle, she asked him if he thought it was true that girls with slender ankles made the best dance partners because they were so light on their feet.

A more experienced and world-weary medic such as George would have put Dulcie in her place very quickly and politely, but this doctor was new to Barts and a bit of an innocent abroad, Sally suspected. Dulcie's outrageous flirting was certainly flustering him. She had got him in such a hot and bothered state that Sally suspected that he was the one who needed a cool soothing hand on his brow, not Dulcie.

Deeming it might be time to bring an end to Dulcie's games and relieve the young doctor's embarrassment, Sally stepped in to say calmly, 'I think Dulcie is worried about her ankles, Doctor, because she's been warned that she could end up with them really swollen with rheumatism if she doesn't take care, and then she won't be able to dance at all. She'll have to sit out with the old maids and watch.'

It was only her own strict standards of professionalism that stopped her laughing out loud at the look on Dulcie's face, Sally acknowledged, firmly controlling her amusement as Dulcie, obviously struggling between maintaining the sweet but helpless pose she had adopted for the doctor's benefit, and telling Sally exactly what she thought of being linked in any kind of way with anyone who was forced to sit out and watch others dancing, was rendered speechless, her face flushed with sheer frustration.

Happily, before the young doctor could be tormented any further, Dulcie was given the all clear. She did, however, manage a final triumphant look at Sally as she got up off the bed. Rearranging her skirt with a flourish that drew attention to her slim legs, as she stepped into her shoes and then pulled on her coat, her parting words to Sally were an ungrateful, 'You want to be careful with them scissors. It was only thanks to me keeping still that you didn't nick me with them, if you ask me.'

Sally managed to stop herself from retaliating with a very firm, 'It was only thanks to my training that I wasn't tempted to do just that.'

But despite all that had happened, Sally was

willing to admit to herself that Dulcie had that way about her that made Sally smile, even whilst she was being her most irritating. Dulcie was a character and a one-off, there was no doubt about that. Her outer shell of tough self-interest shielded and hid a heart that was fiercely loyal to those Dulcie considered to be her friends, and Sally knew how much all the inhabitants of number 13 meant to Dulcie, just as they did to her. There, the house filled with Olive's kindness and love, they had all found a balm that soothed the pain they had suffered from something that had previously either been missing or lost from their lives, Sally acknowledged. Today, though, she didn't want to dwell on such matters. It simply did not do, in her opinion, to overindulge one's emotions. It led to them becoming too demanding and troublesome. Far better instead to focus on the practicalities of life, Sally told herself when she too left the hospital in Dulcie's wake.

Tilly smiled at Dulcie as the latter stretched out her newly plaster-free leg.

'It must be a relief to have finally got rid of that plaster cast at long last,' Tilly commented affectionately.

Dulcie nodded, her blonde hair reflecting the light thrown back from the pretty yellow daisy-patterned wallpaper and the room's buttercup-yellow curtains.

Dulcie loved her bedroom at number 13, although her instinctive defensiveness would never have allowed her to say as much to anyone, much less to her landlady, Olive, who was responsible for her bedroom's fresh sunny decor.

Not that Dulcie hadn't added her own touches to the room, she had, mainly via the addition of some carefully chosen samples from Selfridges perfume and cosmetics counters. On the glass-topped kidney-shaped dressing table, Dulcie had arranged an assortment of elegant-looking glass perfume bottles, the loose ends of their pastel-coloured silk-thread-covered puffers spread out artistically on the polished glass surface, the whole arrangement reflected in the dressing table mirror. There was also a lipstick and compact set in shiny 'gold', set with pretend rubies, and a large box of face powder complete with a pale pink swansdown powder puff. On the back of the bedroom door Dulcie's winter siren suit hung from the coat peg, along with her gas mask box in its bright pink silk cover.

Now, as she always did whenever she was in her room, Dulcie couldn't resist giving it a quick look of pride and satisfaction – her dressing table looked much more expensive than anything any of the other girls had – before she added, 'it's nearly as much of a relief as the Germans not bombing us during the daytime any more.'

'Mrs Windle told Mum that that's because our RAF have shot down so many of their planes during their daytime raids,' Tilly informed Dulcie knowledgeably, adding, 'And I'll tell you some-thing else as well. No one runs any more when the siren goes off like we used to when we first heard it.'

'Well, they should do,' Olive said as she came upstairs just in time to hear what Tilly was saying, 'especially now that the authorities have worked so hard to improve conditions in the shelters.'

An awful lot had been done since the early days of the Blitz in September, weeks ago now, when all those who worked in the voluntary services had seen how poorly equipped the city was both to provide for its homeless, and to tackle the devastation left behind by the bombs.

Now, most shelters had adequate sanitation facilities, there were permanent bunks in many of the underground shelters, special areas had been set aside as children's play areas, and more wardens had been recruited to ensure that life in the shelters was conducted in a respectable and orderly manner.

'Do you know the first thing I want to do now that I've got that plaster off at long last?' Dulcie told them.

'Have a proper bath.'

'Go dancing,' Olive and Tilly spoke in unison, causing Dulcie to laugh.

'You're both right, as it happens. How about it, Tilly? How do you feel about us all going to Hammersmith Palais next Saturday night, if your mum says it's all right?'

Tilly clapped her hands together. Out of sympathy for Dulcie, Tilly and Agnes had put their heads together and agreed that they wouldn't go dancing without her, and the nearest they had got to having any fun had been an impromptu dance in one of the shelters in which they'd had to take refuge, whilst working with their St John Ambulance group.

'Well, I don't mind, just as long as you promise

125

me you'll make for a shelter at the first sound of a siren,' Olive warned them.

'When Drew comes round tomorrow to show you those photographs you were so keen to see, we could ask him to come with us,' Dulcie suggested.

Drew had had Sunday lunch with them twice since Olive had first invited him, and although Tilly had indicated that she felt no particular interest in him – much to Olive's relief, as she didn't want her daughter falling in love at eighteen, especially when there was a war on – it did seem to be Tilly that the young American gravitated towards more than the other girls.

'I'm really sorry but I won't be able to come,' Sally told them when Tilly mentioned their plans to her over their evening meal later.

'That means that she's going out with her chap,' Dulcie told Tilly knowledgeably. Sally smiled good-naturedly. Olive liked George Laidlaw, who Sally had brought home to tea with her one evening at Olive's invitation. Olive had liked him, especially for the way he hadn't responded to Dulcie's energetic attempt to flirt with him, and for his admiration for Sally, which he had made no attempt to conceal. Dulcie hadn't meant any real harm, she was just the sort of girl who wouldn't resist showing off her charms, Olive thought ruefully.

Because Sally had confided the sad story of her past to Olive, following the visit of the good-looking naval officer who had called to see her at number 13, and whose sister Olive now knew was

126

married to Sally's father, Olive knew and understood why Sally never mentioned her home in Liverpool or the people she had loved there, never mind showed any inclination to go back. She did feel, though, that it was very sad that Sally couldn't be reconciled with her father, but she also knew better than to interfere, knowing that if Sally wanted her advice she would ask her for it.

They had all just settled down to listen to the wireless when there was a knock at the door.

'I'll answer it, Mum,' Tilly offered, getting up to go into the hall, only to return very quickly. 'It's Sergeant Dawson. He wants to speak to you.'

Olive got up. Whilst it wouldn't be true to say that she had been avoiding Sergeant Dawson, following from Nancy's unkind remarks about him, Olive admitted that she had been determined not to give Nancy any reason to remind her yet again that the sergeant was a married man. It was for that reason and no other that she felt a little flustered as she went into the hall, forcing herself to resist the temptation to look in the mirror that hung there and pat her hair straight. The sergeant was a tall man even without his helmet, which he had removed, the light in the hallway reflecting on the buttons on his uniform and highlighting the distinguished touches of silver in his dark hair.

'I'm sorry to disturb you, Olive,' he told her, 'You see, there's something I wanted to have a word with you about, in private, like.'

'Oh?' Olive wasn't sure what to say, and she showed the sergeant into the front room.

'Yes. You'll have heard that there's more air-raid wardens being taken on now?'

Olive nodded.

'There's two more going to be needed at our shelter, and I was thinking that maybe you might want to think about applying to become one of them.'

Olive was so completely astonished that she sank down on the sofa. 'Me, an air-raid warden? But I wouldn't know what to do.'

'You'd be trained up properly so you needn't worry about that. You've got the makings of a good warden, I reckon, Olive. I've seen the way you deal with those lodgers of yours and the way they listen to what you say. A good warden has to be able to make people listen. This bombing we've had already isn't going to be the end of it, you know, not by a long chalk.'

Olive had to smile. 'I can't see Mr Baxter welcoming any woman as a warden in his area,' she pointed out.

Sergeant Dawson laughed. 'Old Reg? He's standing down. Getting a bit past it, and with him losing his brother in a bomb in October, it's taken the spirit out of him. He's decided to go and live with his son in Manchester. He reckons it will be safer up there.

'There'll be a wage that goes with it,' he told her.

'A wage?' That would certainly make life easier, Olive acknowledged. Not that there was much to spend money on unless you bought on the black market. 'I don't think Nancy would approve.' She hesitated. 'You know what she's like, and she won't think it a suitable occupation for a woman.'

'No, I dare say she won't, but you won't be the

128

only woman on the unit. Mrs Morrison is going to apply, so her husband has told me.'

'She is?'

'You have a think about it and let me know if you want your name putting forward,' Sergeant Dawson told her, 'although these things take time, and I dare say it will be after Christmas now before anything really happens.'

'Yes. Yes, I will, and thank you.'

'You're welcome.'

He was on the doorstep before Olive could say anything more, his cape swinging from his shoulders as the fog swallowed him up.

Her, an air-raid warden. The girls would laugh when she told them. At least she'd got time to think things through properly if nothing was going to happen until after Christmas.

Christmas! She'd noticed earlier that Sally had been wearing the gloves she had knitted for her the previous Christmas – knitted a pair for each of them, in fact. She'd have to start thinking about Christmas presents for this year soon...

An air-raid warden. Her! Nancy wouldn't approve at all, even if Mrs Morrison was joining as well.

EIGHT

'So what time is your American beau coming round?' Dulcie asked Tilly as the three of them washed up together, Tilly washing, Dulcie drying and Agnes putting everything away.

'He said he'd be here about half-past seven, and he isn't my beau,' Tilly told Dulcie firmly.

Dulcie knew it was a bit mean of her to tease Tilly but she was on edge because, in the morning, she was going back to work after her time off.

There had been many changes during her absence, she knew. Arlene, her old enemy, might have left but, according to Lizzie, who had faithfully visited Dulcie every week, when you added together the number of girls who had left because their parents considered London too dangerous for them to work there any more, and the number of girls who had decided to go into uniform of one sort or another, some of the sales jobs had had to be filled with much older women. Women who, Lizzie had already warned her, were inclined to be rather old-fashioned and stuffy. Then there was the fact that the store itself had been bomb-damaged during an air raid.

'It isn't the place it was,' Lizzie had told her sadly.

So because she was feeling nervous and didn't really want to admit it, Dulcie was taking her

130

anxiety out on Tilly by teasing her about her American. A quite good-looking American, too, Dulcie was forced to admit. Not that he was really her type, with his polite ways, though he had won Olive's approval. Dulcie liked her men to have that certain something added to their good looks, that little dash of danger that sparkled in their eyes. Like it had in David's?

Dulcie scowled as she dried the last plate. She'd asked Lizzie if there'd been any more news about Lydia's husband, but since Arlene, a source of this news, had left, Lizzie hadn't been able to tell her anything. Not that she really wanted to know, of course. Why should she? She could have any man she wanted, and that included Tilly's American.

'Aren't you going to get changed?' she asked Tilly now. 'It's a quarter past and your beau will be here soon.'

'Why should I want to get changed? It's November, the bedroom is freezing cold and the few inches of water we're allowed for a bath isn't enough to get properly warm in. And I keep telling you, he isn't my beau.'

'No, and he never will be if you don't make a bit of an effort and wear something pretty for him. Men like that.' Dulcie looked scathingly at Tilly's neat navy-blue pleated skirt, which she was wearing with a red jumper over which she'd put her apron.

Dulcie herself had, of course, already 'made an effort', changing into a rich amber-brown shirt with a sheeny finish to it that toned with her dark brown eyes and blonde hair, and a fitted brown

131

tweed skirt, both part of the wardrobe that Dulcie had carefully assembled once she had started working at Selfridges. She had a good eye for style and cut, though she had bristled with fury when Arlene had pointed out the first time she had worn her blouse that it could hardly compare with real silk. After that Dulcie had made sure that her blouses were made of silk, even if that silk had to be seconds, or 'bargains' she had found on one or other of London's many markets.

'Still, at least you aren't wearing your siren suit,' Dulcie mocked Tilly.

'There's nothing wrong with a siren suit. I've been really glad of it when we've had to jump out of bed and go down to the Anderson,' Tilly defended herself, adding, 'And Mum worked hard making them for us.'

That was true, and Dulcie knew it.

Olive had got the fabric from a shop that had been closed down after an incendiary bomb set its top floor ablaze. After the fire brigade had soaked all the bales of stored fabric, they had had to be sold off cheaply.

She had made a suit for each of them. Dulcie's was pink and suited her colouring, Olive's own was navy blue and Tilly's was pale blue, whilst Agnes and Sally's were apple green.

'That's the door now,' Agnes told them both unnecessarily, as they all speedily removed their aprons.

'You'd better go and let him in then, hadn't you?' Dulcie told Tilly. 'Seeing as it's you he's come to see.'

She wasn't going to let Dulcie get under her skin, Tilly told herself, as she headed for the front door. She knew she was only being awkward because of her leg. Even so, Tilly did feel a bit self-conscious when she went to open the door to Drew. She felt even more self-conscious when he handed her a box of chocolate bars, even though they did make her mouth water with longing, chocolate being rationed.

'These are for your mom. They're Hershey bars,' he told her.

'Another American tradition?' Tilly guessed, holding the chocolates in one hand whilst she held out the other to take Drew's raincoat and hat, which she put on the hat stand.

Nodding, Drew smiled at her, picking up the briefcase he'd put down as he took off his coat.

Each time Drew had come to Sunday lunch he had brought something with him, usually either flowers or fruit, which Olive had complained was far too generous of him until he had explained to her that his gifts had been obtained from American stores shipped in for the use of American personnel based in London, many of whom he knew.

'Mum isn't here at the moment but she'll be back soon,' Tilly told him, ushering him into the front room. 'She's gone to see Mrs Long, a neighbour of ours who lost her husband earlier in the year and now her son's away so she's by herself.'

'Gee, that's sad,' Drew offered politely.

'Christopher, her son, enlisted recently. He's training for bomb disposal duties.'

133

Drew looked impressed. 'He must be one brave guy.'

'He's not brave at all,' Dulcie piped up. She had seated herself at the most flattering angle to the fire, perching on the arm of the chair there so that when Drew came into the room his gaze would automatically be drawn to her. It wasn't that she was particularly interested in him; it was just that it was impossible for her not to be the centre of young, handsome and appreciative male attention.

'Kit is a conscientious objector,' Tilly explained as she led Drew towards the comfortable chair next to the fire, facing the one Dulcie was perched on, pretending to check her stockings for an imaginary snag, which involved her arching and pointing her foot in a way that showed off the elegant length of her slim legs.

'We're all really looking forward to seeing your photographs,' Tilly told Drew.

The light from the room's standard lamp was highlighting the rich brown of Drew's thick hair, his smile revealing perfect white teeth.

There was something about Drew that was bright and shiny, a something that Tilly wasn't familiar with in British boys. American girls would have recognised it as a preppy college-boy look.

Once the obligatory cups of tea had been made and drunk, Drew opened his briefcase and removed a sheaf of large shiny black-and-white photographs, handing them first to Tilly, who was sitting closest to him on the sofa with Agnes at her other side.

'I took these early on in the first wave of bomb-ings,' Drew explained, leaning across to her. 'See how in this one there's all the hoses from the fire engines? What caught my eye wasn't so much the bombs falling, although that was dramatic enough, but this young kid here.'

'A boy messenger,' Tilly explained. 'The ARP and the fire service use them to get messages across London when the phone lines are down.'

Drew nodded. 'Yes. A kid thirteen or fourteen, no more, and yet he's playing an active role in a war. Back home in America, folks see these photo-graphs and they can't always take it all in. Here's another. See how this doll is lying in the street, its arm and leg missing, and the little girl is bending over it?'

And not far from the little girl the photograph showed a woman's leg, complete with a high-heeled shoe, nothing more, just the leg and the shoe visible beneath a collapsed building. Look-ing at the photograph brought a lump to Tilly's throat. She ached to know if the woman buried beneath the rubble was the little girl's mother, if the little girl knew, if the woman was saved...

'My father writes me that war is about the big picture, but I guess I'm kinda drawn to the small picture.' Drew gave Tilly a self-depreciatory smile and shrugged. 'Of course, I write a piece to acc-ompany the photographs that tells the whole story about what's happening, but I guess I get kinda distracted by what I see. I go out most nights and most days when the all clear's gone, just walking round London, watching folk.'

Olive's return and the presentation of the box

135

of Hershey bars called for a fresh pot of tea and one of the chocolate bars was cut up into thin slivers so that everyone could have a taste.

'Kids back home grow up on Hershey bars,' Drew explained. 'They're an American tradition.'

'How is Mrs Long, Mum?' Tilly asked her mother.

'Very low. She took her husband's death hard, although he was ill for so long, and now that Christopher's been conscripted to such a dangerous service, well, she has a lot of time alone to get anxious about him.'

They were all silent for a couple of minutes, the silence broken when Tilly told her mother, 'Drew's photographs are ever so good, Mum. Look at this one. It's St Bride's Church in Fleet Street.'

'They call it the journalists' church,' Drew informed Olive earnestly, whilst she managed to keep a straight face as though this were news to her.

'I'm planning to photograph the whole of Fleet Street, air raids permitting,' Drew enthused. 'I've already done one of Ye Olde Cheshire Cheese. I did an article on that for back home, writing about how Mark Twain and Charles Dickens had both drunk there, just as reporters are doing now. You hear some fascinating stories. I'm writing down as many as I can. One day I'd like to write a book about Fleet Street and its history.'

'Oh, I do envy you doing something so interesting and exciting,' Tilly sighed.

'Well, you're welcome to come with me,' Drew offered, and looked uncertainly at Olive. 'That's if your mom agrees.'

'Oh, can I, Mum?' Tilly begged.

Olive's instinctive reaction was to refuse. She didn't want her precious Tilly being exposed to any more danger than she needed to be. And that included the company of handsome young men. But then Olive reminded herself that Drew was a polite and obviously well-brought-up boy; a boy who would treat her precious daughter with proper respect.

'Very well,' she agreed, 'providing you both promise me that you will make for a shelter the minute an air-raid siren goes off.'

As much as she wanted to protect Tilly from every kind of danger, Olive knew that her daughter had reached an age when she must start to learn to be responsible for herself. Maternal instinct told her that she could trust Drew to take care of Tilly and make sure that she didn't take risks, and with so much excitement and hope shining in Tilly's giveaway expression, what could she do other than agree?

'Oh, Mum, thank you,' Tilly beamed, flinging her arms round Olive's neck and giving her a fierce hug, before turning back to Drew to demand excitedly, 'I can't wait. When do we start?'

'Next week,' Drew answered. 'We can discuss when properly after church on Sunday.'

As he spoke, Dulcie, who had been glancing through the photographs without much interest, suddenly focused on one of them that depicted five young men, all wearing leather flying jackets, their hair greased back, big confident smiles on their faces.

'Who are these?' she asked Drew.

'Them? Oh, they're some American fly guys who've gotten tired of standing on the sidelines of this war and have come over here to form their own voluntary group of pilots. They've called themselves the Eagles, after the Eagle emblem on the American flag. I bumped into them at a reception at the American Embassy.'

'You went to a reception at the American Embassy?' Tilly queried, round-eyed.

'Oh, I was only there as a goffer for one of the big American newshounds,' Drew told her, 'and when they saw me with my camera these guys asked me to take their photograph.'

Dulcie gave him an arch look, and then demanded with a forwardness that made Olive sigh inwardly, 'Do you know what I think, Tilly? I think we should ask Drew to join us when we next go to the Hammersmith Palais and bring his Eagle friends along with him, introduce them to a bit of proper London social life.'

'Now, Dulcie,' Olive protested, 'you'll embarrass Drew making suggestions like that. I dare say he barely knows these young men.'

After one look at the photograph Olive hoped that he didn't know them very well. Each and every one of them had that look in his eye that immediately put any mother of a young dancing-age daughter on her guard. But it was too late for her to voice any stronger arguments, because Drew was already responding to Dulcie's suggestion with alacrity and enthusiasm, assuring her that his fellow Americans would love to go dancing at the Hammersmith Palais.

138

'We'll go this Saturday then,' Dulcie told him promptly. 'You can meet us there with your Eagle pals.'

Shortly after that Drew took his leave of them, Olive escorting him to the front door, where she thanked him again for the Hershey bars.

He was a very pleasant and personable young man, but Olive was still thankful that Tilly only seemed interested in him as a friend and wasn't showing any signs of having the same kind of crush on him she had once had on Dulcie's brother.

Being back at work was proving to be not much fun at all, Dulcie acknowledged as she and Lizzie sat together in Selfridges' staff canteen having their lunch, and, like everyone else, keeping an ear open for the air-raid alert.

Dulcie's leg ached from standing behind her counter all morning, and since the Christmas rush hadn't begun yet, they hadn't had many customers coming in even on the ground floor. The only one Dulcie had had to serve had been a very smart middle-aged woman with a cold, refined accent, who had complained when Dulcie had not been able to provide her with her favourite scent and the shade of lipstick she wanted.

'Come along, girl,' she had told Dulcie angrily. 'I'm a regular customer here. I demand to see the manager.'

Of course, Dulcie had been obliged to summon the floor manager, who had looked at Dulcie as though he blamed her for the customer's de-manding manner.

'Everything's changed,' Dulcie complained to Lizzie as she spooned up her brown Windsor soup without much enthusiasm. 'And not for the better. I'm surprised we're getting any customers in at all, with those old battleaxes who have replaced Arlene and the others.'

She might not have liked Arlene, but Dulcie liked the middle-aged women, who had taken the place of the pretty young girls who had once manned the makeup counters, even less.

'People are bound to stop coming in to ask for makeup when we have to keep telling them we haven't got any.'

'There's plenty to be had on the black market,' Dulcie pointed out.

'Yes, and most of it has either been brought in illegally by someone working on one of the convoys that come across the Atlantic, or it's second-hand and looted, so I've heard,' Lizzie told her. 'Watch out, Mrs Grange is heading this way.'

Mrs Grange was in charge of the roster of fire-watching duties, which every employee was supposed to undertake, going up onto the roof to watch for bombs and then warn the fire prevention officers.

'Ah, Miss Simmonds,' Mrs Grange announced coming to stand next to Dulcie. 'Good. Now I've put you down for fire-watching duties on Thursday nights, starting this evening.'

'I can't do fire watching,' Dulcie refused immediately. 'I'm not allowed to go climbing stairs. Not yet.'

Mrs Grange pursed her lips. 'Your plaster's off,

140

isn't it?'

'Yes, but my leg muscles are still weak. I've been told not to climb any stairs,' Dulcie fibbed without any compunction. 'It might give way if I was to, see. Of course, I'd like to do my duty and everything but I wouldn't be much good to anyone if I was to go up onto the roof and then my leg gave way and I wasn't able to tell anyone there'd been an incendiary landed. In fact, I wouldn't be surprised if there was a law against me doing it.'

'I see. And how long do you expect it to be before you are able to climb stairs without there being any risk of your leg giving way?' Mrs Grange asked grimly.

'There's no knowing. It will have to be up to the Hospital to say. Of course, with me sharing my lodgings with a nurse, at least I've got her there to keep a lookout for me, if it should.

'Did you see her face?' Dulcie asked Lizzie with glee once they were on their own again.

'She won't let you off easily a second time, Dulcie,' Lizzie warned. 'She didn't like what you said to her, anyone could see that.'

'Well, that's her problem, not mine. Like I said, I've been told not to go climbing too many stairs,' Dulcie told Lizzie virtuously.

'Too many. You told her you aren't supposed to climb any at all, and I know for a fact that you climb them back at your lodgings.'

'Ah, but that's different, 'cos I've got a nurse there to help me, haven't I?' Dulcie insisted, refusing to be outdone.

'Anyway,' she changed the subject, 'have you

141

heard any more about what's happened to Miss Stuck-up Smarty Pants' husband that was shot down by the Germans?'

'*Mrs* Stuck-up Smarty Pants now,' Lizzie pointed out sternly, giving in and laughing when Dulcie pulled a face. 'I don't know any more than I've already told you, and I'm not likely to now Arlene's left, although she did say before she went–'

'What?' Dulcie demanded. Unexpectedly she discovered that her heart had started to beat faster, and she had to struggle not to place her hand over it. It was just because Lizzie was winding her up by being aggravating, that was all, Dulcie assured herself.

Lizzie took a deep breath and leaned closer, to tell her with a purposefully significant look, 'Well, I'm not one for gossip, or talking about others behind their backs – you know that, Dulcie – but from what Arlene let slip it seems there was words spoken between Lydia and her David, before he went off and got himself shot down.'

'What do you mean – words was spoken?' Dulcie could have shaken Lizzie, she was so irritated by the way she was drawing out her story.

'It seems that Lydia never wanted him to join the RAF in the first place and she reckoned he could have stayed out of uniform if he'd really wanted to. I just hope that my Ralph's leave doesn't get cancelled. This will be the first time I've seen him since we got married,' Lizzie finished, reverting to a subject much closer to her heart than Lydia and her marriage.

Dulcie didn't make any response. Everything

142

Lizzie had told her confirmed that she had been justified in not liking Lydia, and that David had been a fool to marry her.

'Sally, have you got a minute? Only there's something I want to tell you.'

'Yes, I've just finished my shift.'

George looked both anxious and elated, his brown hair standing up in spikes as though he'd been pushing his hand through it, his tie slightly askew, and his face flushed. It caught Sally off guard to acknowledge just how pleased she actually was to see him.

George had caught up with her just as she was about to go off duty, coming flying down the corridor after her, calling her name in a way that Matron would have frowned upon.

They'd had a busy shift in the operating theatre. The bombing raids might have eased in intensity, but they were still continuing. People were still being dug out of the wreckage and coming into Barts, needing surgery on their wounds. They'd operated on a young fireman this morning, removing the leg that had been mangled when a wall had fallen on him.

Remembering now, Sally closed her eyes for a moment. His wife was expecting their first child and that child would now have a father who might never be able to work again. Certainly not as a fireman. Instinctively she moved slightly closer to George as if for comfort.

'Well, in that case, if you've got time, how about a walk in Hyde Park?' George suggested hopefully.

143

Hyde Park had become one of their favourite places.

'I'll get my cloak and meet you outside Casualty,' Sally agreed.

She was as quick as she could be but, even so, George was pacing the ground in an uncharacteristic manner when she rejoined him, his head bare and his hair ruffled by the damp November wind.

'Where's your hat?' Sally chided him. 'You'll be cold without it.'

'I don't know. Someone else must have picked it up, thinking it was theirs. You daren't leave anything long in the junior doctors' house. If you do it's bound to disappear.' George's voice was rueful, and Sally smiled up at him as she tucked her arm through his.

Something was on his mind, she could see that, but as they waited for a bus outside the hospital, Sally guessed that George would want to wait until they were in the park to tell her what it was.

Initially it had been strange to see so many different coloured buses on the London streets, sent by various local authorities that could spare them to make up for the number of buses the city had lost to German bombs. When theirs came along, though, it was a traditional red London bus with a chirpy clippie who warned them that there was only standing room.

'When is there ever anything else?' George asked Sally as they stood together strap-hanging in the gathering gloom of the November afternoon.

The park, once they reached it, was virtually empty but for half a dozen boys, standing close to some rhododendron bushes, who stepped out into their path to try to beg a cigarette off them, until a park keeper appeared out of the gloom to shoo them away.

The leaves on the rhododendrons were grey and dusty from the bombings. You could still taste and smell the dust in the air. It seemed to coat everything, its greyness adding to the dull pall of autumn weather that hung over the park, mist shrouding everything. Even the ducks on the Serpentine were huddled together miserably on the bank.

Eventually they found a bench set far enough away from any others to give them a bit of privacy should anyone appear, and sat down together, George lifting his arm to put it round Sally and pull her close to him.

'You know how much you mean to me, don't you, Sally?' he began.

Sally's heart started to thump. Was this a prelude to a proposal. If so, she wasn't ready for it, and wasn't even sure that she actually wanted it. She liked George – more than liked him – but...

'Yes. Yes, I do,' she agreed cautiously, feeling George's chest expand as he took in a deep breath and then exhaled.

'The thing is... Well, the fact is... I've been offered the chance to go and work under Archie McIndoe, the plastic surgeon. You know that he's set up a special unit in Sussex to try to help those poor devils who've been badly burned – RAF chaps, in the main.'

'I had heard.'

'What he's doing is real pioneering stuff. It

would only be a temporary posting, for six months, but of course it will mean me leaving London for that period. I don't know what to do.' He was holding her hand, playing with her fingers through the wool of the gloves that Olive had given her last Christmas.

Leaving London and leaving her, he meant, Sally thought as she realised that he was not after all going to propose to her. She wasn't sure now whether she was glad about that or not, even though five minutes ago she had been very sure that she didn't want him to. What she did know, though, was that the opportunity he had been offered was a testimony to his skill as a doctor.

'You must accept it,' she told him fiercely. 'You have to. It's what you've wanted, and a terrific chance, a wonderful compliment to you, George, although you'll probably try to tell me that it's because you are both New Zealanders. But I know Archie McIndoe wouldn't ask for you to be transferred to his staff if he didn't think you were the right sort and good enough to work with him.'

'It is what I've wanted,' George admitted, looking relieved but still uncertain, 'but I never thought... I didn't have any idea that this might happen. I hate the thought of us being parted, Sally, especially now when we're just beginning to get to know one another properly, but–'

'Don't be silly. Your going to work under Mr McIndoe for six months won't change things between us. Besides, we did both volunteer to work away from London,' she reminded him.

'Yes, I know, but that would only have been to

fill in for someone for a few days here and there.'

Sally could hear in his voice how torn he was, and that touched something unexpected and tender in her own heart.

Dear George. He was such a nice, decent, caring person. With Callum she had created a fantasy inside her youthful head of a man who would be her white knight and who would protect her from all of life's pain just as her parents had done. But with George she often felt that she was the one who had to protect him. Far from worshipping him silently and from afar, as she had done with Callum, with George she felt that they were properly and truly equals. And she liked that, Sally admitted. She liked the warm steady comfortable feeling that being with him brought her. She liked knowing just how much he thought of her without his having to tell her.

'You'll have days off and so will I,' she comforted him.

'Yes.' He looked relieved and much happier now that he had unburdened his concern. 'You could come down and see me,' he told Sally enthusiastically. 'We could have a bit of time together in the country and do some proper walking.'

'In winter?' Sally laughed. 'I'll have you know that I'm strictly a summer walking girl, thank you very much.'

George was looking euphoric. 'I can hardly believe it. I can't wait to write and tell my parents, my father...'

'He'll be very proud of you, George, and justifiably so.'

147

'I haven't done anything yet. McIndoe could send me back before I've completed my first week.' George released her hand to spread his own fingers. 'I don't know myself if I can do it, Sally.'

'But you want to try, and you must.'

'You are just the best girl any man could have,' George told her, 'the very best girl. My girl.' His voice was thick with emotion as he pulled her towards him.

'George,' Sally protested, laughing, 'you can't kiss me here.'

'Who says?' he demanded, before silencing her protest with the warm urgent pressure of his mouth on hers.

It was an emotional moment, an emotional situation for George, she knew. Which was why she didn't resist beyond tensing a little when his hand cupped her breast beneath the cover of her cloak. It was a pleasant feeling, an intimate warm, close feeling, rather than one that filled her with passion, but then Sally didn't think that she was the passionate type.

Being with George felt comfortable and right. There might not be that giddy excitement and longing she remembered from her crush on Callum, often followed by crashing disappointment when the smile she'd been hoping for didn't materialise, but that had just been a young girl's silliness, and the feelings of a girl who hadn't had the wit to recognise what kind of person she was giving her heart to. With George there was nothing hidden. Where she had looked up to Callum as someone older, and had been slightly in awe of him, with George she sometimes felt almost maternal and protective.

'When will you have to leave?' she asked him.

'Soon, apparently,' he told her. 'I only found out about the whole thing this morning. It's all come as a bit of a shock.'

'It's a compliment to you, George, and a sign of how well you're thought of as a doctor,' Sally assured him. 'Now, we'd better get back.'

'I'll write to you with my address as soon as I know where my billet is going to be,' George told her as they headed off, Sally's arm tucked through his, their shoulders hunched against the cold. 'And I'll come up to see you as soon as I get some time off.' He stopped walking and turned to her. 'I'm going to miss you, Sally.'

'No, you won't,' she told him promptly, hearing the emotion in his voice and wanting to cheer him up. 'You'll be far, far too busy learning how to do wonderful things for our poor injured boys.'

She gave his arm a reassuring squeeze.

'Pssst...'

Dulcie came to an abrupt and irritated halt as a lanky, grubby-looking boy of around thirteen or so slipped out of the doorway of a boarded-up building on Oxford Street and stood in front of her.

'Want to buy some shampoo?' the boy asked her. 'Only I reckon with a barnet like yours you will do, and I know just the place where you can get some.' He rubbed the side of his nose meaningfully.

Dulcie glowered at him, and told him sharply, 'Take yourself off, you thieving little tyke. Do I look like I would want to buy stuff that's been looted, 'cos that's what you're flogging, isn't it?'

Instead of looking abashed, the boy grinned. 'Knew you'd be keen, soon as I saw that yeller hair of yours. Looks just like a film star's.'

Dulcie put her hands on her hips and raised her eyes heavenward at this piece of soft-soaping.

Every dark alley in the city seemed to have its own black marketeer lurking in its shadows, most of them willing to sell the roof over their own heads, or rather the roof that had once been over someone else's head, if they thought they could find someone daft enough to buy it, Dulcie thought grimly. She, of course, was fully up to their tricks.

'Do I look like I'm daft enough to fall for your flannelling?' she demanded.

'It's kosher,' the boy insisted with an injured expression, spitting on his palm and then smacking it with his other palm. 'As God's me witness.'

Shampoo. They were down to washing their hair with ordinary soap now at number 13 – even if shampoo wasn't on ration yet, because it was in such short supply – and then trying to put the shine back on it with a bit of vinegar in the rinsing water.

'So where is it then, this shampoo?' she asked.

'Leather Lane Market, Saturday dinner,' the boy told her promptly. 'I'll be standing lookout there, just in case, so I'll keep an eye out for you.' He gave her a wink and a cheeky grin before disappearing like smoke back into the shadows before Dulcie could question him any further.

Shampoo. Well, it couldn't do any harm to go

150

and have a look, Dulcie told herself, especially since Drew was promising to take those good-looking American pilots to the Palais. She'd have to get to the market early, mind. There was no knowing how many girls that scruffy-looking boy had stopped, and if there was some real shampoo to be had, Dulcie certainly didn't want to end up standing at the back of the queue. Lucky that it was her half-day on Saturday. Not that that old trout Mrs Grange had been pleased about that. She'd tried to get the manager to say that Dulcie had to do some fire-watching practices, but Dulcie had soon put an end to that.

NINE

'You all right, Ag?' Ted asked. 'Only you've hardly had a word to say for yourself all dinner.'

Agnes forced herself to smile. 'I was just thinking about poor Mrs Long. She's finding it hard, being on her own. Remember I told you about her husband being so poorly and then dying?'

They were sitting at 'their' table, in the window of the café close to the underground station, alternately buffeted by the raw damp cold air that swept inside every time the door was opened, and the equally damp but warm steamy atmosphere that came from the combination of tea and coffee urns, washing up, and hot food on the other side of the counter.

Ted nodded vigorously before saying, 'If you

aren't going to finish that piece of pie, pass it over here, will you?'

Silently Agnes handed him her plate. 'There isn't much meat in it.'

'Well, there won't be, will there?' Ted pronounced practically. 'Seeing as there isn't much meat to be had. Still, it's nice and cosy in here.' He rubbed his hands together, before tucking into what was left of Agnes's meat and potato pie.

He always saw the bright side of things, her Ted, Agnes reflected. That was what had drawn her to him. That, and the smile he always had on his face.

'I don't know how Mrs Long's going to go on now she's on her own. Proper worried about her Mrs Robbins is.' Agnes had a kind heart and sympathised strongly with her recently widowed neighbour.

'Something's bound to turn up,' Ted told her cheerfully. 'It always does.'

'Your mum doesn't come down to the underground to shelter any more.' Agnes couldn't look at him as she broached the subject that had been causing her so much anxiety as she lay awake at night, worrying that Ted's mother didn't like her.

'She's got this bee in her bonnet about it not being the sort of place she wants the girls to be, on account of some of them others that go down there.' Ted gave Agnes a rueful look. 'I've told her she's worrying about nothing, seeing as I've got them sorted out with that room of their own, but you women, once you've got an idea fixed in your heads, there's no arguing with you.'

If that was why Ted's mum was avoiding the

152

underground, and not because she didn't approve of her, then she'd been worrying about nothing, Agnes realised, feeling light-headed with relief. How daft she'd been not to say something to Ted before.

'Oh, Ted,' she beamed, reaching across the table to put her hand on his.

'You'd better save that until you and me are sitting on the back row of the pictures on Saturday night,' Ted teased her, 'otherwise there's no saying what I might do with you, looking at me like that.'

This time Agnes's 'Oh, Ted' was a sigh of blissful delight, accompanied by a vivid blush.

'I've got to say, I'd rather Mum came down the shelter. It's safer for her and the girls there, no two ways about it, but she won't have it,' Ted continued. 'She's got this daft idea that the Guinness Trust wouldn't approve of her going down the underground. She says that it's only a certain sort goes down the underground for shelter. I've told her she's worrying over nothing but she won't listen. She's worrying herself sick that we might be turfed out of the flat. She keeps on saying that the Trust only let you have one of their flats if they think you're respectable enough. And how we've got to make sure we stay respectable on account of that. Puts a lot of importance on being respectable, does Mum. Always going on about it she is.' Ted paused and then said gruffly, 'I reckon it's on account of her and her mum being taken into the workhouse when she was a little 'un. Her pa died, you see, and they was left destitute. Me mum, her ma, and her little brother all got taken

153

in but her brother, well, he took ill and he never came out. He died there.'

'Oh, Ted,' Agnes whispered compassionately, tears welling in her eyes. 'How awful for your mother.'

'Yes, but you're not ever to let on to her that I told you,' he warned.

'Never,' Agnes promised him fervently.

Agnes smiled when Ted squeezed her hand, but although Ted's revelations about his mother's sad childhood had gone a long way to explaining why respectability was so important to her, they hadn't allayed Agnes's fears that his mother didn't approve of her own background. Far from it. Ted thinking the best of everyone, he didn't mind at all about her not just being an orphan but being abandoned as a baby outside the orphanage, with nothing to say who she was or where she'd come from. But Agnes suspected that his mother would not share Ted's opinion.

Knowing, though, that Ted didn't like her brooding, she told him as cheerfully as she could, 'Mrs Robbins was saying again that you'd be welcome to join us for your Sunday lunch.'

'Well, that's very kind of her, Ag,' Ted replied, 'and I'd like to say yes, but you know how it is. Mum expects me to go to church with her and the girls on Sundays. I reckon she needs me to help keep the two of them in order.'

Agnes nodded. 'Yes, of course.' Her lips felt stiff and the back of her throat ached. 'I dare say I could come to church with you and your family one Sunday, Ted. If you would like me to?' she offered. She'd had to gather every bit of courage

154

she had to be brave enough to make such a forward suggestion. And it was a forward suggestion, even though she and Ted were going to get engaged come Christmas, and even though she knew Dulcie would laugh at her for thinking that.

'I'd like that, Ag,' Ted agreed, 'but like I've told you before, there's not enough room in the flat to swing a cat, never mind set up a proper table and that, like Mrs Robbins has. I reckon that Mum wouldn't like me inviting you round to have our lunch with us on account of that.'

Agnes couldn't look at him, not even when Ted gave her hand a special squeeze.

'Fancy some apple dumpling and custard?' Ted asked her.

Somehow Agnes managed to produce an enthusiastic smile. She knew that apple dumpling was one of Ted's favourite puddings, and that even if the anxiety now invading her tummy meant that she couldn't finish hers, Ted would finish it for her.

'I'm thinking about going to Liverpool,' Sally confided to Olive when she came off home from her shift. 'Mum was buried in November. I'm owed some extra time off and I think it would be right to go up now.'

Olive nodded her head, understanding what Sally meant without her having to explain.

'Not that I'll be able to get any flowers or anything, for the grave, but I just thought...'

'Will you see your dad whilst you're up there?' Olive asked.

'No. There's no point. And ... anyway I just

155

couldn't. Not after what's happened. No. I'll just go to Mum's grave, give it a bit of a tidy and that. I'm the only one she's got to do that now. I should have gone last year but...'

When she couldn't continue, Olive asked her gently, 'When do you plan to go?'

'Next week. I've got some time off owed to me. George leaves for ... for a new post soon. He's got a transfer for six months. He'll too busy starting that to be able to take any time off himself, so I thought...'

'I think it's an excellent idea,' Olive assured her. 'And it sounds as if George is doing well.'

'Yes.' Sally had her hands folded neatly together in her lap but Olive could see that they were trembling slightly so she put one of her own over them.

'I can guess how much you must miss your mother, Sally. I visit my Jim's grave every year on the anniversary of his death, and on our wedding anniversary. Tilly comes with me on his anniversary but on ours I go on my own. It's my chance to talk to him privately, you see, to tell him what's happening, and about Tilly. Some people would probably think I was being silly, but I find it very comforting.'

Sally knew what Olive was trying to tell her.

'I miss the chats that me and Mum used to have so much. Morag used to say–' Sally broke off and looked upwards blinking fiercely. 'That's what makes it all so horrid and hard to bear. Me, Mum and Morag all got on so well together. It was like Morag was my sister. I felt really proud that Mum liked her so much and that Morag got

156

on with her. When Mum was ill, and afterwards, when she'd gone, I thought I was very lucky having Morag to turn to. I thought she felt the same, you see, but she didn't.'

'I know how things must seem to you, Sally, but sometimes our emotions ... well, losing your mother and then what followed must have been dreadfully hard for you, but maybe whilst your mother was alive Morag was all the things you thought her, a good friend to you and to your mother.'

'No.' Sally kept her voice low but Olive could hear the anguish in it. 'No. I can't accept that. She was a traitor to our friendship and to the kindness that Mum showed her.'

She turned to Olive, her distress plain in her expression. 'I don't want to go back to Liverpool, but I keep thinking of Mum's grave, uncared for and...'

'Would it help if I came with you?' Olive asked.

Sally's eyes widened. She'd known already how good Olive was but her offer now made Sally think all over again how fortunate she was to be lodging at number 13.

'It's kind of you,' she told Olive, 'but no. I'll be all right now.'

'Well, if you change your mind the offer is still there,' Olive assured her.

TEN

'Come on, you two. Hurry up, otherwise all the bargains will be gone,' Dulcie called over her shoulder to Tilly and Agnes as she made her way determinedly through the Saturday crowds of Leather Lane Market.

With Christmas not so very far away there was an extra air of energy and determination about the shoppers. Not that Tilly minded the crowds. In fact, she loved the air of pre-Christmas excitement and bustle, pausing by one stall filled with holly decorations, the bright green leaves and red berries so shiny that they looked as though they had been polished.

'Fresh 'olly from His Lordship's estate. Picked it meself, I did,' the stall holder hollered when his sharp gaze noticed Tilly's interest.

'Nicked it, more like,' Dulcie told the other two. She grabbed hold of Tilly's arm. 'Come on, we've got better things to do with our time than stand staring at a bit of holly.'

'It always makes me think of Christmas, and it looks so pretty,' Tilly defended herself good-naturedly, allowing Dulcie to draw her away, and then pulling back as something on one of the other stalls caught her eye. 'Hang on...'

'What is it this time?' Dulcie demanded impatiently, but Tilly wasn't listening. Instead she was reaching for the open box of pretty handkerchiefs, each with one corner adorned with delicate lace. They would make an ideal gift for her mother, who, Tilly knew, would love something so elegant and dainty. But just as she reached to pick up the box, someone else put a possessive hand on top of her own – a buxom florid-faced woman with small, mean-looking blue eyes and an expression on her face that said she was not going to give up her prize, even if Tilly had got to it first.

'Them's mine, if you don't mind,' she informed Tilly with a mixture of determination and sarcasm.

'Actually, I think I picked them up first,' Tilly retaliated, unwilling to be brow-beaten and bullied out of the hankies.

The excitement of a bit of an argument was already drawing a crowd of shoppers to gather round Tilly and the older woman, much to the stall holder's delight, as he started shouting up his other wares to the growing audience, most of whom were paying more attention to Tilly and her adversary than to his stall.

It was Agnes, flushed of face but stalwart in her defence of her friend, who piped up, 'You picked them up first, Tilly,' her comment drawing nods of agreement from those women who had been close enough to see what had happened.

For a minute Tilly thought that she was going to be the victor, but then the other woman called over her shoulder, ''Ere, our 'Enry, come and give me a hand,' and to Tilly's horror the crowd fell back at the sight of the large overweight youth pushing his way through.

'You'd better let her have them, Tilly,' Dulcie

advised in a warning whisper. 'I don't like the look of him.'

Tilly didn't either. He had a mean look about him, his head swaying slightly from side to side, his small blue eyes just like those of the woman, whom Tilly guessed must be his mother. Something about him struck an unexpected chord within Tilly, reminding her of a long ago visit to Smithfield Market with her late grandfather. There had been a bullock being led to the slaughter house, and it had had the same kind of angry hostile look in its eyes. Half cross with herself for being a coward, Tilly relinquished the box, taking some comfort from the murmurs of sympathy for her from the crowd.

'Thanks for sticking up for me, Agnes,' she said as they started to walk away.

'What about thanking me for saving you from getting yourself into real trouble?' Dulcie demanded, all three of them stopping in mid-stride as a young lad came running up to them, dark curls escaping from under his cap, a moth-eaten scarf knotted round his neck over the too-tight tweed jacket he was wearing.

'Me brother said he had another box of them hankies and that you can have them for eight-pence if you want them?' he announced, waving a thin pale blue square box in front of Tilly's nose. ''E said you'd done him a favour getting all them people round his stall.'

Tilly looked back towards the stall, which was now besieged by shoppers, smiling ruefully as the good-looking young man behind it doffed his cap and gave her a wink.

'Don't you go giving him any money until we've seen what's inside. It could be an empty box, for all we know,' Dulcie warned, taking charge.

Happily, though, once the lid was removed they could all see the pretty lace-edged handkerchiefs inside it.

'Hold these for me, please, will you, Agnes?' Tilly begged her friend, handing them over to her whilst she opened her purse to get the money to pay the waiting boy.

'Eightpence for three handkerchiefs?' Dulcie grumbled after the boy had gone.

'I bet they charge more than that for them in Selfridges,' Tilly pointed out.

'Yes, but them as they sell are from Selfridges,' Dulcie retorted.

'They are so pretty, Tilly.' Agnes tried to pour comforting oil on the potentially troubled waters.

'Oh, look there's a label on the bottom that says Harrods,' Tilly squeaked in excitement, when she turned the box over.

'Probably come out of some Chelsea lady's dressing table drawer,' Dulcie sniffed, determined as always to have the last word.

Not that Tilly minded. It had been really kind of the stall holder to find another box for her. Mum would love them, she knew. Her mother did so much for other people, and hardly ever got any special treats for herself.

It was a cold crisp day with ice still shining prettily on rooftops, even if the cold did make one's nose and cheeks pink. Leather Lane Market

161

had originally specialised in leather goods from the many small factories that had surrounded Smithfield Market before the Blitz. The stall holders had obviously taken advantage of shoppers being anxious to make the best of things by filling their stalls with Christmas cheer in the shape of second-hand toys, and decorations. Tilly spotted a stall selling secondhand jigsaw puzzles and games, the sight of them making her smile as she remembered how much she had enjoyed such things herself as a girl. There were still stalls selling leather goods, many of them with signs indicating that what they had for sale was 'bomb damaged' in one way or another.

Several stalls were selling second-hand clothes, among them 'ready darned' sturdy socks, 'a special treat for a serving man's feet'. A solitary clown was attracting a Pied Piper's trail of small children, and keeping them entertained with tricks on sale at a nearby stall, much to the irritation of their harassed mothers, whilst a small troupe of actors in pantomime costume were handing out advertisements for their panto. A man and a woman in Salvation Army uniform were standing outside the door to a small pie shop, and on impulse Tilly broke away from Dulcie and hurried across to slip a few pennies into their collection.

From there, another stall caught her eye, this one selling brightly coloured Christmas stockings made from red felt and sewn with white felt icicles.

'What are you getting those for?' Dulcie demanded, thoroughly exasperated.

'Because I like them,' Tilly told her. Secretly

she was thinking that if Drew and the other boys should spend Christmas Day with them, then it would be fun to make up stockings for them, and if they didn't, well, then they would always come in useful for the church's children's Christmas party.

It was a busy bustling scene, bright with the colours of Christmas, its brave attempt to get into the spirit of the season highlighted by thin fingers of pale yellow watery sunshine. Tears pricked Tilly's eyes. If you closed your eyes and breathed in deeply you could just – *just* – smell the promise of Christmas in the air, even if it was cloaked in layers of dust and despair. They had all come through so much in these last dreadful weeks, Christmas felt like a beacon of hope, a rock, a small haven they must struggle to reach to give them all a small space of time to draw breath for the fight that inevitably lay ahead.

Christmas. Truly Tilly's most favourite time of the year – thanks to her mother, who had always made it such a very special time for her.

'Come on,' Dulcie urged Tilly, taking a fresh firm hold on her arm and on Agnes's as she dragged them with her through the crowd until she found a space to stop and look around purposefully for the boy who had accosted her in the Street earlier in the week.

'What are you looking for?' Tilly asked.

'Wait and see,' Dulcie responded smartly. 'Wait here,' she commanded when she spied the boy lurking by several bicycles that had been left on the corner of one of the streets.

'Dulcie, where are you going?' Tilly protested.

163

'You know Mum said we had to stay together.'

But Dulcie was ignoring her.

'What's she doing talking to that boy?' Agnes asked Tilly.

'I don't know. Maybe she knows him,' Tilly responded.

Having spotted the boy who had approached her on Oxford Street, Dulcie wasn't about to let him go before she had the information she wanted.

'So where's this shampoo you were telling me about then?' she demanded. 'Only if you were having me on...'

'I wasn't,' he promised her, making a cross sign with one grubby finger. 'Cross me heart and hope to die, I wasn't. He's down there,' he told her, gesturing toward the stalls. 'Fifth stall in. Tell him it's the special stuff you want.'

'A book stall?' Dulcie questioned in disbelief.

'It's all right. Dad keeps the stuff hidden away inside the books,' the boy insisted.

'And it's proper shampoo, is it, and not some fake stuff that's being passed off as shampoo?' Dulcie demanded suspiciously.

'It's the real thing. I swear it.'

'If you have been having me on you'll be for it,' Dulcie warned him, before going back to join Tilly and Agnes.

'I've been thinking. What we could really do with,' she told them, oh so casually, 'is some proper shampoo.'

'Proper shampoo? You'll never find that,' Tilly laughed. 'Nancy was telling Mum the other day that even hairdressers are finding it hard to come

164

by. I don't know why though, because it isn't on ration.'

'Maybe not,' Dulcie agreed darkly, 'but there is a shortage, and I know where we can find some. Because a little bird has told me that there's a stall here that sells shampoo.'

'What? Real shampoo?' Tilly demanded eagerly.

Dulcie grabbed hold of her and put her hand firmly over Tilly's mouth. 'Keep it down. Don't tell everyone,' she warned her. 'Come on, this way.'

The stall the boy had pointed out to her was stocked, as Dulcie had already seen, with piles of dusty-looking second-hand books. The stall holder, a thin wiry-looking man wearing a pin-striped suit that was almost as sharp as his narrowed gaze, was standing behind it, eyeing the crowds and smoking a cigarette, his pork-pie hat pushed back on his head. The sight of such a dubious-looking character, far from putting Dulcie off, gave her a grudging willingness to believe what the boy had told her.

Marching up to the stall, leaving the other two to follow her, Dulcie told the stall holder without preamble, 'We want some of your special stock.'

'Keep it down,' he urged her, the cigarette dangling out of the side of his mouth as he scanned the crowd before reaching down behind the counter to where Dulcie could see books piled haphazardly on top of a large tin tray, to keep them off the wet pavement.

'Dulcie, what are you doing?' Tilly hissed impatiently as she watched the stall holder lift a large battered-looking family Bible onto a stool he had pulled out from beneath the stall.

Ignoring her, Dulcie kept her gaze fixed on the Bible, from which, so speedily she barely saw the cover open, he produced a bottle of Drene shampoo. They were permitted no more than a glimpse of it before it was stashed back in the Bible box, as though it was a gold sovereign, not a bottle of shampoo. The stall holder all the while kept his intense gaze moving over the bustling street.

'I want a proper look,' Dulcie announced, reaching out to take the bottle from him.

He was obviously reluctant to hand it to her, and Tilly's eyes widened when, the minute she'd got it, Dulcie uncapped it, first to sniff it and then put a bit on her finger.

'Here, wotch it,' the stall holder protested. 'You ain't bought it yet.'

'No, and we won't be doing unless it's the real thing, and not a bit of something else you've put in the bottle,' Dulcie assured him.

Tilly, though, who had realised that the bottle hadn't been properly sealed, nudged Dulcie in the ribs and hissed, 'Dulcie, I don't think we should buy it. That bottle was open already.'

'Yes, I know,' Dulcie agreed. 'But it's full.' She gave a small shrug. 'I reckon whoever had it first hasn't used more than a capful.'

'Whoever had it first?' Tilly was shocked.

'That's why we've got to check that it's the real thing,' Dulcie explained impatiently in the kind of voice adults normally reserved for very small children. 'It's all very well buying stuff that's been looted from bombed-out buildings, but I'm not

166

paying good money for something that's a con.'

'Looted?' Tilly looked at Agnes and then back at Dulcie. 'That means it's black market.'

'It's no such thing,' the stall holder protested vigorously. 'Smoke-damaged, it is, that's all. Got it off a chap who had a warehouse wot got bombed and caught fire. I'm just doing a bit of a favour for him.'

'A favour for himself, more like,' Dulcie muttered in an aside to Tilly and Agnes, before turning back to the stall holder. 'How much?'

'Tenpence to you, darling,' he responded, giving her a smile that revealed that several of his teeth were either missing or black.

Dulcie, though, wasn't interested in his teeth. 'Tenpence?' she challenged him. 'That's daylight robbery, that is. A bit like the way you got the shampoo in the first place, I dare say,' she added meaningfully.

'Here,' the stall holder leaned across to her, a hard look on his face, 'I don't need the likes of you telling me what's what. If you don't want it, you can go and buzz off, 'cos I'm telling you that there's plenty that does.'

'Three bottles we want, and we'll pay you six-pence a bottle, and they'd better be full,' Dulcie announced, ignoring both the semi-threatening pose he had adopted, and Tilly's impressed gasp at her audacity.

'Sixpence! I've got five kids to feed,' he told her. 'And I won't take a penny less than ninepence a bottle.'

'Sevenpence,' Dulcie argued.

'Look, you've had your little joke, now why

167

don't you clear off and let someone who really wants to do business have a go?' the stall holder suggested, removing the butt of his cigarette from his mouth and grinding it out under the heel of his shoe.

'There's three of us and that's three bottles, three guaranteed sales,' Dulcie told him.

'Four if we get a bottle for Sally,' Tilly said.

'Five if we get one for your mum as well, Tilly,' Agnes added.

'That's if you've got five bottles?' Dulcie challenged the stall holder.

'What? Of course I have,' he told her, diving beneath the counter to re-emerge with four more bottles, each of which Dulcie insisted on opening and testing.

Several other shoppers had paused to see what was going on, a crowd was starting to gather on the pavement, something that seemed to please the stallholder, until a distant shrill whistle had him cursing under his breath.

'Ruddy market inspectors,' he muttered, before telling the girls, 'Come on, give us those.'

'Hold this,' Dulcie told Tilly, thrusting the bottles of shampoo into her hands and then producing her purse. 'Here's half a crown for the five bottles,' she said, pushing the coin towards the man, and then, before he could object: 'Come on, girls, I'm that desperate for a cup of tea I'm spitting feathers.'

Several minutes later, as they sat squashed together in a café made suddenly busy by a shower of heavy rain, Dulcie said gleefully, 'Five for half a crown. That's sixpence each, and they're all full,

I checked.'

'Perhaps they are damaged stock?' Tilly said hopefully.

Dulcie laughed. 'Who cares where they came from? We've got them now and that's all that matters. Come on,' she cajoled when Tilly looked uncertain, 'your mum stocked up her cupboards before the war, didn't she? That's all we're doing now: making sure we've got some shampoo.'

'Mum wasn't hoarding. She was just following instructions from the Government,' Tilly defended her mother. 'It was in all the magazines that housewives had to stock up just in case.'

'And that's exactly what we're doing: stocking up just in case,' Dulcie told Tilly virtuously, adding disparagingly, 'Poo, this place stinks of bacon and wet wool. I reckon we should head back to number 13 and get our hair washed ready for tonight. I just hope that Drew keeps his promise to bring along some of those American pilots.'

It was mid-afternoon before Olive got to hear about the shampoo and its purchase. She'd been out helping to sort through a donation of second-hand clothes, along with the other members of the WVS, ready to distribute to their local rest centre. On her return she found the three girls jostling for space in front of the front room fire as they dried their newly washed hair.

'I suppose we should have turned it down,' admitted Tilly, getting up from the hearthrug where she'd been kneeling with her head tipped forward to dry the back of her hair. Now she let Agnes

169

take her turn in front of the fire. 'But since Nancy told you that even hairdressers are struggling to get shampoo it seemed silly to pass it up, especially when Dulcie had bargained the man down to sixpence a bottle.'

Olive sighed, she'd heard – and seen – enough of what some unscrupulous emergency service workers did in the aftermath of bombing raids not to guess how the shampoo had been come by. Theoretically, no decent person could approve of looting, especially when the looted goods were then sold on at a profit to the looter. But whilst they were working together Mrs Morrison had confided to her that she'd snatched up a handful of stair rods she'd seen lying in the street on her way past a recently bombed out house.

'I know I shouldn't have done,' she said guiltily, 'but my niece is getting married at Christmas and they're desperate for household goods, and I couldn't help thinking that if she didn't have them, someone else would. Now, of course, I feel dreadfully guilty about it. But these clothes we're sorting are all from bombed-out properties. You can tell that by the state they're in.'

What she'd said was true, Olive knew.

'The stall holder said that the shampoo was fire-damaged stock,' Tilly added.

'Well, it's done now,' was all Olive felt able to say.

The front room certainly smelled very pleasantly of shampoo and clean hair, and she supposed that she couldn't really blame the girls for being girls.

Two hours later Olive was beginning to wish that her lodger and her daughter were perhaps not quite so much girls after all, as the whole house seemed to have been taken over by preparations for their evening out at the Palais.

The ironing board had had to be set up in the kitchen so that Dulcie could press the semi-circular black satin skirt as well as the cream silk blouse she was going to wear with it. Not to be outdone, Tilly had insisted on boiling the kettle so that she could steam some very small creases out of the rose-coloured silk velvet dress Olive had had made for her the previous autumn.

Surveying the chaos into which her normally organised and tidy kitchen had been turned, Olive could only reflect that it was just as well that only two of them were going to the dance and not all four.

Two heads of newly washed, pin-curled hair bobbed up and down as their owners giggled and squabbled. Thankfully Agnes, as an officially paired-up young woman, was not obliged to put herself through the Saturday afternoon ritual of 'getting ready' with quite the same intensity as Tilly and Dulcie. She was going to the cinema with Ted.

Tilly, after carefully carrying her newly steamed dress up to the bedroom she shared with Agnes bounced back into the kitchen announcing that she was going to do her nails.

'Not near my skirt, you aren't,' Dulcie warned her. 'I don't want nail polish all over it, thank you very much.'

'It would be better doing your nails somewhere a bit cooler, darling,' Olive felt obliged to point out, 'that way the varnish will dry better. It's like a laundry in here with all the steam.'

'Somewhere cooler. That means the bedroom, and that's freezing,' Tilly complained.

They were having some of Olive's vegetable soup for tea. It would be warming for them, and, she hoped, wouldn't leave a smell that would linger on their newly washed hair, Olive decided, as she watched her daughter, her tongue protruding slightly from between her teeth, as she applied the rose-coloured polish to her nails.

Dulcie had opted for bright scarlet polish for hers, and now, as she finished ironing her silk blouse and put it carefully back on its padded satin hanger, she announced, 'I'm going to go for that Pompadour curls hairstyle tonight. I saw it in a copy of *Woman* magazine that someone had left in the staff canteen.'

'Pompadour curls? What's that?' Agnes asked.

'You've got to draw your hair back from your ears and then pin it into big formal curls on top of your head, and then you tuck the hair from the back under the side curls with some Kirbigrips,' Dulcie explained, adding, 'Of course, I'll need a bit of a hand. Not you, Tilly,' she told Tilly, who looked up from doing her nails and was about to speak. 'Your mum can do it for me.'

'That's very generous of you, Dulcie,' Olive told her, her mouth twitching slightly. You couldn't help but laugh sometimes at Dulcie's wilyness, even though you knew how adept she was at getting her own way, Olive acknowledged.

'If it's still raining when you go out you'll need to tie a scarf over your hair,' she warned Dulcie.

'Oh, I hope it isn't,' Tilly wailed. 'My hair will

go all curly if it is.'

'I thought you weren't interested in Drew,' Dulcie pointed out.

'I'm not,' Tilly insisted, 'but that doesn't mean that I want to look like a fright with wild curls.'

'What I want is to see this table cleared ready for tea in five minutes,' Olive took the opportunity to tell them both.

'I'll do the table,' Agnes offered. 'It won't take me long to get ready.'

When Tilly and Dulcie had gathered up their possessions and were taking them upstairs, Olive used the opportunity to ask gently, 'Is everything all right, Agnes? Only you don't seem to be smiling as much as you normally do. Is something wrong?'

'No. Nothing's wrong. I'm all right really,' Agnes insisted, so quickly that Olive knew that her instincts had been right.

'All young couples have their fall-outs at times, and when there's a war on things aren't always easy. If you and Ted have–'

'It isn't Ted. He's ever so kind. Just the kindest person there could be.'

'But someone has upset you? Is it someone at work?'

'No.' Again Agnes shook her head, but she was now looking agitated and upset, and Olive would have dropped the subject if she hadn't seen the glint of tears in her eyes. Agnes didn't have a mother of her own to turn to – Agnes didn't have anyone of her own to turn to – and that stirred Olive's maternal heart.

Having put the ironing board in its place under the stairs, she said, 'Come and sit down for a

173

minute, Agnes.'

'I'll just finish doing the table. Dulcie and Tilly won't want to be late going out.'

'The table can wait and so can Tilly and Dulcie. Please tell me what's wrong.'

Silence and a downbent head were Agnes's only response.

Olive wasn't going to give up, though. She reached for Agnes's hand.

'Agnes, when you came here to lodge, I promised Mrs Windle and Matron that I'd look after you properly. What do you think they'd have to say to me if they knew that I knew that you were unhappy and I didn't do anything to find out why? They wouldn't be very pleased with me at all, would they?'

'Oh, it isn't your fault,' Agnes said instantly, looking dismayed.

'Then whose fault is it?' Olive pressed her.

She watched as Agnes's thin chest lifted and then fell again, a single tear splashing down her face.

'It's mine,' Agnes half-whispered, half-hiccuped. ''Cos of me being abandoned outside the orphanage and not being respectable. Ted's mum likes things to be respectable, you see, on account of them having a Guinness Trust flat, and because of her ending up...' Aghast at what she had nearly betrayed, Agnes covered her hand with her mouth, her face bright red.

'Agnes, what is it?' Olive asked her. 'Ted's mother has been unkind to you, is that what you're saying?' Olive guessed.

'No. No, she hasn't been unkind to me,' Agnes

174

defended her beloved's mother. 'I wouldn't want you thinking that. It's just, well, I don't think she thinks I'm good enough for Ted. When Ted brought her and the girls down to our station to shelter from the bombs, she never said a word to me. She just looked at me as though ... as though she wished that I wasn't there.'

'Oh, Agnes,' Olive sympathised. 'Have you spoken to Ted about this?'

'No. It wouldn't be right, me saying things about his mum to him behind her back. And besides ... well, Ted's got plenty on his plate with him having to earn enough to support his mum and the girls. I wouldn't want him thinking that I was complaining and letting him down. Nothing's been said at all, and Ted says that the reason his mum doesn't ask me round to have my teas with them or anything is because they haven't got the space, and I know that the reason he can't come here for his Sunday lunch when you invite him is because his mum likes him to help her with the girls on a Sunday. It's just that I can't stop thinking about not knowing where I've come from, and that not being respectable, especially now, with Ted saying how important being respectable is to his mum.' What Agnes couldn't tell Olive, out of loyalty to Ted and therefore to his mother, was just why respectability was so important to Ted's mother.

'Oh, Agnes, of course you're respectable. You're one of the most respectable girls I know. Ted's mother isn't going to hold it against you because you were abandoned.'

But even as she said the words Olive knew that they might not be true. People could be funny

175

about things like that, especially mothers of sons who wanted to marry girls like Agnes.

'I really wanted to make friends with Ted's sisters. I miss the little ones from the orphanage, but when Ted brought them down the underground I couldn't get a word out of them.'

'I expect the Blitz and all the bombs frightened them,' Olive tried to comfort her, but Agnes didn't look very reassured. Then Olive had an idea.

'I'll tell you what, Agnes, why don't I ask Mrs Windle if we can invite Ted and his family to the Christmas party in the church hall? That way you can get a proper chance to talk to his mother and his sisters.'

Agnes's face lit up.

'Leave it with me. I'll have a word with Mrs Windle and then if she agrees – and I'm sure that she will – I'll write an invitation to Ted's mum that he can deliver to her,' Olive promised, pleased to see her young lodger smiling again.

'Here, you can't sit there that's our table,' a shrill female voice objected, as Dulcie slid swiftly into one of the empty chairs round a table on the edge of the dance floor, directly facing the band, and pulled Tilly down into the chair next to her, seconds ahead of the four girls who had been about to sit down themselves.

'Yes, we can. It's our table now,' she said firmly.

'Well, I like that,' one of the girls fumed, glaring at them, but whilst Tilly felt a bit guilty Dulcie merely pulled a face at their departing backs.

'Just in time,' she announced triumphantly. 'I

176

wasn't going to have them beating us to this table. Everyone dancing past can see us here and I'm sure all the boys would rather look at us than at those four. Besides, your Drew will be able to see us here. If he comes, that is.'

'He isn't my Drew,' Tilly insisted automatically.

Dulcie had been right to say that they should get here early. The tables were already filling up, and although they were still attracting glares from the four dispossessed girls, thankfully they didn't seem inclined to do anything other than glower.

Tilly had visited the Hammersmith Palais many times since her first exciting dance here last Christmas, but she still felt a small fizzing sense of excitement and anticipation about being here. It was just about the best dance hall in London, so everyone said, with its good-sized well-sprung dance floor and its popular Joe Loss Orchestra providing the music. It was lovely, too, to see all the other women there dressed up in their dance frocks, the single girls determined to make the most of a few precious hours of relaxation and fun, and those with their partners looking forward to being held close in the arms of the person they loved. These days such happiness was sharpened by the knowledge that all too soon they could be parted by the duties of war. So many of the men were in uniform that the sight of them brought a lump to Tilly's throat. She could imagine how proud and how afraid for them their girlfriends and wives must feel. Just thinking about that made her shiver, as though someone had walked over her grave, as the saying went.

The Palais had not yet been decorated for Christmas, but the gilded columns, reflecting the light given off by the chandeliers and the silver ball suspended over the dance floor, made everything look shiny and exciting. Coming here was a real tonic, a bit of an escape from the grim reality of the war, rather like going to the pictures, only at the Palais you got to create your own fun and happiness rather than watching someone else's on the screen, Tilly decided happily, the bubbles of excitement inside her giving her cheeks a pretty pink glow. Of course, that excitement had nothing to do with Drew. Nothing at all.

People were already giving their table and Dulcie a second glance, and no wonder, Tilly thought generously, modestly unaware that her own pretty face and halo of clustering dark brown curls was attracting its fair share of male attention.

'That bow in your hair really sets off that style,' Tilly told Dulcie, admiring the scarlet ribbon Dulcie had added to her Pompadour curls, its colour matching her lips and nail varnish.

Dulcie looked ever so elegant and grown up, Tilly decided, the black satin skirt showing off Dulcie's narrow waist and the way she had turned her chair so that she was sitting a bit to one side of the table facing the dance floor, showing off her ankles. Tilly didn't feel confident enough to copy Dulcie's pose. She was just happy to drink in the heady atmosphere of the place.

'You'll have to be careful of your ankle when you're dancing,' she warned Dulcie. 'You don't want to damage it.'

Just for a second, Tilly's innocent comment

178

reminded Dulcie of Sally's warning to her when she had been having her plaster removed.

'Dancing won't harm it,' she assured Tilly deter-mindedly. 'Strong, that's what my ankles are, 'cos I've got good ones, see. Here's a waiter,' she changed the subject. 'What do you want to drink?'

'I'll just have a lemonade, please,' Tilly told the hovering waiter.

'And I'll have a shandy,' Dulcie added.

'There's an awful lot of men here in uniform,' said Tilly.

'What do you expect when there's a war on?' Dulcie mocked her. 'Mind you, I don't fancy dancing with some of them with them army boots they've got on.'

'Oh, look, there's Drew.' Tilly raised her arm and waved. 'Over here, Drew,' she smiled and he saw them and smiled back.

'Drew's wearing a dinner jacket,' Tilly told Dulcie, impressed. 'He looks ever so smart.'

Dulcie, though, wasn't particularly interested in Drew. She was looking instead at the three men accompanying him, whom he was directing towards their table. They were all tall and clean-shaven, with that confident look about them, and that slightly swaggering way of walking that air-men seemed to have, but it was the one in the middle on whom Dulcie focused her attention. Just that little bit taller than the others, with slicked-back fair hair, he was surveying their table with the kind of look that told Dulcie that he was just her type: confident, good-looking, and with that element of daredevil about him. Not that she was going to let him know that she'd even noticed him, never mind picked him out as her preferred choice of the three of them. Men like him liked to feel that they were the ones doing the hunting, Dulcie knew.

Drew had reached their table and was introducing his companions. Dulcie deliberately held back to let him introduce Tilly first. She knew that Tilly, with her friendly non-flirtatious manner, was no threat to her own success, even if the three boys were making a fuss of her and paying her compliments.

'And this is Dulcie,' Tilly introduced her, drawing her forward. 'Dulcie, these are–'

'Art, Pete and Wilder,' Drew told her.

'When you said you'd got two pretty girls for us to meet, I kinda thought you might be kidding us,' Art grinned, 'but I was wrong.'

'You sure were,' the one Drew had introduced as Pete agreed enthusiastically.

The third man, the best-looking one with the dangerous air about him, reached into his pocket and produced a packet of cigarettes, opening it and offering it first to Tilly, who refused, and then to Dulcie herself, holding her gaze as he said softly, 'I wouldn't say they were pretty.'

There was a general shuffling of feet and an exchange of embarrassed looks by the other three, but Dulcie didn't allow her gaze to move from the narrowed look she was being given.

'I'd say they were gorgeous.'

The other men laughed, the tension relaxing.

Dulcie took a cigarette and placed it between her lips just like they did in films. When Wilder leaned forward to light it she lifted her lashes to look right into his eyes, again, just like she'd seen them do in films. And as she had practised doing for ages at home in front of her bedroom mirror, until she got the move just right.

'Let's get some drinks over here,' he told the others without lifting his gaze from Dulcie's. 'What will you have?'

'Tilly and I have already ordered,' Dulcie told him.

'Oh, so some other guys beat us to it, did they?'

'No–' Tilly began, but Dulcie kicked her under the table, so that she stopped speaking to give her a bewildered look whilst Dulcie remained enigmatically silent, lifting her chin to exhale the smoke from her cigarette – another mannerism she'd picked up from films.

'So what do you do when you aren't breaking hearts?' Wilder asked her, having scooped up a chair from the other side of the table and then put it down next to hers before sitting on it.

'I work in Selfridges. I'm a makeup demonstrator,' Dulcie informed him, calmly inventing a title for her job without a flicker of guilt.

'I'm really looking forward to going with you when you do your reporting and photographing,' Tilly told Drew happily.

'I'm looking forward to you coming with me. You're a great kid,' Drew responded equally enthusiastically. 'How about Monday? Are you free Monday evening?'

Tilly nodded enthusiastically.

'I'll call round for you,' Drew promised her.

'How will you know where to find the best stories?' Tilly asked.

181

'We'll start off on Fleet Street, in one of the pubs the reporters use. That way we'll get to know what's happening.'

Tilly took a gulp of her lemonade and exhaled a sigh of pure delight. She loved coming to the Palais, of course, but going story hunting with Drew promised to be really exciting and adventurous, a bit like being a girl reporter in the kind of stories she'd read when she was much younger, and something which, if she were honest, appealed to her far more than flirting with boys.

'I'd heard that London has the best-looking babes in England, and now I know it's true,' Wilder told Dulcie.

He was self-confident, this American, with his compliments and his admiring looks, but Dulcie knew his game. For now she was willing to play along with it. After all, she'd already seen the envious looks their table had been given by several other groups of girls who hadn't as yet hooked up with partners. It was also an undisputable fact that Wilder, in his uniform, which he'd told her boastfully he'd had 'custom-made at your Austin Reed store', looked bigger, bolder, and just plain better than many of his British counterparts in their regulation-issue uniforms. Dulcie certainly wasn't going to have Wilder deserting her for a girl he thought might be more appreciative of his flattery – and of him. But if he thought that the evening was going to end with him giving her anything more than admiring looks and compliments, he was going to be disappointed.

Flattery was all very well as a sweetener when it came to men, but Dulcie believed that a little bit of sharpness didn't go amiss in making sure a chap knew that a girl wasn't a pushover. Her lightly mocking, 'And you've met loads of English girls, have you?' wasn't just a small put-down, it was also a way of discovering a bit more about him.

'Sure,' he responded promptly, 'I've met enough to recognise real gold when I see it. I'm surprised you aren't going steady with someone already.'

So she wasn't the only one doing a little digging. Dulcie didn't mind Wilder's question though. It showed that he was interested in more than just a couple of dances.

'I'm choosy,' Dulcie told him, adding nonchalantly, 'I dare say you've got a girl of your own at home somewhere?'

She wasn't going to get involved with someone in uniform who already had a steady girlfriend somewhere else, and who just wanted her to stand in for that girl.

'One girl?' Pete, overhearing Dulcie's comment, laughed. 'He's got—'

Dulcie pretended not to notice the sharp elbow Wilder applied to his friend's ribs, winding him into silence. She had his measure now. He was the type who thought he was God's gift to her sex. Well, she'd soon teach him differently. But first a bit more flattery was called for, Dulcie decided, to smooth away that wary look she could now see in his eyes.

Leaning towards him, she gave him her sweetest smile, accompanied by a wide-eyed, impressed look, as she said admiringly, 'You're very brave, volunteering to fight in a war that you don't have to be part of.'

Immediately the wary look vanished, to be replaced by a self-satisfied grin.

'We can't let you Brits have all the fun,' he told her, 'and besides, we thought we'd come over and show your fly boys how it ought to be done.'

'And boy, are we doing that,' Pete enthused. Slightly shorter, slightly less good-looking, slightly younger than Wilder, he was obviously rather in awe of him, Dulcie recognised. That was good. It proved her judgement was right and that she'd picked the best of the bunch, and the leader of the group.

'Did you see the look on the faces of those RAF pilots in the officers' mess after you'd flown under that Bristol Channel bridge, Wilder? I told them it was nothing and that they should wait and see what we can really do,' Pete flagged up Wilder's daredevilry.

'Did you really do that?' Dulcie asked, opening her eyes wide and looking amazed. She had no idea where or what the Bristol Channel bridge was, and she cared even less, but it was obvious that the three Americans believed that flying under it was something special, but she was prepared to indulge Wilder's vanity by praising him for it – for now.

'Sure I did. Apparently it's off limits to the RAF, but we're American and there's nothing we like more than breaking a few rules, isn't that right, guys?' As he spoke Wilder leaned forward and put his hand on Dulcie's knee.

She let it rest there for a few seconds before crossing her legs, so that he was forced to remove it, before she said archly, 'I hope that one of you

184

boys is going to ask me to dance.'

'Sure,' Wilder agreed, getting up and offering her his hand.

'It looks as though Dulcie and Wilder are getting on well,' Tilly told Drew happily as the other couple got up to dance the last dance of the evening. Tilly was glad that Drew hadn't asked her. They had danced together earlier in the evening – energetic, good fun jitterbug dances that had left Tilly breathless with laughter and enjoyment – but the long slow lights-down, couples-up-close, last dance wasn't something she would have felt comfortable doing. Because of Rick? Tilly's heart gave a small uncomfortable thump at the thought of Dulcie's brother. She was over all that silliness now, she reminded herself. She'd grown up since last Christmas, and all that upset and hurt she'd felt when Rick hadn't asked her for the last dance, but had danced with someone else instead.

On the dance floor Dulcie allowed Wilder to draw her close, but not too close, and the hand he had placed rather too low down her body for her liking she firmly removed to the small of her back, giving him a soft look as she whispered, 'I don't want to take things too fast. You've made me dizzy enough already, with all that dancing, and I think it's important that a girl keeps her feet firmly on the ground around men in uniform. I wouldn't want to lose my balance.'

'There's no need to worry about that,' Wilder whispered back thickly, ''cos I'm sure gonna catch you and hold you real tight if you do.'

'Like you're holding me now?' Dulcie asked, wide-eyed.

'Tighter than that.' Wilder's voice was growing more hoarse by the second, his hold on Dulcie tightening and his breath hot against her neck as he bent his head to whisper in her ear, 'So tight that there ain't nothing that could come between us, if you know what I mean.'

And that was supposed to make her feel safe, Dulcie thought cynically, knowing exactly what he did mean and deciding that things were going a little too fast and too far. She adroitly stepped back from Wilder just as the music finished.

Ten minutes later, after they left the dance hall and were standing outside on the dark street, whilst other dancers hurried past them – some to bus stops, some in the direction of the underground and others obviously intent on making their way home on foot – Drew announced that he intended to find a taxi and escort the girls home.

Wilder immediately objected. 'Come on, there must be somewhere we can go to have some more fun: a nightclub or–'

'We've got away without any air raids so far tonight, but that doesn't mean there won't be any. I'd rather get Tilly and Dulcie safely home than risk being caught in one,' Drew insisted, standing firm, a little bit to Tilly's disappointment. She'd never been to a nightclub and would rather have liked to see what they were like, but Drew was already flagging down a taxi, and then holding the door open for Tilly and Dulcie to get in.

186

'Selfridges, you said?' Wilder called out to Dulcie, grabbing hold of the cab door just as Drew was about to close it.

'Yes,' Dulcie called back. 'Ground floor.'

The taxi driver dropped them off on Fleet Street, not wanting, he said, to risk being caught down a narrow backstreet if the air-raid siren went off.

Although it was well past closing time for the street's many pubs, Drew told the girls that in back rooms in many of them, newshounds and print workers would be enjoying an out-of-hours drink, taking refuge in the pub's cellar, should the siren start, or, in the case of some hardy and reckless individuals, grabbing their notebooks and heading for the newly bombed areas, keen to be the first to get their story.

The smell of fish and chips wafting temptingly from a blacked-out chippy had Tilly's mouth watering so much that she tugged on Dulcie's arm.

'Fish and chips? Well, I'm not going queuing inside for them. I don't want my hair stinking of eau-de-chippy.'

'I'll go in,' Drew offered promptly, so that a few minutes later they were all happily ambling homewards, eating their fish and chip supper as they did so.

They'd just reached number 13 when the siren started.

'They must have been waiting for us to finish our chips,' Tilly laughed, before adding, 'See you Monday, then,' to Drew, and grabbing Dulcie's hand so that they could hurry up the front path together, leaving Drew to head off for the communal shelter close to the church hall.

'That's good timing,' Olive announced with relief as they came in.

'We stopped off at a chippy in Fleet Street, and we got you and Agnes some, Mum,' Tilly told her mother, proffering a newspaper-wrapped parcel.

'We can eat them in the shelter. Come on, Agnes,' Olive urged her lodger. 'You can tell us all about the film whilst we're in there.'

'That's if she actually saw any of it and wasn't canoodling the whole time,' Dulcie teased Agnes, making her blush, as they scurried round gathering up everything they'd need for the night ahead.

'I brought your siren suits down just in case you made it back in time,' said Olive, protesting at the delay when Tilly immediately started to remove her evening dress.

'I'm not risking spoiling my frock by wearing it in the shelter,' Tilly defended herself, breathlessly, as she hurried to undress.

'It won't be much good to you here if the house gets bombed,' Dulcie pointed out, but she too was tugging off her going-out outfit and pulling on her siren suit, before rushing to the back door that Olive was holding open.

'It's those ruddy Dorniers again,' Nancy's husband, Arthur, called over the fence as the Blacks left the house for their own shelter. 'Want shooting down, the lot of them.'

'The RAF are doing their best,' Tilly replied, whilst Olive, ever the protective mother, urged her on with an anxious, 'Do hurry, Tilly, they're almost overhead,' only able to relax once they were all safely inside the Anderson.

The chips Tilly had brought for her and Agnes were good, but Olive knew she would have to air the shelter to get rid of the smell, otherwise it would linger for days. She'd have to wait, though. Nancy was bound to object to her doing something so domesticated on a Sunday.

She'd had a lovely evening, Agnes thought happily as she snuggled down into her narrow bunk bed. Ted had been ever so pleased when she'd told him about Tilly's mum wanting to invite his mother and his sisters to the church Christmas party, squeezing her hand, as they queued together to get into the cinema in Leicester Square, and saying that he'd tell his mum the minute he got in.

It had been a good film, and even better had been sitting in the darkness with Ted's arm around her and his hand holding hers. But best of all had been during the interval when he'd talked about them getting engaged at Christmas and had said that they'd better look sharp and get her a ring so that she could wear it for the Christmas party.

'I've been saving up,' he'd said, ''cos I want you to have a proper diamond ring, Agnes. It's what you deserve.'

A proper ring! Agnes's chest swelled with love and pride as she remembered that moment. She knew that it would be many years before she and Ted could marry, because of his responsibility for his sisters and his mother, but she could accept that, knowing that she had Ted's love.

Of course, she'd told him that she didn't want him spending money on her when he'd got his family to think of, but Ted had brushed her protest aside: he wasn't having his girl not having a decent ring.

By the end of the evening, when they'd walked arm in arm to the bus stop, Agnes had been able to think about Ted's mum without feeling anxious or miserable at all, and tell herself that she'd probably been making a fuss about nothing.

She wouldn't act too keen when Wilder came in to Selfridges looking for her, Dulcie decided. He was the sort who had a big enough opinion of himself already. And she'd make sure that when he took her out they went somewhere decent. Perhaps even a nightclub. Dulcie had never been in a nightclub, but she sensed they would be the sort of place where she could get herself noticed, and where the man she was with could see how lucky he was to be with her.

She couldn't wait for Monday night. It was going to be so exciting going with Drew to look for stories for his newspaper articles. Not that she would let her mother know how excited she was, because if she did she'd probably only start worrying about the possible danger and change her mind about letting her go, Tilly thought wisely.

Church in the morning. How many new names of lives lost would be added to the growing list of those already remembered in their prayers? Olive

190

thought sadly. And poor Mrs Lord – they'd perhaps leave here a bit earlier than usual so that they could walk down to number 49 and ask her if she wanted to go with them. She was so much on her own these days, Olive decided.

Over the city the German bombers discharged their deadly cargo, the four women at number 13 huddling deeper into their bunks as they heard the thankfully distant explosions, punctuated by the even louder sound of the anti-aircraft batteries firing on them.

'That was only a short run tonight,' said Tilly with relief, when, later, they heard the bombers turn for home, her voice drowned out by the sound of the all clear.

ELEVEN

'...and what about that boy who's been hanging around, Sergeant Dawson? I don't like the look of him at all. Sly-faced, he is, and up to no good, hanging around the Row where he's got no right to be.'

They were standing outside the church after the Sunday morning service, Nancy and Arthur, Sergeant Dawson, Olive and Mrs Lord.

'What boy is this?' asked Mrs Windle.

'You'd better ask the sergeant...' said Nancy with one of her disapproving sniffs. Nancy was wearing the paisley-patterned silk scarf she had claimed to Olive must somehow have fallen into her handbag when they had been sorting out some second-hand clothes at the village hall. It was a pretty scarf but its plums, cream and grey colouring didn't really suit Nancy's florid complexion, or her royal-blue coat, Olive thought ruefully. Nor had the somewhat dubious means of acquiring the scarf dented Nancy's belief in her own unassailable moral stance.

Nancy continued acerbically, '...Since he seems to be encouraging him, giving him food and talking to him when by rights he should be sending him on his way. There's places for boys like him.'

It was just as well that Sergeant Dawson had broad shoulders and an equable temperament, Olive reflected, admiring the way in which he responded, calmly explaining to the vicar's wife, 'He's a young lad, who lived with his mother and his gran. They were both killed when the house took a direct hit.'

Mrs Windle had such a kind nature. Olive really liked her. She and the vicar worked so hard for their parishioners. Mrs Windle's dull green tweed coat was to Nancy's knowledge at least five years old, her brown leather gloves thin and worn, her appearance rather like that of the church itself: faded and slightly shabby but in such a way that one could see the genteel elegance they had once possessed.

'So what's he doing roaming the streets? He should have been handed over to the authorities,' Nancy was quick to tell the sergeant, tossing her head so vigorously that without its securing

192

hatpin her Sunday best felt hat could easily have come loose.

'His dad's in the army, and Barney – that's his name – is worried that the authorities will send him somewhere where his dad won't be able to find him when he comes looking for him, so every time we pick him up and take him to the authorities, he runs off the minute their backs are turned.' The sergeant's voice was polite but firm.

'He should be locked up in gaol, then he wouldn't be able to run off.' Nancy was like a dog with a bone.

'Oh, no, Nancy,' Olive was unable to stop herself from protesting compassionately. 'That would be dreadful. Poor boy. How awful for him. I'm surprised, though, that his father hasn't been given compassionate leave to see him.'

'Well, that's the thing.' Sergeant Dawson rubbed the back of his neck in a slightly embarrassed manner. 'It seems that the boy's parents had been estranged, and that has meant–'

'What it means is that the boy's father doesn't want anything to do with him,' said Nancy, her voice sharp. 'And who can blame him? Shifty, deceitful-looking boy, he is.'

It was a cold day with a biting wind, that rattled the now leafless branches of the trees, whipping up what was left of the fallen leaves into small flurries – not the kind of day that tempted any-one to remain outside for too long – but Nancy was obviously determined to have the last word. Mind, Olive thought, if the flush on her face was anything to go by, Nancy was too fired up to feel the cold. Her poor husband didn't look very happy though, his nose thin and pinched.

'Granted he doesn't look very prepossessing, but there's no real harm to the lad,' Sergeant Dawson defended the young boy. 'To tell the truth I can't help feeling sorry for him.'

'I saw you giving him some sandwiches yesterday.' Nancy made the words sound like an accusation rather than an act of kindness. 'That's encouraging him to keep coming round here. This is a respectable area. The next thing we know we'll be having things stolen and sold on the black market. He's just the type to get involved with that sort.'

'Perhaps arrangements could be made for him to be placed with a family close to where his mother and grandmother lived,' Mrs Windle suggested. 'That way, if his father does come looking for him, he'll be able to find him easily.'

'I've tried telling him that, but he seems to think it would just be a trick and that he'd end up being sent off into the country,' Sergeant Dawson told her. 'He's heard from some of the other children, who were evacuated at the beginning of the war and who then came back to London saying how much they hated the country.'

'So where is he living?' Olive asked with some concern, lifting one hand to secure her own hat as a sudden gust of wind tugged at it. Her reluctance to increase Nancy's argumentative streak by getting involved was overridden by her concern for the young boy.

'He's living rough.' Sergeant Dawson told her. 'He won't say where.'

'Oh, poor boy,' Olive sympathised again, discreetly tucking the curls that has escaped from her hat back under its neat brim.

'A nasty piece of work, if you ask me. Not the sort we want round here at all,' Nancy repeated unkindly, her expression daring anyone to argue with her further.

'I can't help feeling that Nancy can be less than charitable at times,' Mrs Windle sighed to Olive a little later in the day when the two of them were on their own at the vicarage, Olive being the first to arrive for a WVS meeting.

'I don't think she always realises how unkind she sounds,' Olive tried to defend her neighbour. 'She's got so used to criticising people that it's become a habit. That poor boy, though. Sergeant Dawson says he's only twelve or so.'

'Oh dear. As you said, poor boy,' the vicar's wife agreed.

'I hope you're going to miss me.'

Sally had gone to the station with George to see him off and now he was standing up at the window of his compartment, looking very boyish and uncertain in a way that made Sally's heart melt with affection for him. She *was* going to miss him, she admitted. She was going to miss him very much indeed. Far more, in fact, than she would have imagined, but she was still glad for him that he had been given such a wonderful opportunity.

'I am,' she told him simply. 'I've got some leave to take because of the extra hours I've worked, and I'm thinking of going to Liverpool. My mother's

195

funeral was in November two years ago,' she explained, 'and I thought I'd like to go and see that her grave's tidy, on the anniversary of her death.'

'You should have said something before. I'd have come with you,' George protested.

'I only decided to go when I heard I'd got this time off,' Sally told him truthfully. 'And you've got to start your new job.'

They'd been early for the train and now the compartments were filling up, four young naval officers filing into George's compartment, the sight of their uniforms reminding Sally of Callum.

'There isn't some Liverpudlian admirer you're going to see as well, I hope?' George teased her, his unsuspecting manner making Sally uncomfortably aware of how much about herself she'd kept hidden from him, since she knew she'd implied to him that with her mother's death she no longer had any ties in Liverpool. There'd been no need for him to know, after all. And there still wasn't. Callum belonged entirely to the past. Talking about him to anyone, but especially to George, could only give him an importance she did not want him to have.

'You're a fine one to talk about admirers,' Sally teased him back. 'I saw the look on that VAD's face the other day when she saw you.'

'What, the tall blonde who looks like a film star?' George asked her enthusiastically.

'No, the small plump one with the lisp,' Sally laughed. Being with George always lifted her spirits.

'I am going to miss you,' she told him fiercely,

for once letting her emotions get the better of her, 'but I'm glad you're going. This is a wonderful opportunity for you, George, working with such a brilliant surgeon, doing such marvellous things for those poor brave men.'

'I just hope I'm up to the job, and that I don't let him – and you – down. I can't help thinking that he's chosen me because we're both Kiwis.'

'Don't be silly,' Sally told him in a rallying voice.

The guard was closing the carriage doors, his red flag tucked under his arm as he made his way down the length of the train. At every window, or so it seemed to Sally, people were clinging to every last second of time they could with those from whom they were soon to be parted.

'I love you, Sally,' George mouthed above the noise of the steam being expelled by the engine as the guard blew his whistle and waved his flag.

'I love you too,' she mouthed back.

The train was starting to move slowly, and then gathering speed.

George was still at the window, cupping his hands together as he yelled, 'I'll write as soon as I get there.'

Dear George. She was so lucky to have him in her life.

Sally waited until the train was out of sight before finally turning to leave the platform.

East Grinstead, and the Queen Victoria Hospital there, where Mr McIndoe, who had become the RAF's 'surgeon' with the outbreak of war, had founded the Centre for Plastic and Jaw Surgery, wasn't so very far away, Sally knew. But

197

right now, having watched George disappear from sight, it felt like a very long way indeed.

There was a war on; there was nursing work to be done, Sally reminded herself briskly, making her way through the busy station, and she remembered the heartfelt promise she had made to her mother's memory to be sure that her grave wasn't left untended. With the anniversary of her mother's funeral so close, now was the time to keep that promise. The fear of seeing Callum and being weakened by her feelings for him, which had kept her away in the past, was no longer relevant. She had George in her life now. She was a very different young woman from the betrayed, angry, helpless person she had been when she left Liverpool – run away, in fact, from the pain she could not bear. Living at number 13, having Olive's wise gentle counsel, witnessing with more mature eyes the blessedness of maternal love there, had helped her to put aside her angry grief and to think instead of the love her mother had given her, the love they had shared, and which had survived her mother's death.

Then there was George, playing his own role in her life. A role she had been reluctant to allow him, fresh, as she had been, from the misery of having to abandon her dream of finding love with Callum. George's steadfast patience had won her round, though, and now Sally admitted she was ready to lower her defences. Her mother would have liked George.

Her mother. Sally exhaled unsteadily. She was stronger now, strong enough to do what she knew must be done. She had a daughter's duty and it was a daughter's love that was urging her to be at her mother's graveside on that all-important date.

Squaring her shoulders, her head held high, Sally headed for the station exit.

TWELVE

'That washing of yours will never dry in this weather. I've been ever so glad that I got my hubby to put me up one of those airing racks in my kitchen. Gets my washing dry in no time, it does. Mind you, I'm not saying that it didn't cost, because it did, but then I've never been one for buying myself or our Linda fancy new clothes instead of spending money on something practical. But then we can't all be the same, can we, and I dare say some folk like to wear their money on their backs.'

Olive was standing in her back garden, trying to peg out her washing as quickly as she could in the sharp brisk wind that was already turning her damp fingers blue with cold. Nancy, on the other hand, with only the washing for two people to have to deal with inside, was leaning on their shared fence, obviously intent on having her say. And when Nancy decided she wanted to have her say there was no power on earth that could stop her.

Ignoring her neighbour's obvious busyness, and before Olive could say so much as a word, never mind react to what she suspected what Nancy's dig at the new clothes she had bought for herself and Tilly when the war had first started, Nancy was off again.

'The clothes I've seen being brought in to be sorted out for second-hand–' she gave a disapproving sniff – 'some of them look like they've come off someone on the stage, not an ordinary decent person.'

'I dare say that some people feel that it cheers them up a bit to have something smart to wear, Nancy. I know that I've been glad that I was lucky enough to buy some good fabric and get some clothes made up for me and Tilly last year.' Olive was tempted to remind Nancy just how she had come by her prized paisley scarf but she didn't really have the appetite for the avalanche of defensive arguments that would inevitably follow the merest hint to Nancy that she was being criticised.

Olive reached down into her laundry basket for a pillow slip. At least the wind was strong enough to dry off her washing, even if right now she was looking forward to putting the kettle on and making herself a reviving brew of scalding hot tea.

'Smart isn't what I'd call some of the things I've been seeing. There was underwear brought in from a house in Chelsea that should have been burned. Shocking, that's what I say. Just a few scraps of silk and lace. Disgusting, it was.' Nancy's lips folded into a grim line. 'And that reminds me. I saw that Mrs Hallows, who's been renting number thirty-two this morning. Dressed up to the nines, she was, and when I asked her where she was going – thinking perhaps that that husband of hers, who she says is in the navy, had perhaps got leave, she told me as bold as brass that she'd just been to the butcher's. Not our butchers, but one on Sparrow Road. Said without the slightest bit of shame that it paid her to go down there on a Monday, and it was obvious what she meant. Reeking of cheap scent, she was, and with her coat open over a blouse with half its buttons undone.'

'Meat's on ration, Nancy,' Olive felt bound to remind her neighbour, as she pegged the last of her washing on to the line and then put her hand on her hip for a minute as she stretched her aching back.

'You mean it's supposed to be. There's always some who are willing to break the law – if it suits them.'

Olive was glad to escape back indoors away from her neighbour. The war was changing people, Olive thought ruefully, as she filled her kettle. In some people it brought out the best, but with others, like Nancy, it seemed somehow to focus their less likeable qualities.

Nancy had been right about one thing, though: she wouldn't get her washing completely dry on a day like today, Olive acknowledged.

Next she'd have to go down to the cellar and fill the coal scuttle.

She'd heard of some people emptying their cellars to use them as shelters, but then others said that cellars were dangerous because you could end up trapped if your house was bombed. Olive's father-in-law had always insisted on

201

keeping the cellar well stocked with coal, and, thanks to the fact that number 13 had always given him a good regular order and been good payers, the coalman had let her have a few extra bags, which meant that she could stoke up the stove to finish drying her washing. Olive did feel a bit guilty about her own good fortune when she knew that other people were going without, but the occupants of number 13 sleeping in damp sheets wasn't going to do anything for the war effort, she told herself.

She poured herself a cup of tea and took a quick sip before getting out her mincer ready to mince what was left of Sunday's roast. The fact that there was a shortage of onions might mean that her rissoles – padded out with potato to make the meat stretch further – would be less tasty than she would have liked, but at least it also meant that her washing wasn't going to smell of onions.

Olive fixed the mincer in place on the edge of the table, and then went into the larder to get the meat. You had to try to see the bright side in these dark days.

Dulcie frowned as she covertly subjected to sweeping scrutiny the entrance to Selfridges ground-floor perfume and makeup department from behind her counter. This involved the much-practised batting of her carefully mascared eyelashes. It was gone four o'clock in the after-noon and the only Americans she had seen so far had been two smartly dressed young women com-plaining about the dearth of stock in the store, comparing it unfavourably to the stores in New York.

She felt like giving them a piece of her mind, she really did. Coming in here and complaining about what British women couldn't get their hands on for love nor money, whilst wearing what Dulcie was ready to swear was Max Factor's newest lipstick shade for the winter. Dulcie suspected she knew how they had come by that! Wilder had boasted openly on Saturday night about how well supplied Americans were by their Government, with all the necessities and luxuries they might want especially shipped in for them.

The two girls Dulcie had seen had been talking about their jobs at the American Embassy, and if the American Ambassador couldn't get whatever he wanted shipped over, then Dulcie suspected no one could. It wasn't right, it really wasn't. That lipstick would have suited her far better than it did them. They looked smart enough, but they weren't as pretty as she was, Dulcie comforted herself. Nowhere near.

A few more weeks and it would be Christmas. Selfridges staff had done their best to give the store a properly festive air, but there was no doubt that the previous year's decorations looked a bit worn and faded, and there were definitely far fewer things on sale, although a special effort had been made in the toy department.

There were men in uniform wandering around the sales floor: a couple of naval officers were carrying brown attaché cases, their caps under their arms; half a dozen army officers, following in the wake of a portly red-faced senior officer with grey hair, a limp and rows of medals. There were even a group of RAF men, obviously up in London on leave and in the mood to enjoy themselves, from the flirtatious *badinage* they had engaged in with several of the salesgirls, including, of course, Dulcie herself. But none of them was Wilder. Not that he'd said he'd call in today, but naturally Dulcie had expected that he would want to prove to her that he was keen on her.

Out of the corner of her eye she saw a couple come in. The man tall, fair-haired, wearing an RAF officer's uniform, was smiling down at the dark-haired young woman at his side. Dulcie almost dropped the duster with which she'd been pretending to look busily occupied keeping her counter immaculately dust free. Her heart gave a terrific bound. David! Only when she looked properly she could see that it wasn't.

'What's wrong with you?' Lizzie asked her. 'You look like you've seen a ghost.'

'More like I'm about to become one myself, with being bored to death on account of us not having many customers,' Dulcie quipped back. 'I thought you said we were supposed to be getting some new stock ready for Christmas.'

'I only told you what I'd heard one of the other girls saying,' Lizzie defended herself.

Dulcie let her disparaging sniff tell Lizzie what she thought.

'You will look after her, Drew, won't you?' Olive, ever the anxious mother, begged the American, as he and Tilly were on the verge of leaving number 13 for Tilly's promised evening out with him to see how he worked.

'Oh, Mum,' Tilly protested impatiently, 'I'm not a baby. I can look after myself.'

But Drew simply said, 'You can depend on it, Mrs Robbins.'

'Honestly you'd think I'd never been out on my own before,' Tilly grumbled, as she and Drew headed towards Fleet Street.

'It's only natural that your mother should worry about you. My mom worries about me. She writes me all the time to make sure I change my socks and don't sleep in damp sheets.'

Tilly laughed.

'It's true,' Drew insisted. 'And it isn't just my mom. I get letters from my sisters, telling me the same thing. That's what comes of being the only boy in the family.'

'They must be fearfully proud of you,' Tilly told him admiringly, 'especially now that you're going to be writing a book.'

'Well, I haven't told them about that yet,' Drew admitted, a strained note in his voice.

When Tilly stopped walking to look at him in the dim beam from her torch, which she was supposed to keep pointed downwards in case the light was seen by a passing German bomber, Drew explained, 'The thing is that my folks – well, my dad – wouldn't approve.'

'Your father wouldn't approve of you writing a book?' Tilly's mystification showed in her voice.

'I guess my dad thinks that his son should–'

'Work in an office or a bank or something?' Tilly guessed sympathetically.

'Something like that,' Drew agreed. He sounded

relieved, because she understood and sympathised, Tilly thought, feeling very grown up to be having this kind of conversation with him.

'I know what you mean. Since the Germans started bombing London I've wished that I was doing something more...'

'More adventurous?' Drew teased her, as they started walking again.

'Something that does more,' Tilly corrected him. 'I'd thought about joining the Auxiliary Fire Service,' she told him, 'but of course Mum would worry, so I can't talk to her about how I feel. It's hard, isn't it, not being able to talk to anyone about how you feel about things? I know I've got the girls to talk to,' she acknowledged when Drew didn't say anything, 'but, well, Agnes will be getting engaged soon, so I don't think she'd really understand. Dulcie is terrific fun, but she'd just pull a face and say that you'd never get her wearing a uniform, and Sally's already doing her bit because she's a nurse. I just feel that I'm not doing enough, Drew.'

Drew reached for her hand and squeezed it. 'You can always talk to me, Tilly.'

Tilly knew then that he understood.

'Perhaps you could work in an office and be a writer – when the war's over, I mean,' she offered, wanting to help him. 'I suppose that's what your father does, is it, work in an office, I mean?'

There was a small pause. 'Yes. That's right,' Drew agreed.

They'd reached Fleet Street now.

'This way.' Drew took Tilly's arm and guided her across the street,

'We'll head for the Ye Old Cheshire Cheese pub first and see what news we can pick up there. It's one of the first ports of call of the most experienced newshounds.'

'Which building do you work in?'

'The Daily Telegraph Building, almost behind us,' Drew answered her. 'They'll be setting up the printers now for the first editions although they'll try to hold the front page for any news of fresh bombing raids tonight. We might be lucky and not have one tonight, seeing as the air-raid siren hasn't sounded yet.'

The normal time for the siren to go off was between six o'clock and half-past.

'I'm going to keep everything crossed that there isn't one tonight.' Tilly told him, as they had to pause on the pavement to wait for several cars to go by, their headlights dimmed as the law required. 'So many cars,' she marvelled.

'It's all those newspaper barons surveying their kingdoms, and then being summoned to see the Prime Minister,' Drew teased her, adding, 'I'm only joking. Most of the cars will belong to top reporters. They get a petrol allowance, and of course they've got to be able to race to the scene of an incident. Come on,' he urged, cupping her elbow, 'we can cross now, but no jaywalking, OK?'

'Jaywalking, what's that?' Tilly asked him.

'It's an American term,' Drew explained, as they dashed between slower-moving cars, to the other side of the road.

Even though it was only a weekday evening, Tilly had still worn her very best coat, feeling that

207

her old coat, which she now wore for work, with its let-down hem and school-girlish style, made her look younger than she was. Luckily it wasn't raining and the knitted beret she'd crammed down on top of her curls was keeping her warm despite the chill in the evening air.

The Cheshire Cheese pub looked every bit a piece of 'olde England' as its name implied, and even though she was with Drew, because she'd never really been in a public house before, Tilly hung back hesitantly as Drew guided her into the passage to one side of the bow-windowed frontage, telling her, 'The door is just here.'

The minute Drew opened the door Tilly forgot her nervousness in the wave of noise, warmth and the smell of beer that rushed out to engulf her. Inside, the Cheshire Cheese was almost as dark as the road outside, the cigarette smoke so dense that it might have been a real pea souper of a London fog. To Tilly, though, the smell of the smoke was as sophisticated and exciting as everything else about the atmosphere she was now absorbing with giddy delight.

'I'll show you round. The whole place is a rabbit warren of rooms and passages,' Drew told her.

He took her through a maze of busy, fuggy rooms and passages, each one of them – or so it seemed to Tilly – filled with men in trench coats, arriving, leaving, talking and calling for fresh drinks, all of them generating an atmosphere that was unlike anything Tilly had ever known.

'It makes me feel giddy just watching them, never mind listening to them,' she told Drew.

'This place, here on this street, is the centre of the world when it comes to news,' Drew told her. 'It's got something that nowhere else has. If printers' ink runs in the blood of those who work on Fleet Street, then printing presses drive their hearts and their minds to a beat that's faster and more reckless than anything else could ever be. There are men – and women – who come in here, who work here on this street, who take the kind of risks to get their story that no sane person would ever dream of taking. Maybe that's what you need to be a good newspaper man – a touch of insanity. Maybe that's why I'd rather be a writer, because I just don't possess it.'

'Drew,' Tilly protested, concerned by the bitterness she could hear in his voice, 'of course you're a good newspaper man. You must be for your newspaper to have sent you over here.'

Drew smiled in acknowledgement of her praise but there was still a shadow behind his smile. That had Tilly, whose naturally sympathetic nature made her want everyone to be happy, change the subject to ask him, 'Which room is best for us to hear news of a good story?'

'All of them,' Drew assured her, with another smile. And this one wasn't shadowed at all, Tilly was glad to see.

'Come on,' he urged her, 'let's grab that table over there. And I'll order us both a drink.'

Tilly was relieved to see that she wasn't the only female in the pub, although the other young women there looked very professional and slightly intimidating, their trench coats cinched in around narrow waists. One of them, Tilly noticed, torn

209

between shock and admiration, was actually wearing a man's trilby pulled down over her blonde hair at a rakish angle, a cigarette dangling from one side of her mouth as she engaged in an animated and what looked like a rather cross – on her part, at least – conversation with the tall, dark-haired, similarly dressed man. He wasn't cross, though, In fact, he was standing looking down at her with what seemed to Tilly to be amusement.

'Do you know those two over there?' she asked Drew, who had returned to their table carrying a half-pint pot of beer and a glass of lemonade.

Drew was smiling, but when he looked at them his smile disappeared.

'Yes,' he told her tersely.

'Who is she?' Tilly pressed him, her curiosity aroused by the sight of a member of her own sex engaged in what even Tilly could tell was essentially a very male world.

'Her name is Eva Ballantyne. She's an American freelance. The guy she's with is Ed Wiseman. He's a top war reporter who freelances mainly for the *New York Times*.'

'She doesn't seem very pleased with him,' Tilly felt bound to say, still watching them as the man removed his coat and dropped it casually across a chair. It had the same distinctive plaid Burberry lining as Drew's raincoat. Tilly remembered that Dulcie had told them all, after one of Drew's visits to number 13, that the coat would have been very expensive and that it was a favourite with Americans.

'She'll be trying to persuade Ed to get her accredited to report in the field, where the fighting's actually happening,' Drew explained to Tilly.

'A woman war reporter?' Tilly's eyes widened, and she gave a small shiver. 'She must be very brave.'

'Bravery doesn't come into it. What Eva's after is her by-line on the front page, and she'll do anything to get it there.'

Drew obviously didn't like the woman reporter, Tilly decided, shaking her head when Drew offered her a cigarette.

'My mother would like you. She doesn't approve of girls smoking. She doesn't think it's very ladylike.' Drew pulled a rueful face. 'Mom comes from a very proper Philadelphia family,' Drew explained, 'and they don't come much more proper than that.'

Tilly laughed. 'Tell me more about your family,' she coaxed him. 'Tell me about your sisters.'

'Well I'm the youngest so that means that they–'

'Are all older than you?' Tilly teased him.

'Older, and bossy with it,' Drew grinned. 'Amy – she's the eldest – she's married and she and her husband live in Washington. They've got two kids, a boy and a girl. Then there's Honor – she's married too – she lives in Boston and she has a little boy. Then there's Lucille and Alice, the twins, who are both engaged.'

'All those girls and you're the only boy,' Tilly smiled.

'Yes.'

Was that another shadow she could see in Drew's eyes?

Before she could say anything, he was being

211

clapped on the shoulder by a burly, smiling, middle-aged man with grizzled grey hair and wearing – predictably, Tilly decided – a Burberry coat, open so that she could see the checked lining.

'Drew! And who is this lovely young lady?' he demanded in a hearty American-accented voice.

'Riley,' Drew smiled at the newcomer. He introduced Tilly, explaining, 'Tilly lives several doors away from my billet, and her mother has been kind enough to invite me round to join them for some of her wonderful Sunday post-church meals.'

'Uh-huh. Nice to meet you, Tilly.'

Shyly shaking hands with the American, Tilly shook her head when he offered to buy them a fresh drink, whilst Drew accepted.

When Riley came back from the bar, placing a half-pint of beer in front of Drew, before sitting down to drink his own whiskey he topped it up from a flask, which he produced from an inside pocket of his Burberry.

'First rule of reporting in the field, young Tilly,' he told her, giving her a wink, 'never go anywhere without a full flask of whiskey. I learned that at my Irish granddaddy's knee. Talking of grand-daddies–' he continued, only to be interrupted by Drew.

'I promised Tilly I'd bring her out with me to see how we go about getting a newspaper story. I'd hoped to pick up some gossip in here about what's new, but...'

'All the American newshounds will be hanging round the American Embassy hoping to be the first to break the big story back home about Joe Kennedy's resignation as Ambassador.'

'But he hasn't resigned,' Drew protested.

'Not yet, but I've heard a strong whisper that he will, which is why I'm off to the Embassy myself.' Draining his glass, Riley stood up.

'If you want a story, Drew, a contact of mine tells me that there's a whole lot of petty criminals getting themselves into uniform – air-raid wardens, auxiliary fire fighters, that kind of thing – so that they can be the first on the scene to get their hands on anything of value in bombed property. I hear there's a waiting list for any kind of civil defence hands on jobs in the better-off areas – Mayfair, Chelsea, and of course the big posh squares.'

'I hate to think of people doing things like that,' Tilly said sadly after Riley had gone. 'Especially people who are in the Auxiliary Fire Service.'

'No one likes seeing their personal heroes tarnished,' Drew told her, adding comfortingly, 'but one bad apple doesn't mean the whole barrel is bad.' He looked at his watch. 'We'd better make a move. It's getting late, the landlord will be ringing time soon, and I'd better get you home before your mother starts worrying. We've been lucky: a whole evening without any bombers coming over. That's a first.'

'We can't go home yet. What about your story?' Tilly protested.

'No bombs means no fresh news, which means no story,' Drew told her.

'Will you ask Riley to put you in touch with his contact so that you can write about the looters?' Tilly asked him.

'I don't know,' Drew answered her. 'It's a matter of balance between revealing what's going on and damaging people's faith at a time when they most need it.'

'Oh, Drew, you are kind,' Tilly told him with admiration as he helped her on with her coat, ready to face the November night chill.

'You mean I'm too soft to be a really good reporter, the kind for whom getting the story matters more than anything else.'

The bitterness and pain in his voice made Tilly feel so sad for him that she tucked her arm through his comfortingly as they left the pub together.

'You are a good person, Drew, and one day you are going to write a really good book,' she told him firmly. 'And that's much more important than being a good reporter.'

'Tilly, I wish I had a tenth of your faith in me,' Drew smiled, pulling his trilby down low over his ears and turning up the collar of his coat, before taking hold of Tilly's hand and, keeping hold of it, pushing it deep into his coat pocket.

Tilly opened her mouth to remind him that she was wearing gloves and then closed it again. There was something nice and warm and really good about having her hand held so firmly in Drew's and tucked into his pocket. It was far more enjoyable than any amount of warmth from a mere pair of gloves.

Neither of them said anything as they headed back towards Article Row. It was lovely to feel so comfortable with a person that you didn't need to make conversation, Tilly thought, as they exchanged smiles as they paused to cross the road.

'I've really enjoyed tonight,' Drew told Tilly as they turned into the Row.

'So have I,' Tilly agreed.

'We should do it again. Go out together, I mean. Only next time I'll take you somewhere better.'

'You mean take me out on a proper date?' Tilly questioned.

They had both stopped walking now and were standing facing one another.

'Yes, if you'd like that,' Drew confirmed.

Would she? It didn't take Tilly long to make up her mind. The rising tide of happiness inside her had done it for her long before she had opened her mouth to tell Drew half shyly, 'Yes, I would.'

'You're one very special girl, Tilly Robbins,' Drew told her in a voice that had a sort of huskiness about it, which made Tilly's heart thump and her pulse race.

'No, I'm not. Not really. But I'm glad that you think I am,' she managed to say firmly.

'Oh, Tilly.' Drew was laughing and shaking his head, and then somehow or other she was in his arms and he was holding her tight. And rather unexpectedly, instead of worrying that someone might see them and demanding to be released, Tilly discovered that she was actually very much enjoying being in Drew's arms and very much wanted to stay there.

'You're a real tonic, as you English say. A beautiful, honest girl, who I think has stolen my heart.'

'I bet you say that to all the girls,' was all Tilly

215

could think of to answer.

Her heart was thudding even more erratically when Drew assured her fiercely, 'No I don't. I've never said that to any other girl. It's too soon, and you're too young. There's a war on, and your mother will think I'm letting her down saying this, but, Tilly, will you think about becoming my girl? I won't rush you into ... anything... Don't worry about that.'

'Yes.' Tilly told him, almost too breathless with delight to speak. 'And I'm not worried, about ... anything.' How could it have happened that she hadn't even realised just how much she would like to be Drew's girl. She had truly only thought of him as a friend until now. Until he had held her hand, until that bubbling, giddy, happy feeling inside her had told her that what she felt for him was more than friendship.

'But I don't think we should tell anyone else yet,' she cautioned him, adding hurriedly, 'It isn't that I want to be deceitful or anything, but, well, we might find out that we really only want to be friends and then...'

'I know what you're trying to say, Tilly, and I do understand, but I must ask your mother if it's all right for me to take you out, and that means that I shall have to tell her something of how I feel about you. It would be wrong of me not to. How about I tell her that we like each other and that we've agreed to take things slowly?'

Tilly nodded. 'But I don't want the girls to know – not yet. It's too soon.' What she meant was that she didn't want to make a fool of herself a second time, like she had done with Dulcie's brother, imagining herself in love with him and daydreaming about him returning her feelings, creating something out of nothing at all and then ending up feeling miserable, although something told her that things would be different with Drew. After all, he was the one who had declared his feelings first.

'How long have you known?' she asked him. 'I mean about me ... about us?'

'From the minute Ian introduced us I kinda knew, but it was when you let me talk to you about my writing that I really knew.'

They were standing in the November darkness, quite alone, with no one to see them.

'I'd very much like to kiss you, Tilly, if that's all right?' Drew told her.

Tilly drew in a deep breath. She had two choices now. She could say no and remain a girl on the edge of womanhood, or she could say yes and cross the bridge that separated being a girl from being a woman.

'Yes, please,' she told Drew shakily. 'I'd like you to kiss me very much.'

And she liked kissing him very much as well, Tilly discovered to her own blissful delight several minutes later when she was still locked in Drew's arms, her own arms around his neck, her lips still warm and tingling slightly from her first proper grown-up kiss.

Of course, it was disappointing after the heady private delight of taking that important step into womanhood to arrive home to find that instead of finding her mother alone so that Drew could ask for permission to take Tilly out 'officially' on a proper date, not only were all three of the lodgers filling the small kitchen, and helping her mother to make an unusually late supper, but that two separate conversations were going on, and Ian Simpson was also there, despite the fact that it was gone 11 p.m.

'Ian was on a late shift, and when he saw me putting the milk bottles out he asked if Dulcie was still up and could he have a word with her to see if Selfridges toy department have got any of the toys his children have put on their lists for Father Christmas,' Olive explained.

'Yes, and I've asked Ian if he would let my brother stay at his house when he comes up to London to see me whilst he's on leave,' Dulcie chipped in, throwing a casual, 'And he can come and have his meals here, can't he?' in Olive's direction so that she felt obliged to agree, whilst quickly looking at Tilly to see how her daughter was reacting to the thought of the return of the handsome young man she had had such an obvious crush on. However, when Olive saw the look that Tilly and Drew exchanged – a silent shared acknowledgement that their news would have to wait – she realised that Tilly was not going to be in the least concerned about Rick.

Of course, Olive wanted to know how the two young people, who had left number 13 earlier as nothing more than friends, were now returning looking at one another with dazzled starry gazes, but she could hardly say anything in front of the others.

'You'll like Rick, Drew,' Dulcie told the young

218

American. 'Everyone does, and he'll be company for you. Oh, unless of course you're going home to America for Christmas?'

'You did say that you might,' Ian agreed.

'I was thinking about it,' Drew acknowledged, 'but there's so much going on here now...'

Again, that shared, love-struck look passed between Drew and Tilly, Olive saw. '...that it makes more sense to stay.'

Makes more sense. Oh, but she'd tease him about using those practical matter-of-fact words, just as soon as they were alone together again, Tilly decided, mentally hugging to herself, the special message in the look Drew was giving her. Makes more sense, indeed! It wasn't anything sensible he'd been saying to her when he'd been kissing her not ten minutes ago, and telling her that even a minute apart from her was a minute too long.

'Cocoa, you two?' Olive asked.

The manner in which her mother said 'you two' made Tilly give her a startled, flushed look as she realised her mother had guessed something was going on.

'I'll take my cocoa upstairs with me and drink it whilst I pack,' Sally announced. Her train for Liverpool wasn't until late tomorrow evening, but she had nervous butterflies in her tummy already at the thought of returning to Liverpool, though she was not going to allow them to deter her from what she believed she had to do.

Agnes stifled a yawn. She and Ted had met up after tea at the café close to the station, making a pot of tea stretch for nearly three hours that had been blissfully free of any air-raid warnings. Poor Ted was worrying about his sisters' Christmas presents...

Seeing how preoccupied Agnes looked, Tilly said affectionately, 'You're very quiet, Agnes.'

'I was just thinking about Ted's sisters,' Agnes told her. 'Ted's feeling bad because the little one has asked for a doll with real hair for Christmas, and the other one wants a dolly's pram. Ted can't afford anything like that, but he doesn't want to disappoint them, so he's been looking round to see if he can buy their toys second-hand. But with so many other people doing the same thing, he isn't having much luck.'

'We can all help him by looking as well, can't we, Mum?' Tilly offered.

'We can,' Olive agreed, 'but, as Agnes has said, with so many parents doing the same thing I don't think you'll have much luck. It's a pity we gave all your toys away, Tilly. You had a lovely baby doll, remember?'

'Yes. Her eyes opened and closed and you knitted her some lovely clothes.'

'I had a doll, but the minute Edith laid eyes on it she wanted it,' Dulcie joined in, 'and of course she ended up getting it.' She tossed her head as the tale of childhood rivalry stirred old memories, reminding Dulcie of the fact that Edith had been their mother's favourite.

In the end, much to Tilly's frustration, it was gone midnight before finally she and Drew were alone in the kitchen with her mother. Ian, much to Drew's relief, had left earlier, saying he wanted to write to Barbara and the children before he went to bed.

Now, almost bursting with what she wanted to say, Tilly reached for her mother's arm, and began, 'Mum, there's something we want to tell you.'

'I rather thought there might be,' Olive agreed, smiling slightly. Tilly might think of herself as a young woman but to her she was still her little girl, her feelings written as clearly in her expression for Olive to see as they always had been.

'Tilly, I'd like to talk to your mom on my own,' Drew announced before Tilly could say anything, adding formally, 'If that's all right with you, Mrs Robbins?'

Olive's heart sank. Surely Drew wasn't going to say he wanted to propose to Tilly? She certainly hoped not. Olive liked the young American, and she could see how Tilly felt about him, but Tilly was far too young and their relationship far too new, for that kind of commitment.

'We'll go into the front room,' she said.

Tilly watched them leave the kitchen, feeling both proud of Drew for being so polite and proper, but at the same time not wanting to be excluded.

In the front room Olive sat down in one of the chairs, not relaxing but sitting on the edge of it, her ankles neatly crossed and her hands folded in her lap as she said quietly, 'Please do sit down, Drew.'

'I guess you've realised what's happened,' Drew told her as he folded his lean length into the other chair.

'I can see that my daughter has stars in her

eyes, like the young girl she is,' was all Olive was prepared to commit herself to.

'I asked Tilly tonight if I could take her out on a proper date, provided you gave your permission. That was all I planned to do. Nothing more, but things sort of got out of hand a little, and before I knew it I was asking Tilly if she'd be my girl,' Drew admitted.

Olive exhaled shakily. It was a relief to discover that it was only as yet her permission for Tilly to be 'his girl' that Drew wanted.

'Tilly is only eighteen,' she pointed out nevertheless.

'We've said we won't rush things,' Drew assured her, 'and I promise you that Tilly will always be safe with me, in every kind of way. I won't deny that as far as I'm concerned I've met the girl I want to be my wife, but I'm not about to rush Tilly or persuade her into something too soon.'

Olive believed him.

'You're the kind of young man that every mother hopes her daughter will bring home, Drew,' she told him truthfully. 'But war makes young people impatient and sometimes, because of that, they make decisions they end up regretting. I am prepared to agree that you can take Tilly out as your girl, but I don't want the pair of you rushing into a more serious commitment, at least not yet.'

In the kitchen Tilly was too impatient to wait any longer, hurrying into the front room to demand, 'Mum, you will let us, won't you?' before going to Drew's side and reaching for his hand.

'Your mom has said that I can date you, Tilly,'

Drew told her, 'and that you can be my girl.'

'Mum,' Tilly said breathlessly, releasing Drew's hand to rush over to Olive and hug her ecstatically.

Of course, after that the young couple had to be allowed to say good night to one another in the privacy of the narrow hall – without the light on – although Olive was reassured about her own judgement of Drew when Tilly reappeared in the kitchen after only a couple of minutes, her face flushed with that look of a girl who has just been very happily kissed.

Olive suppressed a small sigh. It both seemed a lifetime since she had felt the emotions that she recognised Tilly was feeling right now, and yet, at the same time, only yesterday.

'Oh, Mum, I'm so happy,' Tilly told her dancing round the kitchen. 'It's so funny really. Only this evening when Drew and I were walking to Fleet Street, I thought to myself how comfortable I felt with him and how lovely that was, not realising at all just what that meant. But then later, when he held my hand, I just somehow knew, straight away. It was so wonderful, as though everything had somehow clicked into place: so right that I should love him and that he should love me back, and that that had been waiting there for me to recognise it. Don't you think that Drew is just the best and nicest person there could be, Mum?'

'He's a very pleasant young man,' was all Olive would allow herself to say. 'A young man who is sensible enough not to rush into something that's too much too soon, Tilly.'

'I know what you're saying, Mum,' Tilly smiled, 'and we aren't going to rush into anything. We're both agreed on that.'

'Good. I'm glad to hear it,' said Olive.

'I'm not going to say anything to the other girls yet,' Tilly continued. 'We are only going out, after all.'

Looking at her daughter glowing like a lit-up Christmas tree with her happiness, Olive suspected that their lodgers would guess what had happened within a week. Young love, how sweet and precious it was, but war could be cruel, as Olive knew only too well, and young lovers could end up with broken hearts and broken lives ripped apart by that cruelty. At least Drew wasn't in uniform, Olive tried to comfort herself, and thankfully that meant that there would be no tearful pleas from Tilly for her permission to allow them to marry because 'there's a war on and we might only have now'.

The last thing she wanted was for her daughter to follow in her own footsteps to become a young bride and then a young widow. Married at eighteen, Olive had been only nineteen when Tilly was born.

THIRTEEN

Liverpool's Lime Street station was so familiar and yet, at the same time, somewhere where she no longer felt comfortable, Sally admitted. She felt like that because of the memories already aroused by her coming back.

Her train had been slow-moving, stopping frequently, and filled in the main with young men in uniform, especially merchant seamen, no doubt travelling between the ports of London and Liverpool to pick up their next berth. The train had finally steamed slowly into the station just as dawn was breaking.

The city air smelled of the sea, the noise of the gulls overhead reminding Sally that seamen always said the gulls came further inland when the weather was due to turn bad. There was certainly a blustery wind, buffeting those who braved it; most of the people around her huddled into their coats to protect themselves from the icy sting of the rain that had started to fall.

To the west of the station were the docks and Liverpool bar, beyond which lay the Atlantic. The taste of salt sea air on her lips reminded Sally painfully of taking the ferry to New Brighton with her parents for childhood days out, her hands held tightly one parent on either side of her. A happy child, she had never questioned but simply accepted that happiness. What Morag had

225

done, though, had stolen that happiness and those memories from her, overlaying them with the pain it had caused Sally to know that her father could forget her mother so easily.

Wavertree, where Sally had grown up, lay around three miles to the east of the city centre. Originally developed early in the twentieth century as a village on the edge of the city for the middle classes, it had now become part of the city itself. Yet to those who lived there at least, it remained slightly socially above the rest of Liverpool.

Sally's mother had been an active member of her local WI, as well as on the church flower committee at their local parish church of the Holy Trinity. Sally had grown up in a sociable home with a mother who had encouraged her to join in various activities at the church and the local tennis club.

Her mother's grave was in the graveyard of Holy Trinity church, and it was hard for Sally, as she waited for the bus to take her to Wavertree, not to think of the day of her mother's funeral on this, the anniversary of her death.

By travelling overnight and arriving during the morning, Sally had planned to be able to return to London on an afternoon train rather than stay overnight in a city that now held only painful memories for her.

In her mother's memory Sally had chosen to wear the clothes she had worn for her funeral – a black woollen dress under a three-quarter-length black swing coat. She could see herself now, standing in Lewis's department store, staring blankly

226

around, still unwilling to accept that her beloved mother was dead, whilst Morag – treacherous, deceitful, duplicitous Morag – had coaxed her into buying her dress and coat, acting out what Sally knew now had been a fictitious role of friendship.

What a gullible fool she had been, clinging to Morag in her grief, believing that Morag was truly her friend.

The bus arrived, lurching through a puddle to throw up a spray of grey-brown water, so that the waiting queue fell back to avoid it.

'Ruddy driver,' the woman standing next to Sally said grimly with a pronounced Liverpudlian accent. 'He went into that puddle deliberately. Isn't it enough that we've got ruddy Hitler bombing us without some ruddy bus driver soaking us as well?'

No war could dowse the Liverpudlian sharp sense of humour, Sally recognised as she waited her turn to step onto the bus, finding a seat at the back next to two amply upholstered middle-aged women both of whom were balancing worn shopping bags on their laps. Noting the shopping bags, Sally reflected that they must live in the Edge Hill area, not Wavertree. The ladies of Wavertree shopped with wicker baskets, not worn shopping bags. They wore hats and gloves, and in the main had their produce delivered from one of the many excellent local shops on the High Street, travelling into Liverpool perhaps once a week to meet up with friends for afternoon tea in Lewis's and listen to the pianist there.

As the bus lumbered up Edge Road, Sally couldn't help overhearing the conversation of the

227

two women to the side of her. They were having a semi-heated discussion about which poultry stall holder in St John's Market provided the best value for money when it came to a Christmas turkey. Another thing Liverpudlians were good at was speaking their mind, Sally reflected, glad to have the women's conversation to distract her from the sombre and sad purpose of her visit.

By the time the bus finally trundled into Wavertree, it was almost empty. Sally deliberately got off a stop away from the parish church, feeling that she needed the time it would take her to walk there to compose herself for the ordeal she would be facing.

Walking down Woolton Road to its junction with Church Road, Sally could see the eastern end of the church ahead of her. Soon she would be alongside the graveyard. Her footsteps slowed. Inside her head she had a far too clear memory of that other November day when the rain had fallen from a leaden sky as steadily and unceasingly as her own tears as she sat between her father and Morag in the back of the black Rolls Royce funeral car following the hearse. On top of the polished wooden coffin, with its brass handles, the sight of the wreaths and crosses in hothouse red roses and white lilies woven into greenery, the flowers forced into life so that they too could die, had made Sally feel physically sick.

Their bishop had conducted the service, the vicar waiting to greet them just inside the gate to the churchyard. Just before they had got out of the car Sally had looked at her father and seen the tears on his cheeks. Meaningless tears cried for a wife he had quickly forgotten when offered the temptation of a new young second wife. How could he have done that? The church had been full, Sally remembered. It hadn't comforted her, though. Instead she had been filled with anger that someone so well loved had been taken from those who loved her.

Sally had reached the gate to the church. Skirting the church itself, she made her way past the ancient mossy stones belonging to the dead of previous centuries. A gang of workmen passed her, carrying shovels. Sally's heart somersaulted with the threat of nausea. They would be on their way to dig a fresh grave, or perhaps several fresh graves, given the harsh realities of the war.

Her mother's grave lay beyond the old headstones in a quiet part of the cemetery that she and her father had chosen together, the plot large enough for both of them, only now, of course, he had a second wife to choose to lie with for eternity. Angry tears burned her eyes. Sally paused to rub them away and then froze, paralysed by shock and disbelief as she looked toward her mother's grave and saw that it was not abandoned and neglected as she had expected, and that, right now, someone else was performing the task that should have been hers and tenderly laying flowers against the immaculately clean and well maintained marble headstone. Three familiar heads, two of them dark and one silver grey, were bent as though in prayer, whilst from the carefully wrapped bundle one of the three was carrying, a small arm and mittened hand emerged.

Her father, Morag and Callum, with the child

Callum had told her about. They were the last people Sally had expected to see here. The last people she had wanted to see here. They had come to the graveyard just as she had to mark the anniversary of her mother's death. It was too much for her to take in, too much of a shock, too much of an intrusion. She felt an unbearable agony, not just of grief but also of anger, that they would do such a thing. What right, what place did they have here, after what they had done? And to bring that ... that child. Anger, bitter and hot, burned its way through Sally's veins.

As she watched, Callum, tall and strong-looking in his naval uniform, placed his arm around her father's stooped shoulders, whilst Morag rested her head against her father's shoulder. A wave of fierce pain stabbed through Sally's heart as she witnessed their closeness. That was her father, now part of a family group from which she was excluded and to which she was an outsider. Her father standing looking down at her mother's grave with the treacherous friend who had now taken her place.

They had their backs to Sally as they stood beside the grave, and there was no reason for them to turn towards her. They had plainly come to the plot from the other side of the church and could return that way, but whilst her concentration was drawn against her will to the baby Morag was holding, for some reason Callum turned round. They looked at one another. Sally couldn't move, she couldn't speak, she could hardly even breathe. All her faculties seemed to have telescoped into a paralysis that held her rooted to where she was standing.

She saw her father and then Morag, alerted by Callum, both turn towards her. Every tiny movement was recorded by her brain in cruel detail as she saw Morag reach for her father's hand and hold it tightly, his free arm going round the baby, the three of them forming a bond, united against her.

She heard Callum calling her name, the sound picked up and tossed by the keening wind so that it seemed to have a note of stark anguish to it.

That sound broke the spell that was holding her. Sally turned on her heel, starting to walk away and then to run as she heard Callum calling to her again. This time the sound closer. A quick look over her shoulder showed her that Callum was coming after her. He must not catch her. He must not speak to her or touch her. She couldn't bear it. She couldn't bear to have anything to do with any of them. In London she had mentally criticised them for what she had imagined would be their neglect of her mother's grave, but now Sally found that she could not endure the thought of them going anywhere near it. To have seen Morag, that traitor, laying flowers on it was sacrilege of the worst kind. A sob tore at Sally's lungs as she started to run faster. There was a bus at the bus stop, just starting to move off. Sally put on a final spurt of speed, reaching for the bus's hand rail and swinging herself up onto the platform, the effort pulling at the muscles in her arm and earning her a shaken head of disapproval from the conductor.

Through the back window of the bus Sally could

see Callum standing watching the bus disappear. She had escaped from him, from them, but she would never be able to escape from her memories or the pain they caused her, Sally acknowledged as she paid her fare.

Luckily the bus was going back to the city centre, even if the route it was taking was a rather roundabout one. The ride was long enough for the stretched muscles in Sally's shoulder to have started to ache by the time she got off at the bus station to make her way through the busyness of St John's Market as she headed for Lime Street station.

The bag on her arm, containing the things she had brought with her to tidy up the grave, added its weight to the ache tormenting her heart.

How dare Morag have assumed the right to tend the grave of the woman she had supplanted, Sally thought bitterly as she waited for the London train, her normally logical brain overwhelmed by the intensity of her emotions. And taking that baby, as well, adding insult to the injury she had already done to Sally's poor mother. Her mother had loved children, especially babies, her face softening whenever she held one.

Why had Callum called out to her and tried to stop her? What had he hoped to achieve? After all, she had told him how she felt. Had he perhaps wanted to force her to witness her father's new happiness? His new child? His new daughter, Sally recognised, remembering her brief glimpse of that pink-mittened baby hand.

The train Sally had been hoping to catch was

cancelled, and it was over an hour before the next one arrived, by which time Sally felt chilled to the bone and sick of the taste of stewed lukewarm tea. When the train did arrive, as it slowed into the platform the carriages looked as though they were already full, despite the large number of people, especially soldiers in uniform, waiting to board it.

'Looks like it's going to be standing room only,' a young woman in a smart WRNS uniform told Sally ruefully. Both her appearance and her accent suggested that those who said that the majority of girls who went into the WRNS were middle- and upper-class were correct, Sally decided. She nodded in acknowledgement of the Wren's comment, whilst trying not to think that it was girls like these, in their immaculate uniforms, that Callum would be mixing with now that he was in the navy. After all, why should she care who Callum mixed with any more? She didn't.

A few seconds later, one of the group of soldiers clustered round the train door saw them and said something to the others, which had them falling back to form an untidy guard of honour to allow Sally and the Wren onto the train first. Sally hesitated, not sure if their preferential treatment was due to good manners or the smart uniform and undeniably pretty face of the Wren, who had now stepped past the men as though doing nothing more than accepting her due, whilst Sally followed in her wake, offering a thank you for them both.

It was a corridor carriage with compartments off it. Their ascent onto the train might have been swift, but their passage along the corridor certainly wasn't, packed as it already was with other passengers. They had to inch their way along it, Sally's heart sinking at the thought of having to stand, perhaps all the way to London.

However, it seemed that their luck was in because another young man, this time in RAF uniform, spotted them as he stood outside a non-smoking compartment, smoking a cigarette. He turned to look into the compartment, calling out as he did so, 'Pretty girls approaching, chaps – two seats required, and pronto.'

To Sally's amusement, two young pilot officers were immediately ejected from their seats inside the compartment by their fellows, and she and the Wren were offered their seats with a flourishing bow.

'I wouldn't normally accept,' the Wren murmured discreetly in Sally's ear, 'not if I was on my own, it might look too fresh, but since there are the two of us, if you're willing?'

Sally agreed, her original rather less than favourable impression of the other girl revised as she heard her say pleasantly, 'Thanks, chaps. Very much appreciated.'

'Suppose it's too much to hope for you having a flask of navy rum ration stashed somewhere about your person?' one of the pilot officers asked the Wren as she and Sally sat down opposite one another, each squashed between two men seated on either side of them.

It was growing dark outside now. A train guard came round to announce that all window blinds were to be pulled down on account of the blackout, and that if no blinds were there then no lights must be shown in the carriages.

Luckily their compartment did have blinds, although one of the pilot officers tried to pretend that one of them didn't work, teasing the two girls by saying jovially, 'Oh dear, this one's stuck. That means it's going to be to be lights out, I'm afraid, girls.'

The Wren made Sally laugh and went up in her estimation again when she responded with a completely straight face, 'Never mind, I've got exactly the thing that I know will make the blind work.'

'What's that then?' the pilot officer demanded.

'A very long sharp hatpin,' she responded sweetly, her response eliciting guffaws of laughter from the other men.

'She's got you sussed out good and proper, Racey,' one of them crowed.

'They don't mean any harm. They're only boys letting off high spirits really,' the Wren told Sally in a low voice whilst the pilot officers were ribbing one another. 'I've got four brothers so I'm rather used to all that boyish fooling around. They're the reason I'm in this uniform. Our grandfather and our father were both naval men so when they joined the Senior Service I thought I might as well follow suit. Not that mine is much of a life on the ocean waves; more a life on a very uncomfortable stenographer's chair in Bath. I'm Jane, by the way.' She pulled a face. 'Not the best of names, these days, given the racy cartoon from the papers.'

'Sally,' Sally responded, shaking the other girl's

hand whilst she laughed at her mention of the Jane character from the cartoons, who was so famous for shedding her clothes.

'Oh, I'm sorry. I've just noticed that you're wearing black,' Jane apologised. 'I hope I haven't said anything inappropriate.'

'No. I've been to visit my late mother's grave. She died two years ago.'

'Ah. I am sorry. I lost my mother when I was fifteen so I do know how awful it is, but one is constantly aware these days that the sight of someone wearing black could mean that they've just lost someone. Are you travelling all the way to London?'

'Yes,' Sally responded. 'I work at Barts Hospital. I'm a nurse there. And you?'

'To London and then on to Bath. Some of the Admiralty staff are based there, and my job moved with them. A nurse. And you've been in the city through the Blitz, I suppose? I salute you for that. I went up for a couple of days on leave to catch up with some old chums and I was scared to death.'

'Hear that?' Racey spoke up, hearing their conversation. 'We've got a Wren and a nurse.'

'I'm a theatre nurse,' Sally told them, keeping her face as straight as Jane had done earlier, 'so rest assured I shall be able to tell my friend exactly where to stick that hatpin for maximum effect, should it prove necessary.'

The pilot officer who had been standing outside in the corridor smoking now put his head round the open carriage door, obviously having heard her, and said drily, 'Take no notice of

236

them, please, ladies. They're still wet behind the ears, and not really fit to be let out alone. Rest assured retribution will be exacted for any misdemeanours.'

'Wet behind the ears? That's a good one, Quilley, when I've had four kills in ten days, and Smoky over there has had five,' the young man they had called Racey protested.

The man standing in the doorway was slightly older than the others, Sally could see now in the dim light of the carriage, and a flight lieutenant. He also had that look about him she had sometimes seen on the faces of some of hospital's surgeons after they had had to deal with a particularly bad night of bombing victims: a mixture of anger, pain and an absolute grim determination to fight to the last breath for their patients' lives.

Beneath the joshing from the young men in the compartment, Sally could also see their respect for him. She and Jane need not fear that the young pilot officers' behaviour would get out of control with him there.

The train crawled slowly through the darkness, jerking to a halt sometimes for a station with its name blacked out, Sally saw when she lifted the blind, and sometimes for no apparent reason at all. The young men had fallen silent, some of them sleeping, others coming and going to smoke. The journey south was taking far longer than the one north to Liverpool, Sally reflected, checking her watch.

'We'll be pulling into Crewe next stop,' the flight lieutenant, whose name Sally and Jane had now learned was Quillan, told them. 'We'll be there for a good ten minutes, if either of you wants to make use of the facilities or get yourselves a sandwich. I'll keep your seats for you.'

'Thank you,' Sally smiled, appreciative of his kindness and good manners. Her thanks were echoed by Jane.

'That was jolly decent of him, I don't know about you, but I could rather do with a trip to the Ladies,' Jane confided to Sally, 'and I had been rather dreading hiking down the train to find a lavatory.'

'Same here,' Sally admitted.

Their stop at Crewe was just long enough for Sally and Jane's trip to the Ladies, and then to drink a quick cup of tea before they dashed back to their carriage, pausing on the way to buy some sandwiches from one of the trolleys pulled up close to the carriage windows for those who didn't want to risk losing their seats by getting off the train.

The pungent aroma of beer and spirits filling the compartment once the trains set off suggested to Sally that the boys had made use of their time off the train to find a bar, but she didn't have it in her heart to blame the young men for their self-indulgence. Everyone who had read of the bravery of both the fighter pilots and the bomber crews over the summer, when they had fought so hard to win the Battle of Britain, knew how many brave young men had lost their lives.

Mercifully the train started to pick up speed, the motion and the time she had been travelling making Sally's eyes feel heavy.

'Feel free to use my shoulder as a pillow,' the young man to her left offered.

He looked about nineteen, Sally thought, a boy really, and still at that slightly swaggering stage of development of boys of that age. Sally shook her head and assured him with a small smile that she was perfectly comfortable as she was.

In the corridor beyond their carriage some of those passengers who were not fortunate enough to have seats were leaning against the carriage walls. They swayed with the movement of the train, as it gathered fresh speed, whilst others were sitting on kitbags and even on the corridor floor itself.

'Whereabouts in London are you billetted?' Jane asked. 'Only I was wondering if we might share a cab once we get off the train, seeing as it's going to be quite late in the evening before we get in.'

Sally was just about to answer her when suddenly they heard the sound of planes overhead.

'Dorniers,' the flight lieutenant, who had been attempting to do a *Times* crossword announced, repeating in a louder voice, 'Dorniers, lads. Get down, everyone, get down.'

Those were the last words Sally heard. Everything was swallowed up in the explosion of noise that followed: exploding bombs, the screech of brakes, the sound of splintering wood, the screams of the injured in a ghastly nightmare of broken carriages and bodies as the train plunged and rolled, flinging her around inside the compartment.

'Mum, that's the third time in the last half hour you've looked at the clock,' Tilly teased, as the four of them at number 13 sat round the kitchen table, drinking their tea, half listening to the wireless, and half listening for the sound of the air-raid siren.

'I thought that Sally would have been back by now,' Olive responded. 'Oh, no, here we go again.' The air-raid siren had started.

'You just can't stop worrying about us all like a mother hen with her chicks,' Tilly laughed, as they all went into their automatic response to the siren, collecting the things they needed to take to the shelter. As Olive herded the girls in front of her out into the damp night air and down the path to the shelter, she was thinking she was glad she'd spotted those offcuts of flannelette in the market during the summer because they'd make smashing new extra-warm siren suits for them for winter.

Sally was a sensible girl and wherever she was she'd head for the nearest shelter, Olive knew, but she also knew that Sally was bound to have been upset after visiting her mother's grave, and so she sent up a small mental prayer for her as the other three girls ran into the shelter. Tilly and Dulcie were chattering away like a pair of magpies, whilst Agnes lit the oil lamp, its flame casting a warm glow over their young animated faces. Their futures were so uncertain. Life itself was so uncertain. Suddenly Olive wanted to take hold of all three of them and wrap them tightly in her arms, to keep them safe.

FOURTEEN

It was the slow, familiar and deadly warning sound of the rhythmic drip drip of blood that Sally recognised first, a sound to strike horror and fear into the heart of any trained nurse. Dripping blood meant an injured or dying patient. No patient on the wards of Liverpool's Mill Street Hospital ever dripped blood. Mill Street... She wasn't at Mill Street any more, she was working in London. But she wasn't in a hospital now ... was she?

The train... The train had been bombed. Now, with lightning speed, Sally's awareness of where she was and why came back to her. It was pitch-black inside the compartment, and the air was filled with the sounds of groans and cries. People were hurt, injured, and she was a nurse. Something heavy was lying on top of her, preventing her from breathing properly. Sally tried to move and then tensed when she heard a groan. She was pinned down by another person.

She mustn't panic. She was a nurse, Sally reminded herself. First things first. She moved her fingers and then wriggled her toes. All working, thank heavens. The weight – the person pressing down on her – might be making it difficult for her to breathe properly but she *could* breathe. She could breathe, she could think and she could move her fingers and toes. She could hear more

241

groans now, she realised, and people crying out, mingling with other noises: the kind made by houses when they settled down for the night, but intensified, as though... She gave a gasp of fear as suddenly whatever she was lying on shifted. The railway carriage. It had come off the tracks. She could remember now the feeling of it somersaulting over and over, throwing them about.

'Sally, are you OK?'

That was Jane, her voice thin and unsteady, coming from somewhere to the left of Sally.

'I think so,' Sally responded. 'How about you?'

'I think I'm all right as well. There's something on top of me, though.'

'Same here. Mine's a person.'

'Lucky you, I think mine's the luggage rack – and the luggage.'

At the sound of their weak laughter a male voice said, even more weakly, 'That's the spirit, girls.'

'Racey,' they both breathed together.

'Everyone else, speak up, all of you,' Jane commanded. Silence.

'Christ, they can't all be dead. They can't be.'

There was panic as well as disbelief in Racey's voice.

'They're probably unconscious,' Sally said quickly and firmly. 'We need a light so that we can see what's going on.'

'Atta girl,' Jane praised her.

Racey announced in a calmer voice, 'Got a lighter here. Hang on a tick, see if I can get it working.'

Sally felt as though she were holding her breath

during Racey's three frustrating attempts when they could see the click of the lighter but it failed to ignite.

However, once he had it alight Sally almost wished he hadn't.

She and Jane were both lying on what had been the roof of the compartment. Jane did indeed have the luggage rack lying over her, whilst over Sally herself was the body of one of the pilot officers. His neck was broken and there was a spar of broken wood from the carriage sticking out of his back.

'Jesus...' There was a retching sound from Racey and the lighter was extinguished.

Somewhere outside the train, and down below them, Sally could see flashes of moving light. Relief filled her, making her tremble. She closed her eyes and then opened them again to check that she wasn't merely hallucinating. But no, the precious wonderful lights were still there.

'It looks like help's on the way.'

'We could do with signalling that we're here. Anyone got a torch?' asked Jane.

'Mine's in my pocket,' Sally answered her, 'if it's still working.'

Now that she knew that the body pinning her down could not be hurt by any movement from her, Sally asked, 'Are you injured, Racey? Can you move? Can you help me get free? I ought to be doing something to help those who need help.'

'My leg's buggered up, if you'll excuse the language, but I can move. Hang on and I'll try and drag Smarty off you. We called him that because he was always such a smart aleck. Always

243

had an answer for everything. Well, where he's gone now he'll have all the answers, won't he?'

Sally could hear the choke of emotion in the young airman's voice.

'You pull him towards you and I'll try to wriggle the other way,' she instructed him, adding in the kind of voice normally used by the fiercest ward sisters, 'but don't move that leg of yours until I've had a chance to have a look at it.'

Something in that tone must be right, she realised, because Jane gave a weak chuckle and Racey agreed, 'Too right I won't.'

It took them several attempts before finally Sally was able to roll free of the weight of the body, which rolled to the floor with a sickening thump that turned her own stomach.

'Done it,' she said in a loud voice intended to cover up the horrific sound for the other two.

Gingerly Sally sat up. As she'd moved she was pretty sure she felt something sharp underneath her – glass from the compartment's windows, perhaps, or maybe even from the paintings of rural views that had adorned the walls at the back of their seats – and she didn't want to risk injuring herself. She had been lucky, everything seemed to be in working order, but now that the numbing shock of the blast and the derailing of the train was over, she was becoming increasingly aware of cries for help and groans of pain echoing through the darkness. Not from their own compartment, though. Here there was only that persistent sound of blood dripping. She reached into her pocket and removed her torch, exhaling shakily in relief when it immediately came on,

244

then putting her free hand up to her face in horror when she saw the carnage surrounding her.

There would be no rescue for those young men who had travelled with them.

The young man lying on top of her had protected her from the fate that had been his, Sally knew, as she reached out to close his eyes and whisper a small prayer for him. Racey was lying to one side of him with his leg cut open to the bone, the flesh shredded by the glass from the broken window. Hanging out of the window itself was the body of one of the others. Two more had such ghastly wounds to their faces that Sally suspected it was a mercy that they had not lived. Racey was still being sick, moaning their names over and over again.

Jane was trapped beneath the luggage. Sally went to help her and then stopped.

'I know, devilish isn't it? Just like cat's cradle gone wrong,' Jane said quietly when she saw Sally looking at the mess of netting in which she was trapped, not lying down, as Sally had first thought, but suspended by the netting with nothing beneath her other than some very sharp spears of broken wood, beyond which was a yawning jagged gap where the back of the carriage had been. Through it, the night sky was open to her view.

They had been in the last compartment of their corridor train, which meant ... Sally gulped shakily. She could hardly bear to think what that open sky and lack of another carriage meant or what must have happened to those who had been inside it, but somehow she made herself look down through the gap. Below she could see the firefly-like lights of people working, and odd glimpses in those lights of what looked like the tangled wreckage of another carriage, whilst their own carriage had obviously come off the rails and was poised upside down at an angle across the lines on the steep-sided banking. Surely it was going to be impossible for anyone to rescue them without sending the carriage plunging down the steep slope to join the mangled remains of the one already there?

A terrible sense of hopelessness seized hold of her, and, with it, a fear so intense that Sally actually felt as though it was gripping her throat and her heart. A tide of panic and terror surged through her. They were going to die. There was no one to help her help the others. There was no one for her to turn to. She felt as though she was completely alone.

And then inside her head Sally had the most vivid image of her mother, so real that she could almost feel her warm reassuring breath and her familiar touch on her arm. For a handful of seconds Sally simply basked in the image's comfort. The tide of panic and terror that had threatened to overwhelm her had retreated, leaving in its place the kind of steady calm purposefulness she had learned at her mother's knee. Taking a deep breath, Sally flashed her torch over the gaping emptiness that had once been the back of their compartment. From what she could see, they were on an embankment that fell away sharply. The tide of panic wanted to come back but she fought against it, clinging to the mental image of her mother's loving smile, holding her in the warmth of her maternal love. Inside her head, Sally could hear from her childhood the familiar words, 'It's all right, darling I'm here.'

'SOS – Morse code. Use torch.'

Another voice, disembodied, – a paper-dry rustle of sound, no more – had Sally turning her torch in its direction. Flight Lieutenant Quillan was sitting in what had once been the corridor of the train, his hands on his stomach, holding in his intestines.

He was barely alive, but Sally's nurse's instinct had her starting to crawl towards him until he said sharply, 'No. Keep still. Could send us over the end.' He stopped speaking to cough up blood, his blood the source of the steady dripping sound she had heard, Sally realised.

'Quilley's right,' Racey told her. 'Give me the torch. I'm nearest to the window. I'll do the SOS.'

Sally could hardly bear to watch as he fumbled with her precious torch, and then slowly and painstaking flashed out the Morse code signal. At one point, just as he had started on the third sequence of flashes, the torch slipped out of his hands and rolled away from him. Sally thought they were going to lose it but somehow Jane managed to reach for it.

Of course, then Racey had to start signalling all over again but finally it was done, the silence between them stiff with fear and hope until, almost miraculously, they saw a torch far more powerful than their own being flashed back in their direction, followed by the movement of many torches as people ran towards the embankment. Voices, hoarse and harsh, sounded both delighted at discovering them and dismayed at their situation.

'There's someone up there alive.'

'Four of us, tell them,' Sally urged Racey.

But he needed no instructions to cup his hands together and yell, 'Up here, mate, up here.'

'We could do with getting the Flight Lieutenant rescued first,' Sally told the others.

A small muffled sound that could have been laughter, a sigh or a sob, broke from the place where Lieutenant Quillan was.

'You girls will go first,' he told them, a strength in his voice that Sally would have thought impossible, given his mortal injuries.

'He's right,' Racey agreed, his voice much weaker now.

'It could take some time to get me free from my cat's cradle,' Jane's voice was light and controlled but Sally could well imagine how she must be feeling, knowing that she was trapped.

In that instant Sally made up her mind about what would happen, given that she out of all four of them, was neither badly injured nor trapped.

'I am a nurse, you three are my patients,' she pointed out calmly, 'and I don't leave here until all three of you have been safely removed.'

There was a small silence and then Jane reached for her hand and whispered, 'Thanks for that. In truth, I was in a blue funk at the thought of being left here on my own.'

'You, up there. How many of you are there?' a voice disembodied by a loud-hailer demanded.

Cupping her hands together, Sally shouted back, 'Four of us, two who need medical treatment, and one who is trapped. What's left of the

248

compartment isn't very stable either.'

'Don't worry, we'll get you all out. Just hold tight. How bad are the injured? Can you tell?

'I'm a nurse,' Sally responded. 'One man's leg is badly cut, and the other...' she paused and then said firmly, '...the other needs urgent attention and should be rescued first.'

'No. Won't make it. You girls go first.'

Sally flashed the torch in the Flight Lieutenant's direction, taking care to keep the light off his injuries.

'It's over for me,' he continued, every breath he drew a physical effort for him. 'Don't mind, though. Wife and baby already gone. Blitz bomb. No point in trying to hang on.'

He was looking straight at her, his gaze fixed on hers: the gaze of a dying man, Sally recognised helplessly as she watched the blue eyes glaze over.

'Sally?' Jane's hand tightened on her own. 'You know what I wish more than anything else?'

'That we weren't here?' Sally suggested.

Jane gave a small laugh. 'Besides that. I wish that I hadn't been so damned prim and proper and decent, and that when the boy I was going to get engaged to asked me to spend his last weekend of leave with him I had done. His ship was torpedoed three days later, and now this, and it all seems such a waste somehow, "being good". I can't imagine any memory I'd like to have more right now than that of lying in his arms after ... afterwards... I'm sorry,' Jane apologised when Sally didn't say anything. 'I'm being fearfully embarrassing, talking like this.'

'No you aren't,' Sally assured her fiercely. 'We're brought up to behave in a certain way, to do the right thing and to ... to deny ourselves certain things, because that's the way our parents were brought up, but our lives aren't like theirs.'

Down below them, equipment was being gathered, including a fire engine with its long ladder.

In the corridor the Flight Lieutenant drew in a long slow breath and then paused before exhaling it in a telltale rattle.

A searchlight had been set up for the rescue crews to work by, its bright glare making Sally blink and shield her eyes.

'I can see a ladder,' Jane told her, both of them gasping as the action of embedding the long ladder in the embankment next to their damaged compartment set it moving and tilting a little more.

'Hang on, won't be long now,' the man with the loudhailer called up to them, trying to keep their spirits up, Sally suspected. But to her surprise it wasn't very long before two helmeted firemen appeared on the ladder alongside the compartment, their faces smeared in mud.

'We'll get you down first, love, seeing as you aren't trapped,' the one closest to her told Sally.

'No,' Sally argued. 'I'm not leaving until I know my patients are safe.'

A brief nod of his head, and then their rescuers were crawling towards them, two of them working to free Racey whilst the other whistled between his teeth when he saw Jane, calling back down the ladder, 'Two more men up here.'

Sally tried to distract herself from her own

danger by monitoring Racey's groans as he was lifted free of the debris that had been pinning him down.

'The chap in the corridor's a goner. Leave him and get the girl free,' instructed one of their rescuers.

'You don't have to stay with me,' Jane told Sally.

'I want to,' Sally responded, and it was true. Jane may not be a pal, but they had been travelling together. Sally herself could easily have been the one trapped and Jane the one who could have walked away, and how would she be feeling right now, suspended above an almost vertical drop into nothingness in the dark, if Jane had walked away and left her, Sally asked herself.

The men knew what they were doing: two of them were using their axes to cut expertly through the mess of luggage rack and splintered wood imprisoning Jane, whilst a third man stayed below her, holding her steady as they worked. Twice Sally felt the compartment shift. The second time it rocked wildly and sickeningly for several seconds whilst one of their rescuers cursed and then apologised, and they all held their breath. Sally prayed for it to steady and hold firm, easing out a leaky breath of relief when it finally did.

After that the men worked even more swiftly, the banter they had been exchanging earlier was replaced by a tense silence.

Finally, though, Jane was free, and one of the firemen took hold of her in a fireman's lift, heading for the ladder, as another reached for Sally.

Racey had already been carried to safety but

there was one thing Sally still had to do before she could leave now that she no longer had to hold Jane's hand in support.

'Hey, what are you doing? This thing's liable to go any second now,' the fireman warned Sally angrily as she crawled away from him, heading for where the Flight Lieutenant lay.

In death his head had slumped forward and Sally held it gently, as she closed his eyes and whispered a blessing. Only then did she feel able to turn back to the fireman to nod her head and say calmly, 'I'm ready now.'

'Ruddy daft thing to do,' grumbled her rescuer as he hoisted her up and started down the ladder.

Against his back Sally told him, 'No it wasn't. He gave up his seat for us and made his men do the same. If he hadn't then we'd be the ones who are dead now and he could be alive.'

She had no idea whether or not the fireman had heard her, given the position she was in, but it didn't matter.

Never had the earth felt so wonderful beneath her feet, Sally thought when she was finally standing upright on it and was free to see the full horror of what had happened to the train. Crushed carriages littered the steep embankment, rescuers moving amongst the debris, rows of bodies were already laid out on stretchers and ambulances were standing by on the wet road several yards away.

A crashing crunch sound caught her attention and Sally looked up to see the compartment they had been in topple down the embankment, disintegrating as it did so. They had been rescued just in time.

Someone was placing a blanket round her shoulders. A kind, tired-looking St John Ambulance man.

'How many...?' Sally began, and then had to stop before asking again, 'How many?'

'We've found less than a hundred still alive,' he told her, anticipating her question. 'Someone must have been looking after you, love.'

'Yes. Yes,' Sally agreed emotionally, remembering how in the darkness she had been so sure she had felt the warmth of her mother's hand. Others might say, were she to tell them about that feeling, that she had imagined it, but Sally, for all her practical nature, wasn't so sure. In the air around them, rank with the smell of death and destruction, she was sure there was an elusive hint of her mother's Parma violet toilet water.

FIFTEEN

'...and then we – that is, the walking wounded, so to speak – were driven to the nearest station so that we could continue on our way to London.'

'Oh, Sally, what a dreadful experience.' Olive reached for Sally's hand and gave it a small squeeze.

Olive had been due to attend a WVS meeting earlier in the evening, but she was glad now that she had paid attention to what at the time had seemed to be an illogical impulse to change her mind. She never normally missed her WVS meetings but the instinct to stay at home had been so strong that she had felt unable to ignore it.

One look at her lodger's face when Sally had arrived back had been enough for Olive to take Sally into the kitchen immediately and sit her down whilst she made them each a cup of tea, and mentally thanked that impulse – perhaps passed somehow from one mother to another across the ether – so that she could be here for Sally.

Now all Olive could do was listen whilst Sally told her in short, almost reluctant sentences, some of the details about the ordeal she had been through. Sally's voice was shaking as she said, 'Jane – that's the Wren I told you about – and I travelled back to London together, and that helped. Racey, the young pilot officer, should be all right, although I think the injuries to his leg will mean that he's left with a permanent limp, but the others… I'm sorry,' Sally apologised as Olive pushed her own clean handkerchief into her hand. 'I don't know why I keep going on about it. It's best forgotten. I'm being so weak.'

'It's only right that you should want to talk about it, Sally. Right for you and right for those poor young men as well. If I was mother to one of them I wouldn't like to think that the manner of their death was pushed under the carpet. And as for you being weak – no such thing. It takes strength to accept the reality of something so horrible.'

'I thought we were all going to die,' Sally ad-

254

mitted. 'I really did.'

And then, ridiculously, she was behaving like a little girl and not a professional nurse, Sally thought helplessly as she burst into tears and allowed herself to be taken into Olive's arms and comforted.

'I thought I was going to die,' Sally repeated to Olive, once she was able to speak through her tears. 'I felt so alone and afraid, and then somehow it was as though my mother was there. I know that sounds silly.'

'No, it doesn't,' Olive assured her. 'Just before my husband died, I looked towards the end of the bed and although I couldn't see him, somehow I just knew that he was standing there. I could feel his lovely kind nature and his gentleness. There aren't always logical explanations for those things we experience in our times of greatest need Sally, and in my opinion we shouldn't look for them. We should simply accept that what we felt in our hearts was heard.'

'Miss Simmonds, is that dust I can see on the floor behind your counter?'

'It's all this bombing, Miss Cotton,' Dulcie sought to excuse herself. 'Makes ever such a lot of dust in the air. Gets everywhere, it does.'

'That's as maybe, Miss Simmonds, but one place it must not be allowed to get is here in this department. This is Selfridges, remember. See to it that you remove it at once.'

The arctic tones of the floor manager had Dulcie giving her a disgruntled look, as she turned her back and continued on her eagle-eyed inspection of her domain.

'It's not my job to keep the floor clean,' Dulcie complained to Lizzie. 'It's the cleaning staff wot's supposed to do that.'

'If Miss Cotton comes back and you haven't cleaned it up you'll be for it, whether or not the cleaners should have got rid of it. She'll go over your counter with a magnifying glass. Remember when she made Milly from Dorothy Gray clean her counter top so many times with ethylated spirits that she passed out? I'm going for my dinner break now,' Lizzie informed Dulcie, disappearing speedily, leaving Dulcie with no one to complain to, and no escape either from the task of opening the cupboard underneath her counter to remove a small brush and dustpan.

It wasn't right, it really wasn't, her having to get down on her hands and knees in her clean overall just because of a few specks of dust. Angrily brushing, Dulcie was building up a good head of self-righteous steam when from above her a male voice said, 'Hey, I thought you said you were a beautician. Where I come from we call folks who polish floors cleaners.'

Wilder. Dulcie stood up so fast she felt dizzy from the combination of the rush of blood to her head and the rage she felt at being discovered by him involved in such a menial task.

He was wearing his own American Eagles version of a flying ace's uniform: beige-coloured, immaculately cut trousers, and a matching shirt over which he wore a heavy leather thick-lined flying jacket, a white silk scarf knotted casually round his neck. He looked ... he looked exactly what he was, Dulcie thought, and that was far too cocky, and too pleased with himself. That didn't mean, though, that she was going to let some other girl walk off with him, of course. Nor was she going to let him think he could walk all over her, so she smiled mock coyly at him.

'Well, I suppose I am a bit too fussy, but I can't abide my counter looking anything less than absolutely perfect. That's the kind of person I am,' she told him.

'Is that right?' Wilder leaned across the glass counter top and gave her a long slow smile. 'Well, forget the floor cleaning, Cinderella, how about I take you out instead?'

'You mean tonight?' Dulcie asked, intending to pretend that she couldn't make it and that he'd have to choose another night.

But to her astonishment he shook his head and told her with a devil-may-care grin, 'I mean now.'

Now?

Dulcie looked at him. 'But I'm working.'

'You call cleaning floors work? Come on, wouldn't you rather be having fun with me?'

Of course she would, Dulcie admitted inwardly, but even so...

'I can't just leave,' she pointed out primly.

'Sure you can. You can say you got sick and had to go home.' He looked at the watch on his wrist. 'Meet me outside the front entrance in half an hour. It will be worth it, I promise you.'

He'd gone, disappearing into the mêlée of shoppers before Dulcie could refuse. Of course she couldn't possibly do what he had suggested. It wouldn't be right at all. The trouble was, though, Dulcie thought that she was getting tired of doing the right thing, and tired of the war, as well, with its blackouts and its rationing and all the other things that were making life so grey and dull, even without the bombing. She craved nice things – pretty clothes, scent, lipstick – and most of all she craved the kind of excitement that a man like Wilder would bring to her life, she admitted.

'Don't have the hot pot,' Lizzie, who had just returned from her break, warned her. 'I did and there wasn't a scrap of meat in it.'

'Don't mention food to me,' Dulcie shuddered. 'I've been feeling ever so unwell, proper sickly.'

'Well, you don't look it.'

'I might not look it, but I feel it. I nearly passed out when I stood up just now,' Dulcie insisted giving a theatrical shiver. 'Ooohhh, I keep going all hot and cold. I shouldn't be surprised if I was coming down with something ever so nasty.' She *was* feeling slightly light-headed, Dulcie decided, but it was a lightheadedness that came from the surge of excitement now rushing through her rather than anything else. Dulcie liked making her own rules and being the one who decided what she should and should not do. The thought of escaping from the dullness of her work and the heavy supervision of Miss Cotton filled her with a heady sense of power.

'Where are you going?' Lizzie asked worriedly as Dulcie stepped out from behind her counter.

'I'm going for my break,' Dulcie answered her.

'But you just said you couldn't eat a thing.'

'I couldn't. I'm going for a bit of a lie-down.'

'You'll have to tell someone if you're going to do that,' Lizzie warned her.

'I am going to. In fact, I think I'll go up and see the nurse,' Dulcie answered her promptly, as she sped away before Lizzie could ask her any more questions.

Half an hour, Wilder had said. Dulcie judged things perfectly, so that she was walking up behind him whilst he stood outside the store, exactly thirty-five minutes after he had left her, just as he checked his watch and then started to walk away so that she had to reach for his arm to stop him.

The smile he gave her when he turned and saw her held rather more triumph than Dulcie would have liked but on this occasion she was prepared to overlook it, she decided magnanimously.

'So where are we going?' she asked.

'It's a surprise. Come on.'

There was no chance for her to demand an answer to her question, Wilder was already hailing a taxi, and then ushering her into it, the answer given when he leaned forward and told the driver, 'The Ritz Hotel.'

The Ritz? Wilder was taking her to The Ritz for her dinner? No, for her lunch, Dulcie mentally corrected herself, her cheeks pink with excitement and delight as she watched the familiar London streets pass by through the taxi window, until they were pulling up outside the famous hotel.

Having paid off the taxi, Wilder offered Dulcie his arm. Gleefully Dulcie took it. Instead of feeling guilty about the way she had fibbed at work, she actually felt triumphant and glad about what she had done. Because if she hadn't she wouldn't be here, would she, walking into the lobby of The Ritz Hotel on the arm of a good-looking man who obviously knew how to treat a girl as she deserved.

Dulcie's sophistication deserted her, though, once they were inside, and she could see down the long gallery of the hotel through the restaurant, busy now with lunchtime diners, to the hotel's gardens and beyond them to Green Park. But it wasn't the view of the hotel gardens and Green Park that had Dulcie transfixed; it was the opulence of the French château-inspired elegance all around her.

Huge chandeliers dazzled her with their glitter and their light, reflected from embossed wallpaper and gilded furniture so that it seemed to Dulcie that everywhere she looked there was golden light and glamour.

'This way, sir, madam.'

A waiter so grand-looking that the sight of him almost had Dulcie's eyes popping out of her head, escorted them to the restaurant. There, another waiter said to Wilder, 'A table for luncheon for two? Somewhere private overlooking the park? This way, please,' and then led them to a table tucked away out of sight, where Dulcie wouldn't be able to see anyone else other than Wilder.

She was so disappointed that she protested, 'If I'm having my dinner at The Ritz then I want to sit somewhere where I can see what's going on.'

'Of course, madam.'

They were good these waiters, moving so fast that it was almost as though they were on wheels,

Dulcie approved as she and Wilder were led to another table. At this one everyone who came into the restaurant had to walk past them so that it was a bit like having a ringside seat. Not that she was actually allowed to touch her seat. As she made to pull out her chair the waiter was there, quick as a flash, pulling it out for her and then, if you please, putting the serviette across her lap and then doing the same for Wilder.

'See that? That waiter would have made us make do with that poky little table where no one could see us if I hadn't stuck my oar in,' Dulcie informed Wilder in a hissed whisper once the waiter had disappeared. 'It's much better here.'

She had another complaint to make, though, a few minutes later when they had both been handed their menus and she had opened hers.

'There's no prices on the menu,' she told Wilder suspiciously.

'That's because you're my guest and a girl,' Wilder told her. 'It's the person who pays who gets the menu with the prices on it.'

'Why?' Dulcie asked him.

'Because it's the way things are done,' Wilder told her.

'Well, it's not the way I like them done,' Dulcie told him. She stopped speaking to watch as the wine waiter poured a small amount of wine into the glass of one of the four men in military uniform at a nearby table, and then waited as he swirled it round his glass and then tasted it, before nodding his head. However, before she could query what was going on, her attention was caught by a couple coming into the restaurant,

261

her eyes widening as she recognised Lydia. Her companion was an older man who Dulcie didn't know. When Lydia saw her her eyes widened in disbelief. Gleefully Dulcie tossed her head, her delight growing when her old adversary and the man with her were shown to the table she herself had rejected. Well, that was one in the eye for stuck-up Lydia, being hidden away in that corner where no one could see her. Not like her. Everyone who came into the restaurant could see her, Dulcie preened happily.

She'd ordered vegetable soup followed by chicken, the waiter explaining to a less-than-impressed Wilder, when he ordered the soup, a fish entrée and then the chicken, that the rationing rules meant that he couldn't have both a fish dish and another 'main' course.

'What I'd really like,' he told Dulcie when the waiter had gone, 'is a nice juicy American steak. You guys over here don't know what proper steak is, I can tell you.'

'No one asked you to come over here and become a pilot,' Dulcie felt obliged to point out in defence of her country.

'Sure they did,' Wilder argued back. 'Your Winston Churchill is always asking our President to help. Thing is, though, our President won't agree.'

The arrival of their soup brought an end to their argument, Wilder pulling a face over the soup.

'Olive, that's my landlady, gave us Heinz tomato soup for supper the other night, as a special treat,' Dulcie told him, sighing as she added wistfully, 'It was ever so good.'

'Better than this stuff,' Wilder agreed.

'I'll ask Olive if you can come round for your tea one night if you like,' Dulcie suggested. 'Then she can meet you and maybe you can have some.'

She could see that Wilder was looking slightly wary, but Dulcie had made up her mind the minute he had told her that he was bringing her here to The Ritz for her lunch that she and Wilder were going to become an item. A chap who brought a girl to The Ritz for her lunch was definitely worth hanging on to, Dulcie decided as the salty soup made her reach for her wineglass and take another swig, once again grimacing over its taste.

'A nice shandy would have been better than this wine. Nasty sour stuff, it is,' she informed Wilder, frowning reprovingly when he spluttered and coughed.

By the time they had reached the 'pudding' course – apple pie served with thin watery custard – Dulcie decided that she was prepared to overlook the fact that the food was nowhere near as good as Olive's home cooking, because she'd enjoyed herself so much studying the other people in the restaurant, especially the women – the ladies, Dulcie mentally corrected herself, feeling smugly delighted that she was now elevated to that social status since she too was here.

All the other women, no matter what their age or physical appearance, were wearing what Dulcie, with her experience of working in Selfridges and serving so many women of the same class, immediately recognised as 'posh' clothes: fur coats worn over tweed suits, twin-sets, and pearl necklaces on the women under forty, or an expensive-looking brooch on those over forty. One dowager, who had fascinated Dulcie after she had heard her being addressed as 'Your Grace', was wearing so many rows of pearls it was impossible to see the flesh of her neck, and her fingers were heavily beringed.

Whilst many of the men, especially the younger ones, escorting these women were in uniform, some were not, wearing dark suits instead, like Lydia's companion.

All in all she was having a wonderful time, Dulcie decided happily, even if Olive's roast chicken knocked The Ritz's offering into a cocked hat. She couldn't wait to tell everyone at number 13 all about her lunch, although of course she would not be telling them about the fact that she had invented a non-existent stomach upset as an excuse to slope off from work. She felt disappointed when Wilder summoned the waiter and told her, 'I'm afraid we're going to have to call it a day. I've got to be back at base for five o'clock.'

'That's all right,' Dulcie assured him, graciously adding, 'I've enjoyed it ever so much, and you can bring me here again, if you like.'

It was later, in the foyer, whilst she was waiting for Wilder to return from the gents that Dulcie saw Lydia again, sweeping past her on the arm of her grey-haired companion, and so deep in conversation with him that she didn't notice Dulcie. Dulcie had noticed her, though. Dulcie considered herself to be a girl who knew what was what, but when she heard Lydia's companion asking the girl behind the desk if 'their' room was ready yet, her initial reaction was to be so filled with disbelief that she thought she must have misheard.

But then the receptionist smiled and said as clear as day, 'Yes, your room is ready for you now. The porter will show you up. I do hope you enjoy your stay with us, Mr and Mrs Storney.'

Mrs Storney. How could Lydia be that when Dulcie knew for a fact that she was married to David?

'I've just had ever such a shock,' she told Wilder when he rejoined her. 'I've just seen a woman who I know for a fact is married to an RAF pilot calling herself the wife of another man, as bold as brass.'

Wilder shrugged. 'That's what war does for you. Folks feel they have to snatch at every little bit of happiness whilst they can.'

'Well, you'd never get me doing anything like that,' Dulcie told Wilder firmly. 'Passing herself off as a man's wife when she's no such thing. She ought to be ashamed of herself.' Dulcie felt indignant on David's behalf. Indignant and astonished that someone as cold as Lydia should actually want to go to an hotel room with a man who wasn't her husband.

Once they were outside the hotel the doorman hailed them a cab.

'Where to?' Wilder asked Dulcie. 'The store?'

Go back to Selfridges now? Not likely.

'No, he can drop me off at the bottom of Fleet Street.'

Although Wilder was sitting close to her in the

back of the cab, Dulcie didn't realise what he had in mind until he put his arm round her and then tried to kiss her.

Pushing him away, Dulcie retreated to the corner of the cab, trying not to slide on the worn leather seats, before folding her arms across her body as she told him indignantly, 'Here, there'll be none of that, thank you very much. I'm a respectable girl, not the sort that lets a man she's only just met kiss her in the back of a taxi, I'll have you know.'

'I thought we were having a good time together.'

'We were until you went and spoiled it by getting fresh. Just because you bought me dinner that doesn't mean that gives you the right to kiss me,' Dulcie informed him sharply.

'Oh, come on, Dulcie,' Wilder wheedled. 'Take pity on a poor lonely airman and don't be so hard-hearted. I've been dreaming about kissing you from the moment I met you.'

'Then you'll just have to dream on, because you're not going to,' Dulcie responded, but this time her tone was less acid.

'It isn't my fault that I want to,' Wilder told her with a grin, 'not when you're such a pretty girl, Dulcie, with lips that are just made for kissing. You shouldn't have lips like that if you're going to drive a guy crazy by refusing to let him kiss you.'

Dulcie tried to look severe but it wasn't easy when she was being lavished with the kind of compliments she had only previously heard in a film at the cinema. Not, of course, that she was going to let Wilder know that she was impressed. She wasn't that much of a fool. She wasn't a fool at all.

'And you know what?' Wilder was asking her.

'What?' Dulcie responded cautiously.

'I'm going to keep on trying,' he told her, 'because I reckon I'll never forgive myself if I don't.'

'You can try as much as you like,' Dulcie assured him, 'but in this country girls – respectable girls – don't go letting men kiss them unless the two of them are an item.'

The taxi had reached the bottom of Fleet Street and was pulling into the kerb. Wilder was sliding along the seat towards her a determined look in his eyes. Quickly Dulcie opened the door and scrambled out, giving him an equally determined look back.

'See you, sweet lips,' Wilder told her, 'and when I do, I'm going to make those lips mine.'

He could try, Dulcie thought as she slammed the taxi door and the driver pulled away. He could try as much as he liked. A smile curved the lips Wilder had just been complimenting and, uncharacteristically, Dulcie gave a small skip of mingled excitement and determination as she headed in the direction of Article Row. Life was suddenly looking very promising. And fancy her seeing Lydia, and then catching her out like she had. David had been a fool to marry her. What a pity she wouldn't be able to tell Lizzie about Lydia's shameful behaviour, Dulcie thought with disappointment. You'd certainly never get her behaving like that, married or not married.

Everyone knew what happened to a girl's reputation when she started visiting hotel bedrooms with a man she wasn't married to.

SIXTEEN

It was lucky that she'd kept that nearly empty bottle of brandy, Olive congratulated herself, carefully pouring a small amount into the hole she had just made in her Christmas cake with a meat skewer. Her late father-in-law had sworn by a drink of brandy and port for settling upset stomachs, and had always insisted on keeping a bottle of each in the house. Now the flavour and moistness of the Christmas cake which Olive had baked at the beginning of October, would benefit from her late father-in-law's 'medicinal' remedy.

She'd been lucky with her cake, Olive admitted. She'd been worried about it being overcooked when the siren had gone before it was ready, but luckily there'd been a break during the bombing just at the right time so that she'd been able to nip back to the house to remove it from the oven.

Olive had had a busy morning, doing her weekly bake. Not that she was able to bake anything like as much as she once had, thanks to rationing. She had, though, made a couple of trays of currant biscuits thanks to her excellent store cupboard. She'd perhaps take a few down to Mrs Lord after she'd had her dinner – a slice of Spam and the previous night's leftover potatoes and cabbage, fried up together with some of the bacon fat Olive had saved from their precious Sunday morning bacon ration.

Putting her dinner on the table, Olive resealed the Christmas cake in its tin, put it in her store cupboard and then placed the bottle of brandy back on the sideboard in the front room.

One of the curtains hanging at the front room window wasn't quite straight, so Olive went to straighten it, frowning as she thought she heard her back door opening. That was odd. She wasn't expecting any of the girls home at this time. Immediately Olive's maternal anxiety was aroused. The only reason one of them would come home at this time was because something was wrong.

She hurried into the kitchen, where the back door was open and a boy was standing by the table, gobbling up her dinner with one hand whilst holding some of her newly baked biscuits in the other.

The moment he saw her he ran for the door, but Olive was closer to it. She closed it and stood barring the way.

'And just what do you think you are doing?' she demanded.

He was an unprepossessing-looking boy, thin, with a narrow grubby face and untidy dun-coloured hair. His clothes were shabby, there was dirt under his nails and he smelled of smoke.

A memory stirred in Olive's head. 'You're Barney, aren't you?' she challenged him.

The startled look he gave her confirmed Olive's suspicions that this was the boy Nancy had talked about. The boy Sergeant Dawson had felt

269

so sorry for.

'I'm sorry, missus. I didn't mean to eat your dinner, only I was that hungry, and when I saw it just sitting there... It was them biscuits that did it. Looked ever so good, they did, when I seed them through the window.'

'You've been watching me,' Olive accused him. It wasn't a very pleasant thought – one heard such harrowing tales from homeowners about looters and thieves – yet it was hard to feel anything other than pity for this too thin, wary-looking child, even if his manner was slightly belligerent.

'I didn't mean no harm,' the boy defended himself. 'I only come in your garden to get away from her next door. Thought she'd seen me, I did. I know her sort. She'd have me taken away and locked up, and then me dad will never be able to find me.'

Beneath his shabby too small jacket his narrow shoulders were hunched.

'You might as well finish eating that now that you've started,' Olive told him, indicating her half-empty plate.

The hazel eyes widened. 'You mean it?'

Olive nodded. She could make do with a bit of bread and Spam, the boy needed a decent meal, she could see that.

'So what are you doing round here?' she asked him as she filled the kettle and waited for it to boil to make them a pot of tea. There was a bluish tinge to the boy's skin and he couldn't possibly be warm in those shabby clothes. 'Were you looking for Sergeant Dawson?'

The boy was too intent on polishing off her

dinner to answer her.

Olive went over to the back door and locked it, removing the key whilst the boy watched her in silence

'Here's a hot drink for you,' Olive told him, 'and whilst you drink it I'm going to go and get Sergeant Dawson.'

The boy looked towards the door, and then back at her.

'Where did you sleep last night?' she asked him gently.

'I dunno. In some bombed-out house.'

'Do you really think that's what your mother would want you to do, Barney?'

'Her? She wouldn't care where I slept so long as she got her gin, and someone to pay for it. They're no loss to me, either her or me gran. Never wanted me, me mother didn't. Tried to get rid of me, she said, by drinking a bottle of gin and then throwing herself downstairs, only it didn't work.'

Olive fought to conceal her shock at hearing a child talk in such a matter-of-fact way about something so dreadful.

'It was all right when me dad was at home. I wish he hadn't joined up. Ruddy war.'

'You have to have somewhere to live, Barney,' she told him. 'It isn't safe for you to live in bombed-out buildings. I'm going for Sergeant Dawson now. There are people who can write to your father, to tell him where you'll be so that he can find you when he's on leave.'

Olive knew that the sergeant would be on ARP duties because he's said so at church on Sunday.

'I'm not going into no home,' the boy insisted. 'And if anyone tries to make me I'll run off. I can look after meself, I can.'

By living rough and stealing food, Olive thought ruefully. That was no way for a child to grow up.

It was another cold raw day with the almost ever-present veil of smoke and dust hanging in the air.

It didn't take very long for Olive to reach the ARP shelter close to the junction with Farringdon Road. Two ARP officers and a boy messenger were standing outside the sandbagged post, huddled over a brazier and drinking tea. Olive asked for Sergeant Dawson.

'Go in and tell Sergeant Dawson that there's a lady wanting to see him,' the older of the two men told the boy messenger.

'If you've found a bomb in your garden, missus, then it's going to be at least three days before anyone can get to have a look at it,' the other man told her in a war-weary voice. 'The bomb disposal lot lost four men yesterday trying to diffuse a five-hundred-pounder.'

'Olive, Mrs Robbins,' Sergeant Dawson corrected himself as he emerged from the post, putting his helmet on as he did so.

'I'm sorry to bother you, Sergeant Dawson.' Olive moved slightly away from the others as she told him quietly, 'It's that boy, the one you were talking about after church. He's in my kitchen, and I thought...'

'Of course. I'll come round now. I'll just get my coat. Back in a jiffy, lads,' the sergeant called out

272

to the other men, diving back into the post and re-emerging pulling on a heavy great coat.

'In your kitchen, you say?' he said to Olive as they set off to her house.

'I'd left the back door open and my dinner on the table. I suppose it was too much temptation for him, poor boy. I've never seen anyone wolf down food as fast as he did. He is so thin and, like you said, sleeping rough. It can't go on. I've tried to reassure him that his father will be informed where he is by the authorities–' Olive broke off as she saw the lace curtains in Nancy's front room windows twitch as they walked past. 'I think Nancy has seen us. She'll want to know what's going on.'

Although the sergeant didn't say anything Olive could see from his expression that he didn't have a very high opinion of her neighbour. Olive wished she had the courage to gently warn him about the gossip Nancy had tried to spread about him, but in view of the nature of Nancy's unfounded gossip Olive felt that it wasn't a subject she could raise without causing them both embarrassment.

Unlocking the door to number 13, Olive told the sergeant, 'I left him in the kitchen, locked in. I've brought Sergeant Dawson, Barney,' she called as she opened the kitchen door only to turn to the sergeant in dismay. The kitchen window was open and Barney gone – along with the rest of her biscuits.

'I'm so sorry. I should have brought him with me, but I didn't want Nancy to see him and start asking questions.' Start complaining that the boy was a thief and should be punished was what Olive really meant. 'Now I've wasted your time.'

'He can't have gone very far. I'll check the gardens.'

Olive unlocked the back door. 'I'll help you. He won't have gone next door to Nancy's.'

'Looks like he's gone this way,' the sergeant informed her, pointing out the trail of biscuit crumbs here and there on the path that led down the garden.

'He can't have got over the wall at the back.' Olive looked across to her neighbours at number 14, and then back at the sergeant, who raised his finger to his lips and pointed to the door to the Anderson shelter, which was slightly ajar.

Nodding her head to show that she understood, Olive stayed silent whilst Sergeant Dawson opened the door.

Barney had concealed himself pretty well underneath one of the bunks, but not well enough. The toe of a worn shoe and an unfastened shoelace betrayed his whereabouts.

'Come on, out of there,' Sergeant Dawson demanded as he bent down to drag him gently but firmly from his hiding place. 'You're coming with me, my lad.'

'I wasn't doing nuffink wrong,' Barney protested. 'I dunno what she's told you, but it was her that said I could eat her dinner.'

'You should be thinking yourself lucky it was Mrs Robbins' house you went into, young Barney, and not someone else's, and thanking her, 'cos if it had been someone else, right now it could be theft I'm here to talk to you about, instead of trying to help you.'

'I didn't mean no harm. I was hungry and them biscuits she'd made smelled that good. Please don't send me to prison, Sergeant.'

The thin face was screwed up with genuine fear and Olive was filled with fresh concern for him.

'I don't want to press charges against him, Sergeant,' she insisted. 'It's a proper home he needs, not prison.'

'Do you hear that, Barney? I hope you're going to thank Mrs Robbins for her kindness?'

'Thank you, missus,' Barney obliged in a small voice.

'What's going to happen to him, Sergeant?' Olive asked quietly, as they walked back to the house, Sergeant Dawson keeping a firm eye on Barney, who was several feet in front of them.

'I don't know,' he admitted, keeping his voice equally low. 'Like you said, a good home with someone to keep an eye on him, someone who cares about the lad, is what he needs. I'll put in a good word for him with the authorities, but it's up to them where they send him.'

'Perhaps his father could be given compassionate leave to come home and reassure him that he won't lose touch with him,' Olive suggested.

Sergeant Dawson nodded before lengthening his stride to catch up with Barney.

Watching a little later as Sergeant Dawson escorted Barney down the Row, the sergeant's hand resting on the boy's shoulder in a way that was more paternal than imprisoning, Olive wondered yet again just how Nancy could be so mean as to spread unwarranted gossip about their neighbour, even if he had offended her.

Sally rubbed a weary hand over her eyes. Even though it was over a week now since the train crash, she was still being woken from her much-needed sleep by awful nightmares, and not just about the crash itself.

Despite Olive's kindness to her and the company of the girls, she felt dreadfully alone. Images of the small family gathered round her mother's grave found their way inside her head to torment her, no matter how hard she tried to keep them out of it. They had looked so close, the three adults, her father and Morag so protective of their child, and Callum protective of them. If she had died in the carnage of the train's wreckage who would truly have mourned her? Who would have wept for her and felt that their life would be empty without her in it? Who cared about her and loved her with the quality of love she had seen so clearly existed between the three people who had caused her so much pain?

Tomorrow was her day off but she would rather be working, she admitted. At least then she couldn't think about her own misery. She rubbed her eyes again as she crossed the hospital foyer and then came to a halt of astonishment as she saw George coming towards her. At the sight of his face she felt a welling up of emotion. Dear, kind, reliable George. Her George. If he had been with her when she had visited her mother's grave there would have been no need for her to run from the unbearable sight of other people's shared intimacy and happiness. With George she would have had the protective cloak of her own shared intimacy with him to wrap around herself. The unfamiliar intensity of her emotions now made Sally feel slightly dizzy and light-headed.

'I had to come and see you. Letters just aren't the same,' George told her earnestly.

She'd written to him to tell him what had happened, of course, and he'd written back expressing his concern, but their letters had been practical common-sensical missives, and not emotional outpourings.

'George,' was all Sally could say, close to tears, but she managed a smile as he reached for her hand.

'You've lost weight,' he told her.

'I haven't felt much like eating since the accident,' Sally admitted.

'Come on.' Holding her hand, George led her out of the hospital, and then hailed a taxi, telling the driver, 'The Savoy, please.'

'The Savoy?' Sally queried astonished.

'Afternoon tea,' George explained. 'You need feeding up, and I ... I need to talk to you, and it's too cold for the park.'

'We could go to a Lyons restaurant,' Sally suggested, her naturally thrifty soul worried about him spending his hard-earned money on somewhere as expensive as the Savoy, but George turned his head away from her so that Sally had to strain to hear him.

'Things have changed, Sally, and there's something I have to tell you.'

His words, so unexpected, felt like a sledge-

277

hammer blow against her heart, driving the breath from her lungs, and filling her with anxiety. His manner towards her was distant, a yawning space between them as he sat as far away from her as possible, when right now what she wanted more than anything else was for him to take her in his arms with masterful disregard for the proprieties, and kiss her senseless whilst he told her that he couldn't bear them being apart. In short, Sally admitted, what she wanted was for George to exhibit the kind of behaviour that, prior to the accident she would have denied she could ever want. But now, more than anything, she wanted to be protected and cherished, and loved.

But that wasn't what George was here for. She could tell from his withdrawn manner that he had something on his mind.

Dismayed, Sally could only sit tensely in the taxi, feeling as though a blow were about to fall on her as it pulled up in the entrance to the hotel.

Sally, like the others, had heard all about Dulcie's visit to The Ritz in the company of her new American beau, but she felt no sense of excitement or triumph herself as she and George were ushered into the luxuriously appointed foyer by its uniformed doorman.

Nor did she pay any attention to the elegantly dressed women already seated to take tea, their fur coats discarded on the banquettes and chairs surrounding the tables, the discreet hum of refined female voices mingling with the expensive sound of china cups touching china saucers. All Sally's attention was concentrated on George.

278

Again unlike Dulcie, Sally was relieved when they were shown to a table that was tucked away out of direct public view, her tension growing as she had to wait for the ritual of giving and receiving their order to be got through, followed by the pouring of their tea before she could finally be alone with George.

And yet, instead of asking him why he had brought her here, to her own shame at her cowardice Sally then started to ask George about his new job, for all the world as though he hadn't said those weighted words to her in the taxi, she admitted, as he let her ask.

'It's partly because of what I've seen and learned whilst I've been there that I'm here today, Sally,' George told her quietly. 'The men – boys, no more than that in many cases – come in with the most dreadful disfiguring wounds, wounds that rob them of the futures they had expected to have. So many of them have regrets not about what they have done but what they haven't done. That has made me think ... it's made me see... Life is so precious. Happiness, and love are so fragile.' He paused whilst Sally's heart thumped heavily into her ribs with dread as she waited for the knife to fall, the words to be spoken that would end their relationship and set George free to find the happiness he had obviously decided did not lie with her.

'The thing is, Sally... Oh God,' George swore. 'I'm just no good at this. I'd thought that if we came here, somewhere romantic that somehow...'

Somewhere romantic?

Sally's heart was still thudding but for a differ-

279

ent reason now, its beat swinging wildly between hope and a fear of believing in that hope.

'I know we said that we'd wait, that we'd be sensible, that there's a war on, but, Sally...' George reached for her hand beneath the table and Sally let him take it. '...I don't want to be sensible Sally, not after coming so close to losing you, and I damn well don't want to wait living with the fear that because of this war we might never... Sally, will you marry me?'

'Yes. Yes, George, I will,' Sally promised him in a weakly exhaled breath of giddy joy that brought tears to her eyes.

Somehow George was sitting next to her and then he was kissing her and she was kissing him back, and it was every bit as passionate and exciting as she had longed for it to be.

'I love you so much,' George told her. 'When I got your letter telling me about the train, and with what I see every day at the hospital, I knew that despite what we'd agreed I had to ask you to marry me.'

'Oh, George.'

'You're crying.'

'Because I'm so happy. I was afraid that you were going to tell me that it was over between us,' Sally admitted.

'Never. How could you think that?'

'I don't know. I was afraid of losing you.'

'Oh, my precious love, that could never happen. There's a ring,' George said, his voice cracking slightly. 'My grandmother's. She left it to me but if you don't care for the idea–'

'I love it,' Sally assured him truthfully. 'And I'll

love the ring as well. Knowing it was your grandmother's will make it even more special.'

'I hoped you'd say that. Oh, Sally.'

Sally squeezed his fingers as she watched him fight to get his feelings under control.

'I'll write to my parents and ask them to send it. It won't come in time for us to get engaged at Christmas but we could make an announcement.'

'No,' Sally explained, 'Agnes and Ted are planning to get engaged officially over Christmas. Ted doesn't earn very much and he gives most of what he does earn to his mother. Getting engaged formally will be a big thing for them because they've had to wait, and I don't want to take the shine off that for them by us announcing our engagement at the same time. Besides,' she added truthfully, 'it will be nice to keep it to ourselves for a while: our special secret that we can share. I just wish...' Sally bit her lip, then went on huskily, 'I just wish that my mother could have known about you and me, George.'

'Maybe she does,' he told her gruffly. 'And if she does I hope she knows, too, that I'll look after you for her, Sally.'

Another shared look of an emotion that went too deep for words was exchanged between them.

'I don't want a long engagement,' George said.

'Neither do I,' Sally agreed.

They smiled at one another, hesitant uncertain but proud smiles, both knowing that they had taken their first steps down a path that would be theirs to share.

'How long can you stay in London? If you

281

haven't got a room I think that Olive would probably let you sleep on her front room sofa.'

'I've got to go back this evening. I had to barter my next day off with my opposite number just to get up here. We're always busy, but the recent bombing raids over Germany have meant that we're getting an increasing number of new patients. The work Mr McIndoe is doing is marvellous, Sally. He's a genius, a miracle worker when he operates, but there's more to it than skin grafts and rebuilding badly burned and damaged faces. Mr McIndoe believes in treating the whole person. He says that there's no point in rebuilding a chap's face if his desire to live has also been shattered because of what his injuries have done to him emotionally. I'm not very good at explaining the breadth and depth of what he's trying to achieve. You've got to come down and see for yourself.'

'I'd like to,' Sally agreed, 'but it's you I shall really be wanting to come down and see, George.'

'Sally.' His soft groan sent a thrill of emotion singing through her veins.

A December dusk was darkening the streets when they left the Savoy. Sally didn't resist or demur when George took advantage of the privacy of a shadowy doorway, taking her in his arms to kiss her.

'I wish you didn't have to go,' Sally said, kissing him back. Right now she wanted to stay in his arms for ever, feeling the unsteady thump of his heart against her own and the warmth of his body, knowing that she was not alone after all.

'I wish we could be together tonight,' she whispered to him, 'properly together, I mean, George.'

His arms tightened round her.

'Jane, the girl in the compartment with me when the train was bombed, said that she wished ... well, she said she'd always behaved as a respectable girl is supposed to behave, but thinking that she was going to die made her wish... I don't want to die not having known...' Sally trailed off, absently sketching doodles into the thick fabric of George's overcoat with her fingernail in her self-consciousness.

'You've gone very quiet,' she said, after a pause.

'I'm just thinking again how lucky I am. You've echoed my own thoughts so completely, Sally. You've said what is in my heart, but what I felt it wasn't fair to you to say. One hears about chaps who put pressure on their girls by telling them that they're going off to war and might not come back, and I don't want you ever to feel that my love for you is like that, because it isn't.'

George kissed her forehead and then cupped her face in his hands. 'My love for you is for all of you, for all our lives, for everything that we will share, but right now there's nothing I want more than to love you in the most intimate and precious way there is, Sally, to make you mine, to celebrate what we have before life can snatch it away from us. War does that.'

'Yes,' Sally agreed. 'It does.'

They looked at one another, and then George exhaled unsteadily.

'There's never been a time in my life when I've felt happier – or more afraid because of that happiness,' he confided. 'As a man I should be standing here being big and strong and telling you that I'll always be here to protect you and take care of you, but...'

Sally reached out to him. 'That kind of thing isn't appropriate for us or our generation, George. Neither of us can make promises we both know this war may not allow us to keep. It's enough for me – everything to me, in fact – that you love me and that I love you in return. We're true partners in that love in a way that previous generations couldn't be. Our generation are pioneers when it comes to making promises to one another, every bit as much as Mr McIndoe is a pioneer in his field of medicine. I love you, George, for everything that you are, and as you are.'

Of course they had to seal the emotion of the words they'd just shared with another kiss, and then another, but finally it was time for them to part.

'But not for long,' George promised her. 'It will be Christmas soon.'

'But we'll be lucky if we can get leave together.'

'We'll be lucky,' George assured her.

SEVENTEEN

'You did say that Ted's sisters are going to be at this Christmas party, didn't you?' Drew asked Tilly as they walked arm in arm down Oxford Street, avoiding the busy press of Christmas shoppers.

'Yes,' Tilly confirmed. 'Why do you ask?'

'No reason,' Drew assured her, grinning when Tilly stopped walking and disengaged her arm from his to turn and confront him with a mock look of disapproval.

'You're fibbing. I know that there's something you aren't telling me,' she said.

'I can't say any more yet. It's a secret,' Drew insisted.

'There shouldn't be secrets between couples,' Tilly told him sternly.

'Oh, very well then,' Drew gave in. 'I wrote and asked my mom and sisters if they could send over that dolly and the pram that Agnes said Ted's sisters wanted and that he couldn't find, and enough stuff to give all the other kids something now that I'm to be playing Father Christmas at the party.'

'Oh, Drew.' Tilly's eyes sparkled with love and delight. 'How kind you are. They'll all be thrilled. Now I understand why you insisted on us going to Harrods toy department, and why you asked me all those questions about the dolls and the prams. Oh, Drew,' she repeated happily, 'you are wonderful. Agnes was saying only the other night that the only second-hand pram Ted had been able to find was in a very poor state, and the owner wanted far too much for it.' A thought struck her. 'Will they arrive in time, though?'

'I hope so.'

'Your mother sounds so kind. I wish I could meet your family, Drew. Have you told them yet – about us?'

'I've told them all about you and your mom,' Drew assured her. He looked and sounded slightly tense and Tilly lovingly guessed that he was thinking how very far away his family were.

'It can't be easy for you, being so far away from them,' she sympathised. 'I know how much I'd miss my mum and number thirteen if I was the one who was living somewhere else, in another country.' Her heart gave a small hurried thump, and, as though he understood exactly what she was thinking, Drew reached for her hand and squeezed it gently.

'If I'm going to write that book about Fleet Street one day when this war is over then that means that I'm gonna have to make my home over here,' he reassured her.

'You'd do that?' Tilly asked him, her emotions too tenderly touched for her to keep what she was feeling hidden from him. 'You'd stay here?'

When Drew nodded his head and took her hand within his into the pocket of his Burberry raincoat, removing her glove so that he could stroke her fingers within its private intimacy, Tilly couldn't hold back what she was feeling.

286

'But your family is in America, Drew and–'

'You are here, Tilly.'

'Oh, Drew.'

'If you keep on looking at me like that I'm gonna have to kiss you,' he warned her.

Tilly giggled and blushed, reminding him, 'We're on Oxford Street and it's broad daylight.'

'You're right,' Drew agreed immediately and, as far as Tilly was concerned, rather disappointingly. 'I can't kiss you the way I want to kiss you here in public.'

Tilly's heart soared. 'I can't wait for New Year's Eve,' she told Drew in a half-whisper. Her mother had agreed that Drew could take her to Hammersmith Palais on New Year's Eve, to the big New Year's Eve dance there – a dance at which, late in the evening, there were bound to be dimmed lights and slow music so that lovers could get closer to one another.

Despite the war, or maybe because of it, Oxford Street's shops were all making a brave effort to send out a message of Christmas cheer. Their windows were filled with decorative Christmas scenes: Father Christmases on sleighs, reindeer, their antlers adorned with silver bells, merry-faced elves and gnomes; and, of course, in several windows, glittering shiny Christmas fairies, even if a closer look showed that these figures and their costumes were beginning to look a little worse for wear.

They might also be looking slightly worse for wear, but the spirit of the British people still shone strongly as they shopped, determined to give those they loved the happiest Christmas they could. Of course, when you looked closely, there were faces shadowed by loss and fear, but the general atmosphere was one of general busyness and good cheer.

'We must go and look at Liberty's windows on Great Marlborough Street,' Tilly told Drew eagerly. 'It's always so lovely, especially the window dresses with fabrics.' She gave a small reminiscent sigh. 'I remember one year they had a window filled with small fairies wearing pink silk dresses trimmed with marabou. I couldn't believe it when I found one waiting for me under the Christmas tree. Mum had asked the dressmaker to go and have a look at them and make me one. She was always doing lovely things like that for me.'

'She's one of the best,' Drew agreed warmly.

Up ahead of them a street vendor was selling roasted chestnuts, people crowding round his cart waiting to be served, their breath vaporising on the cold air.

A group of burly-looking men in elf costumes were moving amongst the crowd, obviously collecting for a charity. Immediately Tilly opened her handbag, unable to stop herself laughing at the sight of such large men wearing such childish costumes.

'Fire brigade, miss,' one of them announced, waving a hat under her nose. 'We're collecting for a party for bombed-out kids.'

'Here, take this,' Drew insisted, producing two half-crowns, the sight of them making the other man's eyes widen as he gave an appreciative nod when Drew dropped them into his waiting hat.

'That was far too much,' Tilly protested, her heart melting on a fresh wave of love when Drew told her, 'Poor little tykes, I wish I'd given more.'

There might not be any fairy lights adorning buildings and lampposts this year because of the blackout, but the Christmas spirit was still very much in evidence.

Tilly thought happily of the knitted socks she had bought at Leather Lane Market. Dulcie had derided her for buying them then, but now even she had expressed a grudging admission that filling them 'for the boys' to give them on Christmas Day would be fun.

It might be an apple rather than a tangerine they would find in the toe of their stocking, but it was the spirit of Christmas that mattered more than its content, Tilly assured herself, her eyes widening as she spotted a street-seller with a tray of playing cards.

'What is it?' Drew asked when she stopped walking.

'Nothing. You aren't to look,' Tilly told him firmly. 'You have to turn your back and no peeping, otherwise Father Christmas won't come.'

'No Santa...' Drew teased her, and then laughed good-naturedly, doing as she asked so that Tilly could hurry over to examine the packs of cards on the tray supported by a string round the street-seller's neck.

'Good stuff, this is,' he told Tilly, seeing her interest.

'Why are they are in packs of twos?' Tilly asked him. The cards did indeed look as though they were good quality, at least from what she could see of them in their boxes, the lids removed to reveal the contents.

'That's 'cos they're bridge cards,' the man told her. 'Proper posh they are, an' all, and only ten-pence a pack. Bomb-damaged stock, see.'

Remembering Dulcie's warnings when they had shopped together, Tilly told him firmly, 'I'll have to have a proper look at them to make sure they are full packs.'

At first she thought he was going to refuse, but other people were starting to gather round, curious to see what was going on, and with the hope of other customers he gave in and allowed Tilly to remove the packs from the box and inspect them.

The salesman was right, they were good quality, Tilly recognised, and when she looked inside, the lid of the box was stamped with the sign of a royal warrant.

That was enough to have her saying recklessly, 'I'll take two boxes.' It seemed mean to buy only one, which, split in two, meant that two of the boys could have a pack of cards, when the other girls might also want a pack for their stockings. No doubt Dulcie would have called her a fool for not haggling a bit but Tilly didn't care.

By the time she rejoined Drew, waiting patiently on the pavement with his back turned toward the salesman, the cards were stowed away safely in her handbag. It had been a comment by Dulcie that had inspired her when she'd seen the salesman. Dulcie had read out a line from her brother's letter, saying that they were having to play cards with half a pack because they'd lost so many of their cards.

Her mind now fully engaged with the fun of Christmas, Tilly thought happily of the Monopoly and snakes-and-ladders boards her mother had kept from Tilly's childhood, and which came out every Christmas. It would be such fun playing her favourite childhood board games with Drew.

Drew... Tilly moved closer to him, her face rosy and alight with Christmas happiness.

'I'm getting something really special for Mum,' she confided to Drew. 'Dulcie got me a pair of proper leather gloves from a delivery that Selfridges have had in. Whoops!' She laughed as a determined shopper carrying several large boxes, piled so high it was almost impossible for her to see over them, almost bumped into her. Not that Tilly minded when it gave her the opportunity to move closer to Drew.

The sound of carols being sung emerged from almost every shop they passed, further lifting the spirits.

'I love Christmas,' she said to Drew, happily.

'And I love you,' he told her back.

Tilly and Drew weren't the only ones out enjoying the Christmassy atmosphere of London's shops and the relief from air raids that the city was enjoying.

Agnes felt as though her heart was going to burst with pride as she snatched a quick glance at her Ted, looking so smart in his best Sunday clothes, his face so clean and polished that it positively shone, a determined look in his eyes.

Today was the day that Ted was going to buy Agnes an engagement ring. He had been saving up to do so all year, and now finally the time had come. Agnes was wearing her lovely coat that Tilly's mother had had made for her the previous autumn, its soft colour highlighting Agnes's delicate features and colouring, its velvet collar reflecting up the bright winter light around her face, flushed prettily today with the excitement of what lay ahead.

After they had bought the ring they were going to go meet up with Ted's mother and his sisters, for a celebration tea at Joe Lyons. Just thinking about it all made Agnes feel giddy with happiness and excitement.

'How did you get on with that woman who had the doll's pram for sale? The one you told me about the other day? You said you were going round to see her,' Agnes asked, knowing how much Ted was hoping to get his sisters the pram and doll they had set their hearts on.

Ted shook his head and looked glum. 'It was no-go. I thought we'd settled on a price but when I got there she told me that she'd had someone else interested in it and that they'd offered her more. I reckon she wanted to get a bit of a Dutch auction between me and this other person, so I told her that I'd give her three and sixpence for it, like we'd agreed. She said she wasn't going to part with it for three and six, when she knew she could get five bob, so that was that. To be honest, it wasn't even worth half a crown, it was that shabby.'

'Oh, Ted, I am sorry.' Agnes gave his arm a loving squeeze. 'At least you've got the girls a doll, though I know she hasn't got real hair, or eyes that close, like they wanted.'

Ted exhaled and Agnes gave his arm another comforting squeeze. 'The doll looks ever so nice in the clothes that Tilly's mum has helped me to knit. Of course there were only some scraps of wool, on account of the war, so we couldn't make everything to match.'

'You've done your best, Aggie, I know that. Just like I've done mine. Not that I don't feel that that woman has let me down, not selling that pram to me after she as good as promised it to me. I'm not going to let it spoil today, though. Not when you and I have got an important bit of business of our own to conduct.'

When he smiled at her Agnes's heart lifted in a fresh surge of pride and gratitude. She was so lucky to have someone as special as Ted to love her. Sometimes she felt as though her chest would burst, just thinking about how lucky she was and how much she loved him.

'Here's a jeweller's,' Ted pointed out, nudging her. 'Let's go and take a gander.'

They weren't the only couple staring eagerly at the rings on display. In fact, there was quite a crowd of young couples pressing round the window, many of the men in uniform, and some of the women as well. Because of the war many of the rings on display were secondhand, but Agnes, with her starry-eyed gaze, didn't care how worn they were.

The rings were displayed on trays marked with a price, and Agnes automatically positioned herself so that she could look at the trays with the lowest price. She didn't care how little her engagement ring cost. What she cared about was being engaged to her Ted. But then she saw it – the ring, *her* ring – and her heart lifted on a surge of protective love.

'That one looks nice,' she told Ted, fighting to keep the tremor of desire out of her voice as she pointed to 'the' ring.

Ted stared at the narrow band of gold set with a tiny single stone.

'That one?' he questioned. 'But the diamond is so small you can hardly see it.' He'd saved very hard for this moment and he wanted his Agnes to have a ring that showed how much hard work he had put into that saving, a ring that showed how much he loved her.

'What about this one?' he suggested, pointing to a ring on the next tray at a higher price.

Agnes looked at the much larger diamond, wanting to please Ted, but at the same time unable to find anything that appealed to her in the flat yellowy coloured stone.

'It's very nice,' she told him, 'but I really like the other one.' As she looked at it again it seemed to Agnes that the ring twinkled shyly back at her as though it wanted to be hers.

The ring had caught her eye because it looked so delicate and somehow in need of someone to love and cherish it, just as she felt that Ted loved and cherished her. Because of that, to Agnes it seemed that the ring would be a true symbol of their love, but she didn't have the words to articulate any of that to Ted.

'Come on then. Let's go inside,' Ted told her.

They entered the shop on the heels of another couple, the man in an army uniform with sergeant's flashes on his jacket, the young woman on his arm very made up, her hat worn at a very dashing angle, and her checked coat belted tightly round her small waist. She was the kind of woman who immediately attracted attention, a bit like Dulcie, but nowhere near as pretty as Dulcie, Agnes thought loyally. The single tinkle of the shop's doorbell, as they walked in caused one of the three assistants in the shop to look up from the couple he was already serving, whilst at the same time virtually ignoring Ted and Agnes.

Agnes didn't mind. She liked to take her time getting used to things, and the shop overawed her a little, with its overhead lights shining down on the trays of rings, nestling against their black-velvet-covered tray, the diamonds in the rings glittering and shining.

Counters ran round three sides of the shop, the fourth side was taken up by the window. The interior of the shop had that damp, slightly bad-drains smell of older buildings. Couples were standing at each of the three sides, studying rings on the trays laid out in front of them. One of the couples, a young man in naval uniform and a pretty girl with a mass of fair curls, were both looking down at the ring the salesman had just shown to them. 'Is this the one?' the young man asked the girl. When she nodded and the young man slid it onto her hand, Agnes's breath caught in her throat in an emotional response to their obvious happiness.

The ring chosen, they were handed over to another assistant, who conducted them to a screened-off area of the shop, where Agnes presumed they would make their payment. This left a space at the counter free, but just as she and Ted moved towards it, the female half of the couple who had entered the shop ahead of them, and who had been standing at one of the other counters, suddenly pushed past them.

Agnes saw Ted frown, but she was glad that he didn't say anything or make a fuss. Agnes didn't like arguments or unpleasantness. Besides, they weren't in any real rush. No one else had as yet asked to look at the tray on which she'd seen her ring whilst they had been standing outside.

The counter where the other couple had been waiting had now become free. Ted urged Agnes forward, telling the salesman, 'We'd like to see some rings, please. Some engagement rings.' He puffed out his chest with pride. Today was, after all, the culmination of a year's worth of hard work and hard saving, his chance to show Agnes how much she meant to him via the purchase of the engagement ring that would link them together officially in the eyes of the world. Ted loved Agnes; there was nothing he would not do for her. He wanted the world to see that she was spoken for and 'his'. If it hadn't been for the fact that he had had to step into his dad's shoes and become the family's main breadwinner Agnes would have had her ring months ago. Ted, though, had a strong sense of duty and responsibility.

The salesman, dressed in a black suit, a starched shirt and collar, and with a dark coloured tie, his thinning hair slicked back with Brylcreem, inclined his head.

'Would that be a diamond engagement ring, sir?'

'Yes,' Ted answered him firmly, 'a diamond engagement ring.'

'And has madam seen anything she particularly likes?'

'Oh, yes,' Agnes breathed happily, quickly explaining to the salesman which ring she had liked.

When the salesman went to the window to unlock it and remove the tray with 'her' ring on it, Agnes watched him, her attention momentarily distracted by the other couple. They seemed to be quarrelling about something, the woman pushing away the tray of rings in front of her.

Agnes's attention switched back to the tray being carried towards them, her heart in her mouth and unable to speak for excitement as Ted nodded his head to her to point out to the salesman the ring she wanted.

Without the barrier of the window, the ring looked even prettier to her. Agnes already loved it almost as much as she loved Ted, but in a very different way, of course. The ring was so dainty, its small diamond almost hidden in a way that made it even more special to Agnes, without her being able to explain why. She just knew that she had fallen in love with the ring the minute she had seen it.

With very great care it was removed from its bed of velvet. The gold of the ring was fine and delicate, the single small stone so pretty that Agnes's heart bounded into her chest wall.

Ted took it from the salesman and was sliding it

onto her finger when suddenly the woman turned round and said in a loud voice, waving her hand in Agnes's direction, 'You're a cheapskate, Artie, that's what you are. The next thing I know you'll be wanting me to have a little bit of nothing like she's having.' With that the woman marched out of the shop leaving her partner to follow her. Agnes wasn't interested in them though. All her attention was concentrated on Ted, whose ears were burning a dark red. Looking humiliated and angry, he started to tug the ring off her finger.

'No, Ted, don't,' Agnes protested.

'I'm not having anyone thinking that I can't afford to buy my girl a decent ring,' Ted told her.

He'd been pleased initially when he'd seen the price of the ring Agnes had indicated, thinking that with the money left over from what he'd saved he'd be able to put something aside for the future as well as buy Agnes her ring, but now...

'We want to see something else,' he told the salesman. 'Something better.'

'No, Ted,' Agnes protested again, saying almost pleadingly to the salesman, 'I like this ring.'

'If I may say so, sir, when a lady has a delicate hand and finger, then a delicate ring looks best.'

For a moment Agnes thought that Ted was going to refuse to listen.

'Please, Ted,' she begged him, 'I really do want this ring. It's so pretty. The minute I saw it I felt that it was just there waiting for me.'

She could see from the set of his mouth that Ted still wasn't happy but he gave in and finished sliding the ring onto her finger.

Agnes gave a happy sigh as the ring slipped on.

It fitted her perfectly, just as though it had been made for her.

'The stone might be small but it is good quality,' the salesman assured them both, his expression relaxing into a hint of a smile as he looked at Agnes, her face all prettily pink with happiness.

'If you're sure it's what you want?'

Ted could see how much Agnes liked the ring. That was one of the things he loved about her: the fact that she was so honest about her feelings. The other woman's words had rankled, though, and hurt his pride. Right now he wanted to see his Agnes wearing the biggest and shiniest diamond ring there was, just to show everyone how much he loved her.

Agnes, though, was stroking the soft slightly worn gold of 'her' ring with a tender smile on her face as she watched its small diamond twinkle up at her.

'This is the one I want, Ted,' she repeated.

The salesman was looking at him, so Ted gave an abrupt nod of his head. Agnes removed the ring and handed it over to the salesman to take away, but as he started to do so he stopped and turned round.

'There's a wedding ring that goes with it, if you're interested. Came in as a pair, they did, but Mr Goldstein, who owns the shop, separated them.'

'We won't be getting married yet,' Agnes informed him, giving Ted a proud smile as she explained, 'Ted's got his family to look after, you see.'

299

'We might as well have a look at it,' Ted over-ruled her. 'No sense in not doing.'

The wedding ring was duly produced, and they could both see that it fitted together perfectly with the engagement ring.

One look at Agnes's face was enough to have Ted saying firmly, 'We'll take them both,' his pride restored at being able to do so.

'Oh, Ted,' Agnes breathed ecstatically, so that he straightened his back and walked tall as he left her to go and pay for the rings.

'And then the salesman put the rings in ever such a lovely box, on account of Ted buying both of them together, didn't he, Ted?' Agnes told Ted's mother excitedly, her face flushed with happiness, as the five of them – Ted, and her, and his mother and two sisters – sat together in Joe Lyons. Of course, with it being a Saturday and so close to Christmas, the café was busy. Agnes had to raise her voice a little to make herself heard above the noise and bustle, with the smartly dressed 'nippy' waitresses whisking to and fro, serving afternoon teas and clearing and resetting tables. Ted's party had had to queue at the door to get a table, but luckily not for very long, and now, whilst they waited for their order of tea and teacakes, Ted had begun to tell his mother about their successful shopping trip.

'Mum said that she doesn't know how our Ted can afford to go buying engagement rings.' Ted's younger sister, Sonia, suddenly piped up, causing the three adults to fall silent.

Agnes could feel her face burning with dis-

300

comfort as she avoided looking at Ted's mother.

'I can afford it 'cos I've saved up for it, that's how,' Ted told his mother firmly.

'That's all very well, Ted, but I don't like to see you going without, just to buy a fancy engagement ring,' Mrs Jackson said. 'You could have done with replacing that old winter coat of yours this year, and the girls are growing out of theirs as well.'

'There's plenty of money in the kitty for new coats for the girls, Ma,' Ted responded. 'I've already told you that.'

The nippy arrived with their tea and teacakes, but Agnes's happiness had evaporated every bit as quickly as the steam escaping from the teapot when Ted's mother opened the lid to give its contents a good stir.

'So where is it then, this ring?' Ted's mother demanded once she had poured the tea.

'We'd perhaps best not get it out here, Ted,' Agnes suggested in a low voice. 'You can show your mum later at home.' She didn't want to see her precious ring exposed to Ted's mother's critical gaze, and somehow she felt that it *would* be a critical gaze, the same as the critical not-good-enough-for-her-son gaze she felt that Ted's mother was fixing on her.

Her hand shook slightly as she lifted her teacup to her lips.

EIGHTEEN

'...and Drew's managed to get a special Father Christmas suit so that he can hand out the presents to the children at the Christmas party, seeing as the one Sergeant Dawson used to wear has been lost.'

'Yes, Tilly, you've already told me that several times already,' Olive pointed out to her daughter, who was hopping excitedly from one foot to the other as she waited for Olive to finish putting on her coat, prior to the two of them setting off for the church hall for the Christmas party.

Olive was a loving mother who liked Drew, but Tilly, like all young women freshly in love, could barely manage to say a single sentence without somehow or other managing to include a reference to Drew in it. Not that Olive wasn't grateful to Drew for offering to step in at such short notice when Sergeant Dawson had been unable to play his normal role of Father Christmas because he had to be on duty instead. She was, and she was even willing to agree that Drew would be a very good Father Christmas.

'We're going to be late,' Tilly protested.

Olive raised an eyebrow, remembering how last Christmas Eve Tilly had complained that attending the church party was dull stuff compared with the delights of going dancing at the Hammersmith Palais. That was what young love did to you though, Olive knew: it coloured everything that included your beloved in a rosy glow.

Olive and Tilly were the only two occupants of number 13 making their way to the party from there, but the others were also going to attend. Agnes was meeting Ted and his mother and sisters at the tube station, and going straight to the church hall with them. Sally was going direct from the hospital, where George, who had managed to get leave over Christmas, was going to pick her up, whilst Dulcie, who had announced that Wilder would be escorting her to the party, would be meeting him outside Selfridges when she finished work, the store expecting to be busy since it was the last day to shop before Christmas.

Tilly had been lucky in that she had only had to work in the morning, returning home at dinner time, and offering to help her mother with her busy Christmas preparations in the kitchen.

Olive, though, sensing disruption to her carefully laid Christmas cooking plans, had suggested instead that Tilly wrap the Christmas presents Olive had hidden away for her lodgers.

With that task done, Tilly was now anxious for them to get to the church hall, all the more so since she knew about the surprise Drew had arranged for the children with the help of his mother, and her friends. She was longing to see the expressions on the faces of the children when they received their unexpected gifts, especially Ted's two sisters. That, of course, was not the prime reason why she was urging her mother to hurry. It was the prospect of being with Drew himself that excited her the most. She hadn't seen him since

303

the weekend because he had been busy writing an extra column for his newspaper back at home about how war-struck London was facing Christmas.

The weather had turned cold, and secretly Tilly wished it could be a white Christmas, especially since Drew had told her about the white Christmases in Philadelphia, where his mother came from.

Olive and Tilly had already received a large Christmas card from Drew's parents, thanking them for welcoming Drew into their home, and Olive had sent one back – a much smaller one, but still a very nice one, Tilly felt, with its scene of a Dickensian Christmas.

At last her mother was ready to leave. Olive had already made one visit to the church hall earlier in the day to take down the food she had made as her contribution to the party, along with some small gifts for the children's bran tub, and a pair of fingerless gloves she had knitted for Mrs Windle, who complained that when she had to stand in for the church organist her fingers were so cold she could hardly find the keys.

The church hall was busy with those members of the WVS who had helped to cook, bake and otherwise provide the buffet meal that was now laid out on trestle tables, the plates of sandwiches covered by carefully dampened tea towels so that the bread wouldn't dry out and curl up.

The hall's wooden floor had been brushed and then scrubbed. Coloured garlands, patched here and there with different colours where they had broken, swung gently in the air from the constantly opening and closing door. In addition to the garlands, paper chains made by the children attending the party had also been hung up, some of the 'chains' stuck together rather haphazardly.

A large Christmas tree stood at one end of the room, decorated with tinsel and coloured tree lights in various shapes and colours. The tree had a group of excited children standing round it, with an even larger group surrounding the bran tub, with it's hidden presents. The faded red velvet curtains pulled over the blackout fabric covering the windows added an extra festive touch to the room.

Tilly had come to Christmas parties here as far back as she could remember, first with both her grandparents and her mother, and then with her grandfather and her mother. Now, of course, there were just the two of them. Tonight, though, their small family would number three and not two, even if Drew's inclusion in that family could only exist inside her own and Drew's hearts for now. They had, after all, promised her mother that they wouldn't get too serious about one another.

Tilly smiled a secret tender smile. It just wasn't possible for her not to get serious about Drew when he was such a special person.

As though her thinking about him had magically conjured him up, Drew came in through the doors that separated the church hall from the outer vestibule, his face breaking into a smile the moment he saw Tilly.

'I didn't think you'd be here for ages yet,' Tilly

told him after they had exchanged a brief public hug. 'We've only just arrived. Mum's gone to have a word with Mrs Windle.'

'I didn't want to leave it too long in case some other Father Christmas got here before me and stole my girl,' Drew laughed.

'Have the toys all arrived then?' Tilly asked. 'I know you were worrying that they might not.'

'Don't worry. We got everything sorted out, although not quite as I'd planned.' He bent towards her ear and whispered, 'It's your present that matters most to me right now, Tilly. I've got something I want to give you later, a special present, just between us.'

There was an urgency in his voice that had Tilly drawing back to look at him. She could see his love for her in his eyes, and she was about to ask him what her special present was when he gave a small warning shake of his head and told her in a louder voice, 'I could do with some help finding somewhere to put the stuff I've left in the foyer. Including my Father Christmas suit.'

The sound of her mother's voice came from behind Tilly: 'We'll both give you a hand. There's a small room off the kitchen where you can put everything and get changed later when all the children are here.'

Drew hadn't been joking about needing some help, Tilly acknowledged several minutes later as she and her mother stared at the mound of brightly wrapped presents standing in a corner of the vestibule on a red sledge.

'What on earth...?' Olive began.

But Tilly broke in, enthusing, 'Isn't it wonder-

306

ful, Mum? Drew wrote to his mother and sisters and asked them to have a collection of no longer needed toys so that all the children here could have something.'

'How very kind of them, Drew. But how did everything get here so quickly?' Olive frowned. 'I do hope it wasn't taking up space on a ship that could have been used for–'

'No, no, they didn't do that,' Drew assured her.

Tilly was relieved to see her mother's frown disappear.

'Did a pram and a doll come for Ted's sisters?' she asked him.

'Yes,' he assured her.

'Drew, they'll be thrilled,' Tilly told him, giving him a shining-eyed smile.

Tonight at midnight, after Ted's mother had taken his sisters home and after she and Ted had been to the midnight carol service here at the church, Ted was going to give Agnes her engagement ring and then they would be officially engaged. Agnes sighed happily to herself as she opened the church hall door for Ted and his mother and the girls.

Ted's sisters, who had been chattering excitedly about Christmas all the way from the underground station, had gone all shy and quiet now they had seen families they didn't know greeting one another as they headed inside.

Olive, who had been keeping an eye out for their arrival, immediately made her way towards them, giving them all a warm smile and saying welcomingly, 'You must be Mrs Jackson, and these two pretty girls must be Marie and Sonia. I'm Agnes's landlady, Olive Robbins. We're so glad you were able to come. I know that Agnes is looking forward to having a chance to get to know your girls a bit better. Ted, why don't you take the girls and show them the Christmas tree with Agnes whilst I take your mother and introduce her to Mrs Windle?' She turned back to Ted's mother. 'Mrs Windle is our vicar's wife. She'll be playing the piano later on for the children's games and then the dancing...'

And so Ted's mother was borne away, leaving Ted and Agnes to take his sisters over to the tree, where Agnes was soon introducing them to some of the other children whom she knew from seeing them at church with their parents.

One of them, a sturdily built boy with red hair, announced importantly, 'Father Christmas will be here later. Well, he isn't the real Father Christmas, of course, because there isn't—'

A sharp dig in the ribs from the older girl standing next to him had the boy coughing, whilst she continued in a voice that warned anyone against arguing with her, 'He's helping the real Father Christmas because he'll be busy delivering everyone's presents.'

'George, you look as though you haven't slept for days,' Sally told her boyfriend with concern as they stood together in the hospital foyer.

'I haven't,' he admitted, 'or at least not very much. I volunteered to stand in for three of the other chaps to make sure that I could get this time off to be with you.'

308

'Oh, George.' Sally shook her head. 'Somehow I don't think Mr McIndoe would approve of you doing that.'

'Luckily we're pretty quiet. Mr McIndoe likes the men to live their lives as close to normal as possible so all ops other than the most urgent are suspended over Christmas. And the families of those patients who can't go home have been invited down to spend Christmas with them. It's hard sometimes to watch them watching the door for visitors, half hoping, half afraid. Some of the wives and girlfriends can't face what's happened to them. Only a few,' he added when Sally made a small sound of distress.

'I had a lovely letter from your parents this week,' Sally told him. 'You must have given them a very improved version of the real me, George. They seem to think I'm some kind of saint.'

'I told them that you are the most wonderful girl and that I love you,' George informed her. 'And I said that they would love you too, which they will.'

Arm in arm they left the hospital, heading for the bus stop.

'I'd like to drop my bag off at Ian Simpson's first, before we go on to the party, if that's OK?' George told Sally.

'Yes, of course it is,' she assured him. 'I've got a key for you. Ian gave it to me before he left for the country. I've never seen a man loaded up with so many Christmas presents.'

Sally shivered, taking the opportunity provided by the icy cold wind to snuggle closer to George as they waited for the bus.

'Olive's going to have a houseful tomorrow for Christmas dinner, seeing as she's invited Drew, and that young American that Dulcie is seeing, as well as you,' she told him.

'Our first Christmas dinner together,' George smiled. 'But most definitely not our last.'

Outside Selfridges, as the staff leaving streamed round them in the gloom of the late December afternoon, Dulcie quickly found Wilder. He was wearing his leather flying jacket with its American Eagle badge, a white silk scarf thrown nonchalantly round his neck. It was no wonder that other girls were pausing to give him a second look. Dulcie felt very pleased with herself because he was waiting for her. Not that she intended to let him know that she'd noticed those admiring looks.

Instead she greeted him with a frown and demanded, 'What's that?' as she looked at the square box Wilder was holding in its bright red and silver Christmas wrapping paper, tied with a matching red and silver ribbon. Both the paper and the ribbon were new and expensive, suggesting to Dulcie that they and the gift inside the box must have come from America, since paper and ribbon were luxuries hard to find in London. Earlier in the week she had watched Olive carefully ironing the paper she had saved from last Christmas, and now although she wasn't going to let Wilder see it, she felt a thrill of satisfaction at knowing that what she guessed must be her present looked so very obviously smart and professionally wrapped.

'It's for you,' Wilder informed her, handing the box over to her.

'I can't open it until after midnight. It won't be Christmas until then,' Dulcie told him.

'I'll just have to take my thank you kiss before you open it, in that case,' he responded boldly.

Again a small thrill ran through her body, but this time it was the kind that came from the excitement of doing something that you knew was dangerous.

Tossing her head she demanded, 'Who says that it deserves a kiss?'

'Of course it does. I wouldn't give a girl something that didn't.'

'A girl', not 'my girl', Dulcie noted.

'And I don't give kisses to men just because they give me a present,' Dulcie responded, but she kept a firm hold of the box as she did so.

'Tell me again where we're going?' Wilder demanded.

'To a Christmas party at our local church hall,' Dulcie reminded him. 'Then you're staying overnight with Drew at Ian Simpson's, and then you're having Christmas dinner with us at number thirteen tomorrow.'

'Come on, open it,' Wilder tried to persuade her.

'Not until after midnight,' Dulcie refused. 'Look, there's our bus. Hurry up otherwise we'll miss it.'

The children had played Pass the Parcel, and dived into the bran tub to retrieve the small stocking fillers provided and wrapped up by Olive and the other WVS workers. Soon it would be time for the buffet and then the grown-up dancing, but first Father Christmas had to arrive.

Now they were watching and waiting, wide-eyed with excitement, Agnes delighting in the relaxed happiness she could see in Ted's sisters' faces. With their mother's attention occupied by Olive, Agnes had finally had a chance to get to know the two girls and now they were smiling happily at her and chattering away nineteen to the dozen.

In the room off the kitchen, Tilly and Dulcie were in fits of giggles over Drew's struggles with his cotton wool Father Christmas full beard. Wilder, who had been co-opted in to help man-oeuvre the heavy parcel-laden sledge, stood to one side with his arms folded, looking irritated and bored.

'Come on, it's time to go, otherwise we're gonna have those kids making a mass attack on us in here,' Wilder announced, his patience finally running out. Unfolding his arms he leaned down to push the sledge from behind.

The sledge started to move. Tilly ran to open the door, a signal to the vicar to clap his hands and demand silence from the children for the arrival of Father Christmas.

The sight of the awed expressions on the faces of the children young enough still to believe in Father Christmas brought a lump to Tilly's throat and filled her with pride that it was Drew – her Drew – who had volunteered for the role.

'Look,' one little voice piped up, 'Father Christmas has got a sleigh.'

'That's not a sleigh, it's a sledge, innit, and he ain't got no reindeer, has he?' an older boy replied cynically.

But it didn't matter, and neither did the absence of the reindeer. The children who had been hanging back surged forward *en masse* when Drew kneeled down beside the sledge and reached for the first present.

'Jimmy Smithers. Is there a Jimmy Smithers here?' he called in a deep Father Christmas voice.

As luck would have it, it was the older boy who had made the cynical comment who stepped forward, his face a picture: a mixture of disbelief, wariness and hope.

The WVS ladies had carefully written down a list of all the children who were expected to attend the party several weeks earlier; in the main, children who had been evacuated but who for one reason or another had now returned home. Labels had been written with their names on them. Thanks to Drew and his mother and sisters, each child would receive a toy, the labels having been placed on them by Mrs Windle and her team of helpers while the games of Pass the Parcel were taking place.

Tilly found that she was holding her breath, every bit as excited as the watching children, as Jimmy Smithers took his present.

Jimmy looked more bored than excited as he unwrapped his gift. He was at that age where boys felt they had to behave with a certain cockiness, but then once the wrapping had gone and he was staring down at the box in his hands, he dropped to his knees, totally engrossed in removing its contents, his disbelieving, 'It's a Hornby Double 00 engine, and it's brand new,' bringing the other children to cluster round him in excitement. Then Drew seized control of things and called out another child's name.

Within half an hour the floor was covered in discarded paper whilst an increasing number of very happy children were gazing starry-eyed at their presents – presents of far greater size and value than were normal for such an event.

Now there were just a handful of presents left. Ted's sisters, who had been leaning against Agnes's knees in silence, looked at one another with excitement when Marie's name was called out, before turning to their mother for permission to go up.

'I think you're going to need a bit of help with this,' Drew told her in his gruff Father Christmassy voice, but before he could ask for help Ted, who had seen the size of the large box being pushed towards his sister, was already on his feet, picking it up to carry it over to the table where the three adults were sitting.

'Open it!' Sonia demanded excitedly, but Marie shook her head.

'Don't you want to see what's inside?' Agnes asked her.

'Yes,' she admitted, 'but I'm afraid that it might not be what I asked Father Christmas for.'

Agnes felt a tug on her heartstrings. She recognised that awful feeling of anxiety that came from knowing that a present couldn't possibly be what you really wanted, mixed with not wanting to let others know that you were disappointed.

'Sonia Jackson,' Drew called out, looking towards their table.

More confident than her older sister, Sonia immediately ran forward, giving Drew a wide smile. 'I know what my present is,' she told him. 'It's a dolly with real hair and eyes that close.'

'Poor little tyke,' Ted murmured to Agnes and his mother. 'She's too young to know how much dolls like that cost.'

'Come on,' Sonia urged her sister, having returned with her present. 'Race you to open your present.'

The box containing Marie's gift was so large that Agnes offered to help her remove the paper, getting down on her knees to do so, when Marie nodded her head.

After the paper was finally removed, though, Agnes was every bit as disbelieving as Marie when they saw the picture of a doll's pram on the outside of the box. Marie's face went pink, then white. She looked at Agnes as though not daring to hope.

'See, I told you it would be a dolly,' Sonia cried out triumphantly, holding out for inspection a lovely 'baby' doll that not only had soft brown hair, and bright blue eyes, which did indeed open and close, but that also cried 'Mama' when her middle was pressed.

Ted had taken Agnes' place on the floor, to open the cardboard box, but it wasn't pleasure Agnes could see in his eyes when he lifted out the doll's pram, although his sister was speechless with delight.

'Ted, what is it?' Agnes asked him worriedly.

'Where's this stuff come from and who's paid for it? That's what I want to know.'

315

'Tilly told me earlier that Drew had asked his mother and sisters to ask round amongst their friends for toys their children had grown out of,' Agnes told him.

'This stuff isn't second-hand, it's new,' Ted told her. 'Charity, that's what it is, and I'm not having it.'

'Ted...' Agnes protested. She had never seen him like this before, looking so angry. Not like her lovely Ted at all.

'Ruddy American, thinking he can come over here and patronise us, telling folk that we can't afford to give our kids Christmas presents.'

'I'm sure that Drew didn't mean anything like that, Ted. I expect he just wanted to help. I suppose it's my fault really, because I told Tilly how much the girls wanted a pram and a doll, and what a problem you've had trying to get hold of them.'

'Trying to afford them, you mean. There's plenty available for them with the money to buy them.'

Agnes was getting more upset by the minute. 'Oh, Ted, you could have afforded them too if you hadn't bought me an engagement ring.'

'...and we can put my dolly in your pram and then–'

Ted's mother interrupted Sonia's happy plans, announcing grimly, 'And who's going to carry a thing like that up and down the stairs to the flat, I'd like to know, never mind where it's going to go? Waste of money, it is, when the pair of you need new winter coats.'

Agnes felt her heart sink even lower. It was her

fault that Ted was cross, and her fault that his mother was cross as well. She thought of the carefully knitted dolls clothes she had wrapped up for Sonia, and the blankets and sheets she had made from some offcuts of fabric Olive had given her, just in case Ted had been able to buy a second-hand pram for Marie, and wished that instead she had got the girls something service-able like new gloves and scarves.

The wrapping paper and toys had been cleared from the floor, the buffet eaten and Father Christmas had reverted to being Drew before Olive was able to find the time to take the young American by the arm and lead him into a quiet corner of the room.

'That was very generous of you and whoever else supplied them, Drew,' she told him quietly. 'I know that those presents you gave the children were not secondhand; they were new. New and rather expensive.'

Drew's face burned self-consciously as he moved his weight from one foot to another.

'Gee, I hope I haven't offended anyone, Mrs Robbins,' he said worriedly, 'only when I wrote my mom and sisters, my mom told her friends that she lunches with and ... well, to cut a long story short, they decided that it would easier to wire over the money for me to buy the kids their presents than to collect some second-hand stuff and then get it shipped over.'

'That was very generous, Drew,' Olive re-peated, privately thinking that whilst some of the parents might have been surprised to see their children receiving such expensive gifts, the joy with which their children had received them had quickly made up for their qualms, as more than one mother had already told her.

'We might not be in this war with you officially, but there's plenty of folk back home who aren't comfortable with that. I guess this was just a way of showing you folks here how we feel,' Drew continued.

'And it was a very kind way, as well. No parent likes to see their child being disappointed at Christmas. We adults might understand how important it is that essential materials for the war are given precedence over everything else, but children don't. I have to admit that my initial feeling was one of concern. I knew your motives would be good ones, but people's pride is easily bruised, and all the more so when they have very little. However, as so many of the mothers have already said to me, it was a true joy to see the children's faces when they unwrapped their presents.'

Olive could see from the look on Drew's face that he understood both what she had said and what she had not said. She waited a few seconds and then covered his hand with one of her own. He was such a very nice kind young man. Exactly the sort of young man that she would welcome as a future husband for her precious daughter? Olive's heart gave a small anxious thump. She didn't want Tilly to marry young, especially not in wartime, but young hearts were impatient and clamoured with the strength and longing of their feelings, as she knew all too well. All around them the sounds of young voices filled with excitement and happiness filled the faintly dusty air of the hall. It seemed only a few blinks of her eyes ago that Tilly had been a child herself. Part of her half wished that she still was. A mother could protect a young child by knowing what was best for her. But a mother couldn't necessarily protect her child from war, Olive reminded herself, acutely aware of the grief she had witnessed in mothers who had lost children.

This was Christmas, she reminded herself. This was a time for being grateful for everything that she had to be grateful for. Tilly loved Christmas, and she loved Tilly.

'Please do tell your mother and her friends when next you write how appreciative we all are for their kindness,' she told Drew, removing her hand from his. 'Did you choose all the presents yourself?'

'Sort of. I wanted to ask Tilly to help me but there wasn't really time, so I took that list you gave me of all the kids names and ages, and Ian and I went to your Harrods to get everything, including thank you gifts from me to his kids for letting me stay in their house.'

'Well, the pair of you did very well,' Olive praised him. 'Jimmy's face when he saw that engine is something I'll remember for a very long time.'

It wasn't like dancing at the Palais – how could it be when her mother was sitting a few yards away chatting to some of the other mothers, whilst Mrs Windle valiantly bashed out a popular dance tune on the piano – but at least she was in Drew's arms, Tilly thought happily.

319

'You're so kind and I'm so proud to be your girl,' Tilly whispered to Drew as they circled the floor together.

'I'm the one who's proud to have you as my girl,' Drew corrected her, bending his head to her ear. 'About this special present I've got for you, Tilly, that's if you'll have it...'

'I can't wait for tomorrow,' Tilly responded happily.

Drew shook his head. 'This isn't a present I can give you in front of anyone else, especially not your mom.'

Soft colour flushed Tilly's face, her eyes widening and her lips parting. This was new territory indeed but it was one she was very willing to explore – with Drew. So without hesitation she began breathlessly, 'I'd love to, but if we try to sneak back to Ian's so that we can be on our own, Mum is bound to notice.'

'No, it's nothing like that,' Drew told her, flushing a little himself, as he realised what she had thought he meant. 'Not that I wouldn't like...' His voice became semistrangled with emotion as he told her, 'When the time comes for that, Tilly, it will be somewhere special, and something that we've talked about and planned, both of us together, not me suggesting... No, it's just...' He looked down at his right hand and for the first time Tilly realised that he wasn't wearing his graduation ring.

'There's a custom that a guy sometimes gives his girl his graduation ring to wear on a chain round her neck. It signifies that they are a couple. I'd like you to have my ring, Tilly. That's if you

320

want to wear it.'

'Oh, Drew.' Tilly's eyes shone like stars, and Drew held her closer. 'Of course I want to wear it. You're right though, Mum will only worry that we're getting too serious too quickly if she knows. Besides,' Tilly added with new emotional maturity, 'some things should only be between us and for us, as a couple.'

It was over an hour later after the midnight carol service when they were all making their way back to number 13, that Tilly and Drew could finally take advantage of Olive being deep in conversation with Sergeant Dawson, who had come off duty in time to attend the service, to slow their walk to put some distance between themselves and the others. They were all heading for number 13, and the mince pies and sherry Olive had promised to celebrate both Christmas and Agnes and Ted's engagement.

'Keep still,' Drew warned Tilly as he reached behind her to fasten around her neck the gold chain he had just slipped from the velvet pouch he'd had in his pocket.

The ring felt warm, warm and heavy and meaningful, a symbol of their private commitment to one another and the future they both knew they wanted to share, Tilly thought as she lifted it to her lips to kiss it, her fiercely passionate gaze fixed on Drew as she let the ring and chain disappear to hide beneath her blouse.

'Tilly, come on, hurry up,' Dulcie shouted back to them. 'It's gone midnight and I want to get back so that I can open my present from Wilder.'

'Is there any news about the boy Barney, Sergeant Dawson?' Olive asked. She suspected that Nancy would have something to say on Boxing Day about the fact that she had walked home from church with the sergeant, but Olive's anxiety for the boy she had found in her kitchen was greater than her concern about Nancy's meanness.

'As it happens there is,' Sergeant Dawson answered her. 'I've had a few words here and there and it's been agreed that the lad will come and live with me and Mrs Dawson. Of course, Mrs Dawson took a bit of persuading, but I reckon it will help cheer her up a bit having a young lad around, although I've warned him it will be straight back to the council if he gets himself into any trouble with the good folk of Article Row.

'Oh, I'm so pleased,' Olive told him. 'You've got just the right way with him, I think, and a boy like that needs that.'

'Well, I don't mind admitting to you that I've taken a bit of a liking to him. He's got spirit and brains, even though he uses them for the wrong things at times. The lad's never had what you'd call a proper home, by all accounts, and I reckon that now he knows that his dad will be able to find him, he'll settle down a treat.

'He'll be coming home with me when I come off duty tomorrow morning. I've managed to persuade Mrs Dawson to let me put up a bit of a Christmas tree for him. There's all our lad's books and toys up in the attic still, but, well, naturally Mrs Dawson doesn't like anyone touching his things, so I was glad of young Drew's offer of the extra toys he'd got just in case there were more children at the party than expected. A nice lad, he is. The right sort and no mistake.'

'I'm very pleased for you and Mrs Dawson, Sergeant,' Olive said as they reached number 1.

'It will do us both good. Perhaps breathe new life into the house and into us, having a lad around again. Not that young Barney is anything like our lad was, of course.'

'Of course not,' Olive agreed, understanding everything that the sergeant hadn't said as well as everything that he had.

If she was surprised that Mrs Dawson seemed so ready to accept Barney then she certainly wasn't going to say so to Sergeant Dawson and risk putting a shadow over his obvious happiness. She wasn't Nancy with her acid comments, after all. Even so, she had to admit that she did have some misgivings about how it would all work out, given that Mrs Dawson had shut herself away from them all. But no, it was Christmas Day, a time for hope and belief and joy, not a time for doubt.

'Happy Christmas, Sergeant,' Olive smiled.

'Happy Christmas, Mrs Robbins,' he returned, and they exchanged smiles before Olive herded her group of young people together, urging them towards number 13.

'I'm sorry about the doll and the pram, Ted,' Agnes whispered humbly as they walked together.

'It's not your fault.'

'Yes it is. I was the one who told Tilly about the girls wanting them.'

'No, Agnes. That isn't what I meant. What I

meant is that it's my fault that I couldn't go to ruddy Harrods and buy them for them myself, just like I can't afford to rent a better place for them and Mum, and like I can't afford to give you a proper engagement ring.'

'You are giving me a proper ring,' Agnes protested emotionally. 'I won't have you saying any different. You're giving me the only ring I want. Drew didn't mean any harm,' she told him, sensing his anger softening a little. 'Tilly just told me that he asked his mum to send over some second-hand toys but she and her friends sent money instead, 'cos they feel guilty that we're at war and they aren't.'

'When I saw that kid's face when he unwrapped his train...' Ted shook his head. 'Always wanted an engine like that meself, I did. Of course, it was out of the question. That lad will never forget this Christmas and getting that train. I suppose I'm just feeling out of sorts because I wanted to be the one to give the girls their dolly and pram,' he confessed reluctantly. 'Makes me feel like a poor kind of brother not to be able to get them the Christmas present they wanted. They don't ask for much, after all.'

'Ted, you are the very best kind of brother, and when they grow up, it won't be the dolly and the pram they remember, it will be the love you've given them and the hard work you've put into keeping your family together. There's nothing more important than family, and knowing ... knowing that you're part of one.'

Hearing the sadness in her voice, Ted pulled her closer to him. 'You have got a family, Agnes.

324

Don't you fret about that.'

'I don't think your mother likes me very much.' Agnes was aghast at what she'd let slip out. Now Ted would be cross again.

But instead he simply pulled her even closer. 'Ma isn't always the easiest person to get along with. It's on account of her losing Dad and worrying about losing the flat, and everything. But don't you ever think that you don't come first with me, Agnes, or that I don't know how lucky I am to have you.'

Their quick awkward kiss snatched in the darkness might not have seemed romantic to anyone else but to Agnes it meant everything when she added it to what Ted had just said to her.

Everything was going to be all right. In fact, everything was going to be perfect.

In Ian Simpson's front room, Sally smiled as she looked down into George's sleeping face. As though he was conscious of her concentration on him, even in his sleep, he stirred and then opened his eyes, exclaiming in a confused voice, 'Sally?' and then groaning as he sat up and apologised, 'I fell asleep, didn't I? I'm sorry. We'd better get off to this party, hadn't we?'

'It's a bit too late for that,' Sally laughed. 'It's just gone midnight.'

When George looked even more abashed she told him softly, 'It isn't too late for this, though, or too early. In fact it's exactly the right time. Happy Christmas, my dearest darling George,' she told him. And then she kissed him.

It was a good ten minutes before they spoke

again, George's voice soft with love as he warned her, 'This isn't a good idea, you and me with the house to ourselves.'

'I don't think we'll have it to ourselves for very much longer. The others will probably be back soon. Mind you, we ought really to go to number 13 and toast Ted and Agnes's engagement.'

'You should have woken me up earlier.'

'I didn't have the heart. You looked exhausted. You were fast asleep almost before you sat down,' Sally laughed as he helped her on with her coat and they headed for the front door.

In the front room of number 13, Ted dropped down on one knee in front of Agnes the minute Olive had shown them in and closed the door, leaving them alone together.

Overwhelmed by such a romantic gesture, Agnes put her hands to her flushed face and whispered his name.

His hand trembling slightly, Ted removed the jeweller's box from his trouser pocket and opened it, saying gruffly, 'Agnes, will you do me the honour of–'

'Oh, yes, yes, Ted, I will,' Agnes breathed ecstatically, not allowing him to finish, but holding out her left hand instead so that Ted could slip the ring – 'her' ring – onto her finger.

Looking down at his downbent head with its mousy hair, Agnes felt a rush of love and pride. She was surely the luckiest girl in London to-night. She certainly felt as though she was.

Ted was getting to his feet, dusting down the knees of his trousers, even though, thanks to

Olive's excellent housekeeping, there wasn't a speck of carpet fluff on them.

'That's that done then,' Ted announced in a relieved and satisfied voice, before planting a smacker of a kiss on Agnes's mouth. 'It's official now. You and me, we're engaged.'

'Yes.' Agnes felt dizzy with delight.

Someone was knocking on the door, and then it opened to reveal Olive standing there with a tray of glasses of sherry, with Tilly, Dulcie and Sally crowded behind her.

'Can we come in?' That was Tilly.

'Let me see the ring,' Dulcie was demanding.

'Agnes, you look so happy.' Sally's smile was calming and kind.

'Congratulations, Ted. We wish you both every happiness,' Olive announced, putting down the tray so that she could join the girls, who were all admiring Agnes's ring.

The diamond was so small but very pretty, Olive thought, relieved that Dulcie for once had been tactful enough not to make the kind of Dulcie comment that could have hurt Ted's pride and marred Agnes's obvious joy. Watching Agnes reminded her so much of her own engagement, which had been here in this very house and in this very room, with her husband's mother pursing her lips and looking rather critically at her.

'To Ted and Agnes,' Olive toasted once everyone had got a glass of sherry.

'Ted and Agnes,' everyone echoed. Then it was back to the kitchen for mince pies, warm from the bottom of the oven where Olive had slipped them, somehow managing to find room, despite the fact that the oven was almost filled by the turkey she'd put in when they had come back from church.

Watching Agnes finger her ring, a look of dreamy delight in her eyes, Tilly had to fight the temptation to touch Drew's ring, where it hung from its chain concealed beneath her clothes.

George reached for Sally's hand. If he'd had his way they'd have been celebrating their own engagement tonight, but of course Sally, being the wonderful caring person that she was, hadn't wanted to steal Agnes's limelight.

Never one to enjoy someone else being in the limelight, Dulcie seized the opportunity to open Wilder's present to her. It was, after all, after midnight and Christmas Day. A satisfied smile curved her lips when she opened the gift-wrapped box to find inside it a shiny gold compact with a D picked out on it in sparkling brilliants. Inside, the compact had two compartments and a pretty swansdown powder puff. There was a lipstick case to go with it in exactly the same design. Dulcie, who knew exactly how much such luxuries cost, preened as she gave Wilder an approving smile. Hers would be the most expensive present any of them received, and it was only right that that should be the case. After all, she was the prettiest of all of them.

She bestowed another smile on Wilder as a reward for his generosity.

'Happy Christmas, everyone,' Drew toasted them all with the remains of his sherry.

'Happy Christmas,' they all chorused back, whilst Tilly gathered the girls together and whispered, 'Let's give the boys their stockings now, shall we?'

Dulcie rolled her eyes. Privately she had thought Tilly was being a bit babyish when she had first suggested that they should fill the stockings she had bought from the market with silly bits of nothing, but when Sally had laughed and nodded her head and Agnes had gone all soft and damp-eyed with emotion, Dulcie, not wanting to be the odd one out, had felt obliged to go along with Tilly's plan.

It was Sally who volunteered to go upstairs and collect the stockings. She smiled tenderly to herself as she picked up George's. Some things were beyond price, and now, in the privacy of her room, she used up a whole sheet of her precious writing paper to write: 'To the man I love – I promise to visit you every time I have enough time off,' and then adding several kisses and signing it, before folding it and placing it into a matching envelope, which she carefully sealed, writing George's name on the front. She tucked the envelope as far down the stocking as she could amongst the other small gifts she had gathered: a book of poems, all penned by New Zealanders, she'd found in a secondhand bookshop; one of the packs of cards Tilly had generously shared with everyone, two sticks of liquorice – George's favourite sweet treat – and, of course, the obligatory handknitted socks, nice and thick to warm his poor aching feet, along with one of Olive's carefully hoarded apples.

Although she had been as quick as she could, Tilly was hopping impatiently from foot to foot by the time Sally returned downstairs, her arms piled high with the four well-stuffed stockings.

Witnessing the look of barely suppressed excitement and anticipation on Tilly's face, Olive's heart filled with a mixture of love and nostalgia. In her heart Tilly was still her little girl, the little girl she had filled so many Christmas stockings for, and yet the reality was that Tilly was now a young woman, carrying on one of the traditions Olive had created so lovingly for her. Gripped by the maternal ache of her own emotions when Drew was the first of the young men to step forward – a twinkle in his eye and an expression on his face that said that not only did he understand his role but also that he was fully prepared to play it – Olive was torn between gratitude for the fact that Tilly was involved with a young man who so obviously thought a great deal of her, and anxiety over the growing strength of feelings she suspected that Tilly and Drew had for one another.

'What's this?' Drew demanded, giving Tilly a teasing look as she took his stocking from Sally and started to hand it to him.

'It's from Father Christmas,' Tilly told him, trying to keep her face straight, 'but you can only have it if you've been good.'

The sound of Drew and Tilly's laughter as they mock-wrestled with the stocking had the three other young men coming forward so that they too could receive their stockings.

Whilst Dulcie's manner was studiedly off hand and 'grown up' as she handed Wilder his, when he discovered the pack of cards tucked inside it and immediately started to shuffle them, acknowledging that they were 'a real nice pack', she immediately dropped her pose and told him firmly, 'I knew you'd like them.'

'Liquorice?' George smiled at Sally. 'My favourite.' But it was the look in his eyes as he read the special note she had written for him that said what he was really feeling, and the touch of his hand as he reached for and squeezed hers.

'We always have Christmas stockings at home. It's one of our traditions.'

'And now it will be one of ours,' Sally promised him. One day, one Christmas, please God, a long time from now, when their own children were old enough to understand, they would gather round their own fireplace and she would tell them about the first Christmas she had shared with their father. But not perhaps about the note she had written for him. Some things were too special and private ever to be shared with anyone else.

The second Christmas of the war, Olive thought painfully. Twelve months in which there had been so much to bear and so many lives lost: Dunkirk, with those poor young men coming back looking so beaten and defeated; the Battle for Britain, when the country had held its breath, knowing that only the skill of the few stood between them and German invasion, and then the start of the Blitz.

How much more destruction and death would the coming year bring?

'Mum, can I have another mince pie. Please?'

Automatically Olive switched her thoughts from her private anxiety to the reality of the present. Her home was filled with young people who were safe and well and happy, and that surely was worth celebrating and worth being thankful for. A true Christmas gift to be appreciated and welcomed. The very best of Christmas gifts in fact.

This Large Print Book for the partially sighted, who cannot read normal print, is published under the auspices of

THE ULVERSCROFT FOUNDATION